Breathless

USA TODAY BESTSELLING AUTHOR

LEX MARTIN

Copy editing by RJ Locksley

Cover by Najla Qamber Designs

Model Photographs by Perrywinkle Photography

First Edition

ISBN 978-1-950554-11-9

ABOUT THE NOVEL

Joey...

I wouldn't say I ran away *exactly*—twenty-two is too old for that.

I'd call it self-preservation.

I have one objective: protect my heart from the boy next door who has no clue I've loved him my whole life, even with a front row seat to his revolving bedroom door.

My escape plan almost worked.

Except I left one thing behind.

Logan Carter hijacked my heart, and now it's time to get it back. This time for good.

Logan...

I wouldn't say I've been lying this whole time—not about everything.

Not about how much I miss my best friend, and definitely not about how pissed I am that she left with hardly a goodbye.

She's the last person I ever expected to ghost me, and her absence left a gaping hole in my chest.

When Joey Grayson steps off that bus, I know I'll do anything to keep her home, and that means finding out the truth.

But I'm not sure how to tell her my truths when I'm living so many lies.

∽

Breathless is a standalone companion novel to the *USA Today* bestsellers *Shameless* and *Reckless*. Each book features a different couple.

As always, to Matt & my girls

"My very soul demands you."
– Charlotte Bronte, *Jane Eyre*

PROLOGUE

Joey

BEFORE TONIGHT, MY MOST SIGNIFICANT SEXUAL RELATIONSHIP HAS been with my shower head.

Let me just say it takes guts to purchase a removable shower head from DeLuca's Hardware Store when Mrs. DeLuca's eyeing you like she knows you're going to blast it against your privates when you get home.

Unfortunately, bravery has been fleeting in my life, but that was one of my more courageous moments.

So is this one.

For some reason, though, I'm not feeling the relief I thought I would.

And I'm not talking about the lack of an orgasm.

This—hooking up with Trent—is supposed to be about me letting go of the past, of someone I can't have, and forging ahead. Of living my life instead of always feeling like I'm trapped in the back seat of someone else's journey.

Trent is trying his best. Going slow and speaking softly. Being gentle.

And the sex is... fine.

Except my body aches, and not in pleasant ways. But a girl's first time doesn't always feel good, right?

I blink, wondering if I'm supposed to feel so numb. So disconnected.

But like I've just been hit by a car and it's taking my body a few seconds to process the pain, the dam of emotion finally breaks.

One tear. Then two. Until a whole river cascades down my face, my conscience objecting to what I've just done.

Objecting to the man hovering over me with his brow crinkled in concern. Because he looks all wrong. Smells wrong. Feels wrong.

Black hair instead of dirty blonde. Brown eyes instead of blue. Smooth hands instead of rough.

"Joey, sweetheart. Are you okay?" Even the way he talks to me is wrong.

I shove him off me, wincing when he exits my body, and curl into the pillow that smells like the rest of this hotel. "Yeah. Just had too much to drink. Sorry." I try to muffle the sob by burrowing deeper into the bedding.

His hand runs along my spine, a gesture to soothe me, I'm guessing. Trent's a good guy. It's not his fault I'm in love with someone else. In fact, we bonded over our mutual heartache. He's recovering from a bad breakup. It was his idea for me to "break the seal" and use him to forget Logan.

Not that Logan was ever mine.

Trent probably just wanted to get off. I can't blame him. A sure-thing hook-up with a twenty-two-year-old virgin with no strings attached? What red-blooded man declines that? No one I know.

But this is supposed to help me cut ties with Logan. That's

what this trip to Florida has been about. To grow up and get over him.

I needed to do something. What self-respecting woman in this day and age spends her whole life pining for the boy next door when he's made it clear she's not his type? That he loves her as a friend. That he sees her as his bud. His sidekick. Maybe even a little sister.

I cry harder. Because I know—as certain as I'm sure the sun will rise in the morning, despite the dread burning in my soul right now—that Logan loves me. As a friend. That even after not talking to him for months, he'd probably take a bullet for me. That he'd likely be pissed I gave it up to some guy I've only known for a few weeks after spending a lifetime waiting to give myself to someone I love.

Well, I got tired of waiting.

After years of watching my best friend hook up with other women, I finally grew a backbone. I only wish it felt better.

It doesn't matter because Logan will never know what I've done.

I've been friend-zoned, and I'm ready to move on.

And by the time I see him at his brother's wedding this summer, I hope my heart has let go of him too.

1

LOGAN

Secrets are the most damning thing about small towns. Secrets and lies.

I would know.

I stir my cup of shitty gas station coffee and watch another bus enter the dusty Texas depot, dropping off another ragtag group of people. They disembark, squinting into the soul-searing July sun as they stretch, probably wishing they'd forked over the extra cash to fly coach into Austin.

If Joey had told me she was taking the fucking bus from Florida, I'd have given her the money for a flight.

I shake off the pang of regret and anger that thrums through me every time I think of her. No, if she wanted my help, she'd have returned any one of my texts in the last six months.

Anxiety twists in my gut. Worry over how she's doing. Fear that she traveled so far by herself. Irritation that I feel so helpless when it comes to this girl.

As the bus driver tosses suitcases from the side compartment of the Greyhound, one man picks up his bag and starts to stroll away, except he pauses, looks around, and yanks off something from his hand.

His wedding ring.

See what I mean? Secrets.

An SUV pulls into the parking lot a minute later, and he waves at the driver. A pretty young thing exits her vehicle and races into his arms. I'm guessing that's not his wife.

I roll my eyes, a wave of anger settling in with the coffee and nerves churning in my chest.

Is it really so hard to keep your promises, asshole?

Reason two hundred why I don't have a girlfriend—if you can't be focused on a relationship, if you can't be committed and faithful, then don't have one. It ain't that difficult.

Reaching over to the dash of my truck, I crank up the air conditioner.

A smack to my shoulder makes me jerk, and my buddy Patrick motions toward the clock. "For the third time, what time does her bus get in?"

My heart jackhammers against my sternum. "Ten more minutes."

"No offense, but you look kinda fucked up. You okay?"

I shrug, not bothering to mention I forgot he was in the truck. "Just want to get this over with."

He laughs and gives me a teasing look. "I'm sure Joey would love to know that's how you feel."

My hands tighten against the steering wheel, years of frustration whirling below the surface, but I shove that shit down. "Joey doesn't know I'm coming. She thinks Tori's picking her up."

She asked my brother's fiancée, who's also her good friend, to give her a ride. If I'm being honest, it stings. But how could she ask me when she wouldn't answer the fucking phone?

Patrick's eyes widen. "Dang, son. This oughta be fun."

I press the heels of my palms into my eyes, exhaustion from the last week taking its toll. "Cody wasn't feeling well this morning, and Tori had to take him to the doctor. Otherwise..."

It pains me to finish the next sentence, so I don't. But the truth is I wouldn't have had a clue Joey was coming home today if Cody hadn't gotten sick.

I figured she'd be back soon since my brother Ethan and his fiancée Tori are getting married in two weeks, and Joey is one of Tori's bridesmaids, but no one gave me any specifics. Tori's been strangely silent on the topic of my best friend. Or former best friend.

Fuck.

I rub my chest, over the ache that started when Joey left with barely a word as to why. One minute we were taking holiday photos with my family, and then, *poof*, she was gone. She left me a vague text—something about needing to get on with her life, which really fucking confused me—and then moved her grandmother to be near their family in Florida. I knew her uncle had offered to help relocate Rosalie, but Joey never seemed eager to go.

Until last December.

When her brother put their grandmother's house up for sale last spring, I nearly went ballistic until I remembered she'd be back for the wedding.

Not sure how it went from Joey and I talking almost daily to me getting ghosted by the girl who's been my shadow since we were kids, but that's what happened.

Yeah, I'm pissed. At her for treating our friendship like it means nothing to her. At myself for not knowing what's going on with her. Because obviously something is wrong for her to up and leave like her ass was on fire.

I've always prided myself on being there for Joey when no one else was. I thought we had something special. Something meaningful. We're each other's one call from jail, for fuck's sake.

My Netflix binge buddy when I genuinely want to watch a movie and relax. The one woman who makes me want to try to be a better person.

Patrick nods at me. "You coming to the bonfire?" When I don't say anything because I'm too deep in thought about this mess with Joey, he groans. "Come on, man. It's been ages since you've gone out with us."

It's my first night off in weeks, and all I want to do is order a pizza, grab a beer, and veg out in front of my flatscreen with Joey, if we can get over whatever the hell happened between us this year.

"Don't tell me you're ditching us for another chick?" He snickers. "Which one you been hanging out with? Felicia, Deb, or Anna?"

I have no clue who he's talking about, but that's because I'm a liar, and I can't keep my shit straight anymore.

"Sure. One of them." It's the only way to get him to shut up. I can't explain what I do with my time without untangling a lie too big to stuff down once it's out.

My phone buzzes on the console between us, but before I can pick it up, the name flashes. I mute it and jam it in my pocket.

A quick glance at Patrick tells me he saw more than he should've. He lifts his eyebrows. "A new one, huh? Is she a babe?"

I don't respond because there's no way to answer that question in an appropriate way. Not sure when I became an "appropriate way" kind of guy, but I can't deny the last few years have fucked me up.

He hums in the back of his throat. "Been meaning to ask you... You wouldn't care if I asked Joey out, would you? Bro code kinda applies because you're BFFs or whatever weird platonic thing you have going on, and you get ragey when guys hit on her, so I thought I should ask. But she's been looking so damn hot on her Instagram, it got me thinking."

"Ragey" is fucking right. The last thing I want is one of my idiot friends jerking her around. He'd probably dine-and-dash her like the rest of my friends, and there's no way I'll put up with that bullshit. Joey's not a casual sex kind of girl.

Don't get me wrong. I love women who are into casual sex. They're pretty much all I've sampled in a horizontal sense, but I know enough not to mess with anyone who wants a ring on that finger. And I say don't fish in that pond if you're only lookin' to catch and release.

My eyes narrow. "And you think you're good enough for Josephine?" Because I know Patrick won't bother to wake his lazy ass up when Joey gets locked out of her house in the middle of the night or needs a ride home after pulling a double shift at the salon. And my girl deserves someone who'll man up for her.

He starts to mumble a response, but I throw my hand up. "Back up. What Instagram? Joey has an account?" She hates IG.

His eyebrows pop up. Probably because never in the history of Joey and me has Patrick known something about her before I did.

Reaching into his pocket, he palms his phone and clicks around, and then I'm looking at the beautiful girl with the face I know as well as my own.

Damn, I miss her. Never thought I'd miss that little squirt so much.

She was always trailing behind me and her brother Silas when she was little. With lopsided pigtails and a toothy grin. Always tripping and scraping her knees or elbows. Always needing help climbing up the slide or wanting a push on the swings.

Silas and I are four years older. We used to be best friends until our families had a falling out. Then it was just me and Joey.

Whatever happened between our parents somehow didn't affect our friendship, though I can't blame her for sticking with me instead of Silas since he's a dick. After all, *I'm* the one who crawled down an abandoned well to get her when she fell in as a kid, and not her dumbass brother, who was standing right there.

I scroll through three or four photos, marveling at her golden tan and smooth skin. Staring at the freckles dotting her cheeks. Looking a little too long at her plump bottom lip and the way her flowy top clings to her petite body.

My eyes drift to her lips again. To the delicate curve of her neck and the way her necklace dangles between her perky, round breasts.

But years of kicking my own ass to not let things get weird between us force my attention above her neckline. To her eyes.

Joey has the most expressive gray eyes, the kind that soothe and cajole and caress. These photos don't show the depth of her eyes.

Somehow, she's different. Distant.

It sends a shiver up my spine.

What's happened to my best friend?

Except I don't have time to snoop more because her bus pulls into the station.

2

JOEY

THE CLOSER THE BUS GETS TO OUR DESTINATION, THE HARDER MY heart pounds. Sweat builds down my back and under my arms even though I have the air conditioner vents aimed at my face.

After twenty-seven hours on a cross-country bus, I have no illusions about how I look. Ratty hair twisted into a crazy bun. No makeup. Circles under my eyes. And I'm so on edge, I've barely been able to eat or sleep despite being exhausted. Not even the bodice-ripper on my old Kindle is enough to keep my attention.

Thank God Tori is picking me up and not Logan, but I know I can't avoid him forever.

You don't want to avoid him forever, dummy.

That's the worst part—the eager, hungry piece of me that's dying to see him.

I tuck both of my hands under my thighs so I don't bite my nails. Some beautician I'd be if I showed up to Tori's wedding with hands looking like they'd been gnawed off by a gremlin. My hair situation is bad enough at the moment.

When I left Texas, I wasn't thinking I'd be returning so soon. Tori and Ethan's wedding crept up on me. I booked this bus ticket in February, and back then, July seemed like plenty of time to get my life in order and my emotions on lockdown, but with every passing mile, my anxiety ratchets up like I'm about to walk off the gangplank of a pirate ship instead of visiting old friends.

"Sweetheart, would you like one of these?" asks Mrs. Reynolds as she holds out a bear claw from 7/11, the cellophane crinkling in her weathered hand.

"No, thank you, but I appreciate it."

I've had the good fortune of sitting next to a very kind elderly woman for the last twenty hours, and although she looks like the kind of person who snuggles her grandbabies and sings them lullabies before bedtime, she threatened to chop off the balls of the thug who harassed me for a blow job back at that Port Arthur rest stop.

"You haven't eaten anything all day. You nervous 'bout seeing that boy?"

When two southern women sit next to each other for this length of time, they're bound to tell each other their life stories, even if there is a fifty-year age difference.

"Yes, ma'am. I'm nervous." I swallow, wishing I had some water. "I thought I was doing the right thing when I left. I was just so hurt, you know? And I didn't want to say anything to him that I'd regret, so I... I didn't say much at all, but now I'm wondering if I should have. Logan's always been there for me, and it's not like he *knew*..." I can't blame him for not knowing things I've never said out loud.

Tears well in my eyes, and I fan my face with my hand because, dang it, I don't wanna be a snotty mess when we get to the bus station. Although Tori won't care. She'll wrap me in her arms and tell me pervy jokes until I laugh.

Somehow, I manage to keep it together as Mrs. Reynolds

pats my hand. "What about your brother? I bet he'll be happy to see you."

You'd think, but no. Silas has always viewed me as a pain in his ass.

Sniffling, I shrug because I can't handle any more depressing stories today. "You've been kind to listen to me ramble about my family's troubles." I give her a smile, a genuine one because talking to someone aside from my cousin Dawn back in Florida has made me feel better.

The bus pulls to an abrupt stop. With all of my chattering, I hadn't realized we'd arrived.

When I stand, my muscles and joints protest from being confined. I can't wait to fall face first into my bed. After changing the sheets. Because there's no telling who Silas let sleep in my bed since I've been gone.

I check my phone, frowning when I notice my brother hasn't returned any of my messages. Silas and I lived in my grandmother's house until I relocated her to a facility in Florida to be near my uncle's family.

None of us were expecting her to pass so soon. One morning, she just didn't open her eyes again. I haven't really known how to process her death. While I'm grateful her suffering is over, every time I stop to appreciate that I have more free time, I'm racked with guilt.

As I step out into the painfully bright sun, Mrs. Reynolds nudges me. "Is that your young man there?"

"No, he's not—"

I stop mid-sentence because, *oh, God*, there he is.

Logan Carter. The boy next door and my lifelong crush.

And he looks mighty ticked off.

"Can I give you a word of advice, dearie?" Mrs. R asks as she waves toward an older gentleman heading toward us from the other side of the parking lot. "Tell him how you feel. What's the worst thing that can happen? Maybe he doesn't return your feelings, or maybe he does. Either way, the ground isn't going to swallow you whole. And who knows? He might need to hear it from you to make a difference." She squeezes my shoulder. "Life's too short not to say what you mean and live the life you want."

With those parting words and a hug, she's gone.

All around me, people talk and retrieve their bags, but my feet are glued in my flip-flops to the searing hot concrete as I watch Logan stalk closer. He's beautiful, with those mesmerizing blue eyes, that messy, dirty blond hair, and the easy grace of an athlete from a lifetime of riding horses. He's wearing jeans and a faded Port Aransas T-shirt, my favorite of his, that says "love at first bite" with an image of a shark that's taken a chunk out of a boat.

Even though I want to look away, I can't. It's been too long since I've seen him, and I want to soak him in. Every cell in my body screams to run to him. To get closer. To throw my arms around him and tell him what's been burning in my heart since I was a girl.

In my head, it's one of those rom-com montages where the heroine runs gracefully across the screen with the sun silhouetting her from behind. In that moment, the guy realizes how much he needs her and opens his arms as she throws herself into his body. He twirls her around and around until they kiss. And then it cuts to a scene a year later where they're married with babies and surrounded by furry farm animals.

I press my hand across my eyes with a self-deprecating laugh because I'm obviously delusional. Maybe I *was* mugged back at that rest stop, and I'm lying on the ground somewhere dying. That's the only way to explain how I could be fantasizing right now about the guy I left the dang state to avoid.

"Josephine."

His rough voice cuts through my racing thoughts and does what it always does—before I can even peel my hand away from my face, goosebumps erupt on my skin and my nipples harden like little traitors begging to get out of a jail cell.

This is the problem. My head knows I'm an idiot for being in love with Logan, for wanting someone who's never wanted me, but my body has never gotten the memo.

He sighs. "Joey, come on."

My heart thrashes against my ribs like a fish that's been beached at high tide. How far is Mexico? I could make a run for it.

"Damn it, would you please look at me?"

Finally, I open my eyes, and my breath catches because he's so close, and in the breeze, beneath the familiar scent of Texas cedar welcoming me home, I smell him—his ocean-crisp soap and leather and clean sweat. Cinnamon gum and coffee.

My eyes dart down to our feet where his black boots tower ominously close to my flimsy flip-flops and pearlescent pink nail polish.

One rough finger tilts my chin, and I lift my eyes up his muscled thighs, perfectly encased in washed-out denim, up his slender waist and broad shoulders, and pause on his square jaw and the firm set of his lips.

Lips I've always longed to kiss.

Lips that have kissed many, *many* other girls.

But never me.

Because maybe I'm not good enough. Or old enough. Or pretty enough. Or smart enough. Or big-boobed enough. Or whatever it is that keeps me firmly parked in the friend zone.

With that final twinge of pain, a good reminder that I need to get my shit together and not let myself swirl down this drain of self-loathing—because no man is worth me questioning my value—I clench my jaw and make eye contact.

We stare at each other, his blue eyes stark while they study me beneath tight brows.

Even though I've daydreamed of a thousand snarky things I want to say to him, they blow away in the breeze when he breaks into a breathtaking smile and wraps me in a hug.

"Missed you, brat. Can't believe you ghosted me." Holy crap, I'm in the air, just for a minute, but my feet lift off the ground as he mumbles, "You ever do anything like that again, and I will spank your ass. You hear me?"

I'm laughing against him with my nose pressed to his neck, and he's chuckling too as he holds me tightly, and for this space in time, nothing bad has happened between us. There are no hurt feelings. No misplaced emotions or unrequited crushes. He's just the boy I grew up with who's always had my back. The one I've always loved in one way or another. The boy who's always kept my secrets.

In this safe place in his arms, I make myself a promise. To tell him how I feel. To lay it all out and tell him why I left.

Even if I have to let him go in the end.

3
_____

LOGAN

It's so good to see Joey, to breathe in her sweet floral scent, to feel her against me and know she's back home, safe and sound after all this time apart, that it's hard for me to let her go.

A throat clears next to me, and I reluctantly set her on the ground. She looks exhausted but beautiful. She's wearing a bright yellow shirt and khaki shorts, the light colors showcasing her great tan, one she probably got from spending time at the beach with her cousins. Somehow her legs look long, even though she's a tiny thing.

Gone is the adorable tomboy who used to follow me and Silas everywhere. Joey is all grown up—has been for a while— but seeing her now after being gone for the last several months seems to highlight the fact that she's not a little girl anymore.

Swallowing, I lift my gaze off her lush body because nothing good can come from that. Instead, I study the giant mass of blond hair knotted on top of her head.

I look for streaks of purple or blue or hot pink that might be tucked away, but I can't see any of her usual unicorn colors. She must've gone with something safe for the wedding.

Patrick shoves me out of the way. "Josephine Grayson, it's been too long."

When he swoops her into his arms and twirls her around, making her laugh, I have a sudden urge to punch him in the nutsack.

"Put her down, asshole. She's not a doll."

He gives me a look. "Why can't I pick her up? You did."

"'Cause she's my best friend. Not yours."

He sets her on her feet and gives me another playful shove. "Whatcha gonna do? Whip it out and pee a circle around her so no one else talks to her? Huh?" He jumps around the parking lot like he's going to mock-fight me.

A small hand lands on my chest, and I look down to catch Joey trying not to smile. "Guys, stop talking about me like I'm not here."

I pull her into a head lock, smiling when she lets out a squeal. This is our standard operating procedure. "Oh, you finally decided to grace us with your presence, Itsy Bitsy?" When she was six, she played a spider in the school play, and sometimes I need to give her shit about it.

As I drag her to my truck, she screams, "Shotgun!"

Patrick curses, and I laugh.

"Am I seriously getting booted?" Patrick's face scrunches up like this is a surprise to him as he folds himself into the back and I give Joey a boost into the passenger seat.

"Joey gets shotgun." I shut her door and walk around the front of the cab, relishing the sight of her in my vehicle. Damn. She's a sight for sore eyes.

But Patrick won't shut up. When I climb in, he's at it again. "Bro, she's been gone. For six months. Don't I get any credit for sticking around your sorry, mopey ass all that time?"

"Josephine always gets shotgun. That's just how it is, man.

Sorry." Even though I'm trying to keep things light, being reminded of her leaving sucks the air out of the truck.

I can tell Joey senses it too because she looks down at her lap where her hands are twisted together.

"Hey." I tug on the sleeve of her T-shirt until she makes eye contact. "I don't care what happened. Why you left or why you didn't call me." I sigh and glance away. "I mean, I do care, but I want you to know I'm not mad that I didn't hear from you, okay? I'm just glad you're home."

Have I racked my brain trying to figure out if I did something to hurt her? To push her away like that? To make her run across the damn country?

Yes to all of those questions. And I aim to find out the truth at some point.

But for now, I just want my best friend back.

I stare into those stunning gray eyes that somehow make time stand still. "You can tell me anything. I'm not going anywhere. Because you're stuck with me." I clear my throat and glance at the parking lot. "While I'm laying it all out there, I should say how much I missed you. Patrick was right. I was a little mopey."

Thanks, asshole, for pointing it out.

Joey's eyes get misty, and it guts me because I figure whatever made her hightail it to Florida *is* a big deal. But if this is how I get to keep my girl, by laying off and chilling out, then this is what I have to do.

"Missed you too, Logan. I'm sorry that I—"

I shake my head, and she gets my meaning. No apologies.

Joey is always the first to apologize for shit that's not her fault, and I can't bear the thought of her doing that right now. I might not know why she left, but she obviously felt she needed to, and I respect that. But the last thing I wanna do is hash that out with an audience. This is between her and me. That's it. Later, when it's just the two of us, we can have a heart-to-heart.

The idea of losing Joey the way I lost my friendship with Silas—randomly, like the universe has nothing better to do than fuck me over—makes me willing to do almost anything to smooth this over with Jo.

Without a second thought, I grab her hand to reassure her, threading my fingers through hers. Something I've never done before, and the intimacy of it makes me pause.

Sure, I've grabbed her hand in the past. I held her hand all the time when we were kids because she couldn't cross the street otherwise, but this is something different.

She seems to notice it too, studying our intertwined hands, her small, smooth fingers engulfed by my big, rough paw that's spent too many hours in the barn grooming horses and shoveling shit.

A tinge of pink flushes her cheeks, and when she glances up and aims her smile at me, it hits me in the solar plexus.

Patrick coos behind us. "Aww, bro. You so sweet. No wonder all the buckle bunnies wanna fuck you."

I roll my eyes and reluctantly pull my hand from Joey's so I can start the truck. Glaring at Patrick through the rear view mirror, I mumble, "Why do you have to ruin everything?"

I hate when he does this, talks about other girls in front of Joey. I've played the field from time to time, but never in front of her.

Plus, I'd have to be a moron to not know she had a crush on me when we were kids, but she probably would've liked whichever one of Silas's idiot friends pulled her out of that well. I figured she was over it by the time she dated that Mason douchebag in high school, but I've always felt like it would be a dick move to parade women in front of her.

I might have to act like I spend my spare time screwing

around so no one pays attention to what I really do, but that doesn't mean I want Jojo thinking I'm that guy.

I should tell her the truth.

The thought loops in my mind. I almost can't remember a time when this shit didn't weigh me down.

But one lie begets another, and I don't know how to untangle them from the mountain of deceit I've been hiding from everyone. Especially when some of those lies aren't my secrets to reveal.

If there's one person in this world I want to tell, though, it's Joey.

We drive in silence as I try to shake off the funk I always get into when I stew over this crap.

It's not until we're on the highway that I think to ask where I should drop her off. "Where we headed, Bitsy? Back to my brother's?" I'm sure she and Tori have a lot to catch up on. Ethan and Tori want her to come for dinner tonight, but I'm wondering if she's too tired to socialize after that bus ride.

Joey digs through her purse and frowns as she stares at her phone. "What? No, I'm staying at my grandma's."

Patrick and I exchange frowns in my rear view mirror.

There's so much wrong with what she just said, I don't know where to begin, but I don't have to because Patrick is already opening his big mouth.

"Can't, baby doll. Silas sold the house a while back."

I bristle at Patrick's nickname for her, because he's never acted so infatuated with Joey before, though I have to admit she does look incredible despite her recent road trip.

Gripping the steering wheel, I chance a look at her, and her expression says it all.

No, she didn't know her brother sold her family's home.

Motherfucking Silas.

Guess I'm not the only one keeping secrets.

4

JOEY

MY EYES GLAZE OVER AS WE WIND THROUGH TOWN BACK TO THE Carter ranch. I'm trying to keep it together until I can lock myself in a bathroom and cry.

How could Silas do this? He said he'd keep an eye on the house until I got back. He knows how much our home means to me. I don't have many fond memories of my whole family together, but the few I have were there.

By the time it was just my grandma, Silas, and me, I could almost block out the bad things that had happened there.

I roll down the window, needing air.

"Hey." Logan grabs my hand, but I keep my head turned because I can't look at him when I'm this close to the edge. "Sorry, Jo. I figured Silas told you, or I would've." He squeezes my hand. "It'll be okay. We'll figure this out together. My mom and Ethan will know what to do."

This is why Logan has always been my person. He swoops in to punch my bullies and rescue me out of wells.

Why can't I just love you like a friend? It would make my life so much less complicated.

When he talks like this, I can almost forget what happened at Christmas time.

Like someone slams the brakes, my heart lurches at the memory.

I want to ask him why he said the things he did. Why he cleaved my heart in two. But if I do, that would prove his point—that I'm clingy and have no life—and I still have a little pride left that prevents me from laying it all out there, especially with Patrick hanging on our every word. Granted, I was never meant to overhear Logan's conversation on the River Walk, but that doesn't make it hurt less.

Yes, I want to apologize to Logan for not communicating with him more. I never meant for him to worry. At the time, I wondered if he'd even care, but now I know those were my emotions talking. I was so hurt, and that pain blinded me from the obvious—that he cares... as a friend. A friend who needs space.

Grim, still feeling like someone kicked my puppy, I hold out as long as I can before I start sneaking glances at him as he drives.

I take in his rugged good looks. His messy hair that dangles over his eyes and makes him roguishly flirty. That perfect nose and square jaw that's lightly dusted with stubble. Those sexy lips I've longed to feel against my skin. His tanned forearms roped in muscle.

I could go on and on, but enumerating his handsome physical attributes is only making this worse.

Pulling up to the ranch brings an unexpected smile to my face. Even the old wooden sign makes me happy: Carter Cutting Horses, est. 1960.

Logan and his brother raise, train, and compete champion cutters, horses that are used alongside cattle to "cut" one from the herd if it's injured. They inherited the business from their father when he passed away several years ago. Ethan was graduating from college at the time, and Logan was a senior in high school.

I slide out of the truck and stare at the beautiful house that sits surrounded by acres and acres of farmland and fenced-off areas for horses.

Although I've always said I live next door to the Carters, it's more like two lots over, and since their property is ginormous, it's a good twenty-minute walk. My grandmother's house looks more like a shack compared to this ranch, but Bev and her family never treated me like a charity case. Even though I was.

Logan motions toward the barn as we head up the walkway. "Wanna ride Cinnamon Pie some time? She misses you."

The mention of my favorite horse banishes the gloom that had settled over me on the drive here. "Heck, yes, I do."

Patrick laughs along the other side of me and tosses his arm over my shoulder. "I love how you don't curse. It's so cute."

What every girl wants to hear. How cute I am. Pint-sized. Adorable. The little sister they always wanted.

I roll my eyes and shove his arm off me. "You won't think I'm so cute if I knee you in the balls."

The boys snort, and I'm chuckling when Logan pulls me to his chest, so that my back rests against him. I'm expecting another chokehold, because somewhere in that dense head of his, he thinks I'm his peanut-sized MMA partner, but he keeps his forearm gently pressed to my collarbone. Almost like... like he's holding me.

I will myself to take a deep breath in hopes it'll stop my heart from pounding out of my body.

"See. *My* best friend." Logan's voice, low and grumbling in my ear, makes goosebumps break out on my skin.

For a moment, I'm so confused how this could be the same person who said those things about me. If he needs space, why is he being so affectionate? Did he really miss me that much? Did he have a change of heart?

Like this, it's easy to appreciate his incredible physique and strength. Against me, his stomach flexes, and I don't have to strain my imagination to envision that crazy eight-pack. Logan is a lean, athletic machine.

And so dang sexy.

I want to close my eyes and relish being in his arms, but I'm already too close to purring and rubbing against his leg like a stray cat.

Coughing, I extract myself from Logan and Patrick's pissing contest and head into the house.

He's just taunting Patrick. That didn't mean anything. It never does.

The moment I'm inside, Mila sees me from the kitchen and screams. Ethan's seven-year-old daughter races toward me and jumps into my arms, nearly sending both of us hurtling to the floor.

"I missed you *sooo* much, Joey!" she squeals in my ear.

"Missed you too, munchkin."

Another set of arms wrap around my waist, and Cody, Mila's little brother, grins up at me.

"Dude. You're covered in chocolate."

His smile widens as he presses his face into my shirt. Ugh. Gross.

I laugh and squeeze the kids, overwhelmed by how excited I am to see their sweet faces. I've known them since they were babies. Held them in my arms as infants. Changed their diapers and patched up boo-boos.

Mila's hair is longer, and Cody is so big, I swear he swallowed a tree.

I've never been gone this long without seeing them, and the realization of how much I missed in those six months sends a sharp twinge to my heart. That knife twists when I consider how much more I'll lose when I head back to Florida like I've planned.

Because, really, what are the odds that I tell Logan about my feelings for him and he sweeps me off my feet and tells me he loves me too? Only in the movies. I might be naive, but I'm not dumb.

Blinking back a whirlwind of emotion, I squeeze the kids tighter.

"Good to have you back, Joey," a deep voice calls out to me.

I grin up at Ethan, who's always been like an older brother to me. He's four years older than Logan, and where Logan is the wild, party boy, Ethan is the stalwart family man.

I drag the kids with me to greet their dad, and then I'm the one squealing when I see my friend Tori.

"There's my maid of honor." She hauls me to her for a quick hug, somehow managing to avoid the chocolate. She grimaces when she gets a closer look at my clothes. "Codybug, please apologize for sliming this girl with pudding."

"Sorry, Aunt Jojo." Two dimples pop out on his chubby cheeks.

The little booger doesn't look the least bit apologetic. I laugh and brush those thick blond locks out of his face and kiss his forehead. "It's okay, dude. I'm not gonna melt."

He'll be four next month, but you'd never guess it from his height. I shouldn't be surprised, though. The Carter men are all over six feet tall.

"I huwt my arm." He holds it up to me for my inspection.

"Aww, sorry, buddy." I kiss his elbow for safe measure.

Behind me, a throat clears. "Hey, Joey," Patrick calls out. "I have a booboo too that's swollen. Been keeping me up at night. But kisses might make it feel better."

I turn in time to catch Logan elbow his friend in the gut, and

Tori snickers. She loops her arm in mine and pulls me down the hall. "Come on. Let's get you changed."

Once we're out of earshot of the boys, I tug Tori to a stop. Shame, hot and familiar, flushes my cheeks. "I need to do laundry," I whisper. "I'm not sure I have anything clean to wear."

After giving my cousin a huge down payment for our new business, I didn't have much left. I had to work overtime last week so I could scrounge the money to afford this trip and didn't have time to wash anything. With the exception of some underwear, everything in my suitcase is dirty. I thought laundry would be the first thing I'd do when I arrived at my grandma's house.

Which your brother sold. You have some real winners in the family, Jo.

Tori shrugs. "No prob. I'm sure I have something you can borrow."

In her bedroom, she digs around her dresser and tosses me a tank top and jean shorts. Because I have chocolate handprints on my rear too.

I eye the clothes in my hands warily. Tori is taller than I am, but I have more junk in the trunk. "Not sure I'm gonna be able to squeeze into your shorts."

"Try them. If not, I'll find some sweat pants or something. It's just so hot."

In the ensuite bathroom, I change into her clothes and then go wide-eyed when I catch myself in the mirror. "Tor, I can't go out in this!"

She sticks her head in, looks me over, and gives me a thumbs up. "Looking good, mama."

"My boobs are gonna pop out of this top if I bend over too far."

She scoffs. "You're fine. You have a great body, and it's not like you're prancing around in a bikini on your way to church." When she senses my turmoil, a worried expression crosses her face. "I need to do my own laundry or I'd offer you something else. I can grab you one of Ethan's t-shirts if you're really uncomfortable."

For some reason, wearing another man's clothes feels weird. Especially when they belong to my friend's fiancée.

"This is fine." I don't want to be any trouble.

She gives me a reassuring smile and then glances at the bedroom door behind her. "Didn't mean to throw you under the bus earlier by having Logan pick you up, but Cody had an earache that wouldn't go away, and I had to take him to the pediatrician."

"It's okay. I appreciate the ride. Is Cody okay?"

After she assures me Cody is fine, she studies me a second. "Did you guys talk on the way over here?"

I know she wants Logan and me to resolve our issues, which are basically my issues. "Not really. He kinda said we could let bygones be bygones, and we left things at that."

Nodding, she reaches for me and gives me a big hug. "I'm not pushing you one way or the other, but I do think you'll feel better if you tell him what happened and clear the air."

When she lets me go, we sit at the edge of her bed. "You're probably right, but if I tell him what happened at Christmas, then I have to tell him everything else, and that's hard for me. It's embarrassing." And pathetic. I'm quiet for a moment. "I didn't mean to hurt him when I left. I was upset and confused."

"I was upset when you told me what happened too. It's a miracle I didn't maim him on your behalf." She gives me another reassuring squeeze. "And you don't have to be embarrassed. You feel how you feel. There's no shame in caring about your best friend. You have the biggest heart of anyone I know, and he's damn lucky to have you by his side."

My face flames, and I laugh awkwardly. Sometimes I still feel like that gawky teenager who doesn't always know how to talk to people.

"If I haven't told you lately, I'm really honored to be in your wedding." I bump her shoulder with mine. "Thank God Logan made Ethan hire you that summer." Tori and I became fast friends when she came to work at the ranch two years ago.

"If you'd told me on the day I interviewed that I'd be marrying Ethan Carter, I'd have laughed in your face."

She swears she hated him when they met, but I think it was lust at first sight with a heaping side of denial.

"And now you're getting married!"

We look at each other and squeal like maniacs.

While my own love life is a train wreck, I couldn't be happier for Tori and Ethan. Tori is like a sister, and Ethan's always treated me better than my own brother.

Our powwow is interrupted when Mila calls for her in the other room.

"I gotta go make sure no one is burning down the house, but are you sure you're okay with my clothes?"

"Sure. Yeah." I mean, I think I am.

"Trust me when I say you look beautiful." She trots off with my soiled shirt and shorts to toss them in the laundry, and I take a minute to wash my hands and face in the bathroom because I feel grimy after that bus ride.

Staring at my reflection, I tug on my top to stretch it a little. I work out enough that I'm toned everywhere I should be, but showing this much skin makes me nervous from years of being told horrible things by my parents.

I shake my head, hating that I'm being dramatic. Tori wears tanks all the time, and she looks fine. My boobs aren't *that* much bigger. I just... won't bend over. And I'll probably be sitting most of the time for dinner this evening, so it's not like anyone will even notice my rear.

I can do this. No one here cares what I'm wearing.

I almost smile at the rebellion. If my father could see me now, he'd break out his shotgun to scare off any boys who looked in my direction.

Of course, he'd have to actually be here to do that.

And degenerate fathers who ditch their families don't get a say in what their daughters wear.

Straightening my shirt, I make up my mind.

I'm done living by other people's rules.

5

LOGAN

WE'RE SHOOTING THE SHIT IN THE KITCHEN, SITTING AROUND THE bar when, three big gulps into my iced tea, I choke.

What is Joey wearing?

At first, all my monkey brain can process is skin. Golden skin. Smooth planes with faint freckles. And curves. So many fucking curves.

Despite my hacking cough, I still manage to ogle the woman, who's now decked out in what have to be Tori's clothes. Because I have never seen Joey put so much on display. Even when we go swimming, she always wears a giant T-shirt over her suit.

I'm not judging. Women should wear whatever they want. I'm not some Neanderthal. I'm just not used to my friend in this context. The limited clothing context.

As I stare at her, two words come to mind: *Mouthwatering tits.* Damn, she's stacked.

Is it hot in here? I take one more gulp of my tea, feeling like I got struck in the face by a two-by-four. How have I not ever noticed that my best friend is alarmingly attractive? It's like my head always knew this, but the rest of me is only now catching on.

Awkwardly, she tugs at her tank, to pull it away from her stomach. She's shy, and judging from the flush crawling up her neck, she's feeling it now too.

I wonder where else she gets flushed.

Not cool, dude.

I'm about to turn away when I catch a glimpse of her round little ass in those snug shorts. Fuck me.

My cock agrees with a hearty nod.

Clenching my eyes shut, I think of all the disgusting things I can. Like that time Patrick puked up eggs through his nose after going on a bender. Or how much horse shit I have to shovel when one of our ranch hands calls in sick. Or when my nephew crapped all over my lap when he was two.

Better.

My dick stands down enough that I can lean back in my seat, but now I'm wary. Joey and I have spent tons of time together over the years, and I've never been so affected by her presence.

Is that why I was acting like a tool out on the front stoop, grabbing her and telling Patrick to piss off? I've been a dick to him all day for no good reason, except maybe he's right... I'm feeling territorial about Joey. More than my typical BFF concerns.

I'm gonna need something stronger than tea to wrap my head around this.

Sure, I've missed her. Been upset with her for disappearing on me. Wanted to straighten things between us, but the thoughts hurtling through my brain have more to do with exploring that tight little body rather than reuniting with an old pal.

And that's a line I've never crossed. But given how my friends and family constantly encourage the "Team LoJo" relationship, it's no wonder my thoughts are going haywire.

I've had her firmly placed in the little sister category for so long that even when she grew curves, I've always tried to ignore it.

Except...

Except for that one spring.

A flash of a memory from my senior year breaks out of the box I keep all the shit from that time locked down.

Of her laughing. Of us talking in the barn. She was only fourteen and so fucking beautiful. It was always her eyes that got me. Pierced me down to my soul—the way she looked at me. The way she trusted me.

And as someone once pointed out, women should never trust me.

No, the year my father passed away changed everything, and there's no going back.

Angrily, I thrust my hand into my hair and lock the past away where it's been for the last eight years.

"We need food!" Mila chants, and I pause my mental bullshit long enough to give my niece a noogie.

This thing with Joey will pass. I'm just tired. Been working seventy-hour weeks, here at the farm and at a side gig that's not such a side gig anymore.

Something's gotta give.

My sanity, it appears.

About an hour later, we're all settling around a mountain of food at the dining room table—the kids, Ethan, Tori, Joey, Patrick, and myself—when the front door creaks open and my mother yells, "Is she here?"

The moment Mom spots Joey, Beverly Carter's in motion

again. Our very own whirling dervish is a silver-blonde ball of energy with a dust cloud behind her feet. My old fears subside as I study my mother's level of energy. She's having a good day.

"Darlin', you are a sight for sore eyes!" My mom collides with Joey in a fierce hug, beaming with delight.

Over the years, I'm pretty sure Mom wanted to trade one of us in for Jo.

I reach for the bowl of mashed potatoes before I hand it to Patrick, who takes the seat next to me. When he's done, I scoop some onto my nephew's plate and then push Cody closer to the table so he doesn't end up with food all over his lap.

Leaning over to him, I whisper, "You feeling better, little dude? Heard you had to go to the doctor."

"He gave me dwops." He points to his ear and smiles. "All bettuh."

I give him a high five.

Today, he's my shadow, mimicking me every time I reach for my drink or take a bite. When I make a silly face at him, he imitates me.

"Eat your dinner, goofball. Or it'll get cold."

Five minutes later, my mother is still gushing over Joey like she hasn't seen her in years. "Child, my garden has missed you! I swear everything wilted after you left."

Hell, *I* wilted after she left.

I smile as I watch my mom and Joey bond over the vegetable garden they always worked on together.

Joey pulls out her phone. "I saw this really cool technique for growing fruit trees we could try. Since you've always wanted peach trees..."

I zone out, content simply to have Jo back in our house, but then my mother starts fawning over her again. "Look at this gorgeous hair. I miss the pink you had in last winter, but I love this shade too!"

Next thing I know, my mom's talked Joey into taking her hair out of the bun, and then her thick, golden locks are spilling over her shoulders and down her chest. Across that tiny tank top and amplifying that killer cleavage.

Fuckkk.

I stare, slack-jawed, like I'm watching one of those models on Instagram shake out her hair before she vamps for the camera.

But Joey doesn't vamp. She blushes fiercely and glances down, somehow looking more enticing through that veil of shyness.

Patrick bumps me, murmuring under his breath, "Think I just came in my pants, bro."

I press both of my palms into my eye sockets until I see stars behind my lids as I try to right this ship.

One, I won't kick Patrick's ass for having the same thoughts I'm currently entertaining.

Two, I won't give into the urge to wrap a blanket around Joey.

And three, I definitely won't haul her, caveman-style, back to my place.

Thankfully, after my mom stops doting, Joey tucks her hair back up into that big twisty knot, an action which I avoid watching.

Across the table, my brother's having a private conversation with Tori. Well, it ain't private enough because they're making goo-goo eyes at each other, and I can almost hear Marvin Gaye crooning *Let's Get It On* in the background.

Their love for each other is so palpable, I'm almost jealous.

That's another reason I can't unload my secrets. My brother believes in love. Believes in those happily-ever-after stories my parents fed us as kids. All this despite Ethan's disastrous first marriage.

Tori made him believe in fairytales again, and I'm not gonna be the one to burst that bubble. For his sake and Tori's, I hope they're the exception to the rule. They're happy, and that's all that matters to me.

Blowing out a breath, I stretch my neck from one side and then the other, realizing how tense I am and that I probably just need to get laid. It's been months since I've been with anyone, and between the family business, Joey returning, my brother's wedding, and all the shit that shouldn't be my responsibility but is, I'm wound tight.

Of course, that would require time I don't have to socialize in ways I'm not interested in.

Whatever the solution to my wayward thoughts, one thing is clear—I need to stay away from Joey until they subside. And that shouldn't be too hard. She'll probably bunk here where my mother will monopolize all of her time until Ethan's wedding.

I'm not sure how long I tune out and mindlessly gulp down dinner, but my mother's next question makes me pause with my fork halfway to my mouth.

"Joey, honey." My mom's voice carries over everyone else's. "When are you headed back to Florida?"

Unease crawls up my spine. I've been so preoccupied with her return that I hadn't thought about her leaving again.

She shrugs, her eyes catching mine before she looks away. "Probably in two weeks, so a few days after the wedding."

Twin spikes of pain and hunger launch through me. Pain that this visit will probably be the last time I see her in the foreseeable future, and hunger for something I can never have and shouldn't want.

I grip my fork and, before I can help myself, blurt out, "Why aren't you staying longer?"

After a long silence, Joey sighs. "I was barely making ends meet here. At least in Florida I can work for my cousin, who's opening a new salon."

"But that's 'cause you were paying everyone else's bills." Her good-for-nothing brother would rack up debt and let his little sister deal with it, like she didn't have her hands full enough with her grandmother, who had early-onset dementia. One minute Rosalie would be lucid and the next she'd be calling Joey by her mother's name, the mother who died when Joey was twelve.

My heart swells for her. Jo's been through so much, but you'd never know it. She's always so sweet and loving despite the hand she drew in life. No wonder my family grafted her on like she's one of ours.

"I just think it'd be easier if I left." The resignation in her voice kills me.

I consider all the times she's given me pep talks, and I wanna be that same voice of optimism for her. "What if you got a job in Austin? It would probably pay more than staying local." Our town is barely a speck on the map.

"And where am I supposed to stay?" Now she looks pissed, not at me necessarily. I mean, I don't think. "Silas sold the house. I'm guessing Gran's Buick isn't sitting in the driveway waiting for me. What am I supposed to do? Ride a bike to work in the Texas heat? Borrow one of your horses and hoof it to work?" She laughs, unamused and sounding much older than her twenty-two years. "I'm tired of everything being so difficult. Don't you ever want life to work out? For the universe to tell you that you're on the right path because the dominoes line up? And I'm not talking about working hard. I mean not always feeling like I'm swimming upstream all the time."

Patrick sets down his fork. "Did you know that after salmon swim upstream, they lay their eggs and die?"

I narrow my eyes at him. Seriously?

"What? It's true. I saw this documentary on National

Geographic. Most go back to the place they were born to kick the bucket." He slurps up a giant bite of mashed potatoes. "And apparently you can eat them once they're dead. It's not weird or anything, like barbecuing roadkill. That is, if the salmon aren't gobbled up first by a bear or beaver."

Everyone stares at him.

Mila turns to her dad. "What's roadkill? And have we barbecued it?"

Ethan gives me a look like this is my fault.

Needing to redirect this conversation, I motion between my mother and brother. "Is there any way to challenge the sale of Rosalie's house?"

The expressions on their faces say it all. Ethan's brows pull tight. "Doubtful. The new family's already living there."

My mom pats Joey's hand gently. "I was so sorry to hear about your grandmother. She was a lovely woman. When I heard the news, I lit a candle for her at church."

"Thank you. That means a lot to me."

"Sorry, Jo. I know that had to be hard. We all loved Gran." I clear my throat. It killed me to not be there for her when Rosalie died.

But then again, I didn't find out until weeks after she passed when Tori mentioned it.

I might still be a little butthurt Jo didn't tell me herself. Fine —I'm pissed about it, but I know that's immature, so I try to think of something more consoling to say.

"Silas is an ass for selling that house." Yeah, I might need to work on my condolences.

God, I am a fuck-up.

Thankfully, Joey's expression tells me she knows what I mean.

I point at the kids before they get up in arms about the curse word. "For your information, 'ass' means 'donkey.'"

Mila tilts her head, staring up at her dad, the oracle of wisdom and all things holy in her eyes. "So I can say 'ass' if I mean 'donkey?' Like, 'look at that big ass crossing the road?'"

Ethan glares at me, and I laugh under my breath.

"What I don't understand," Tori mulls aloud, drawing away the ire of my brother, "is how Silas had the authority to sell that house."

We look to Joey, and she shakes her head. "Maybe Silas was on the deed. There's no telling what he had Gran sign. At least this time he wasn't forging her checks to cash her social security."

"I'd like to give Silas a piece of my mind and maybe a foot up his ass." Tori slaps a hand over her mouth and looks between the kids. "I mean donkey! Dang it, sorry, guys. I'm a bad girl."

She has a mouth worse than mine, but it's one of the reasons I like her so much. But Ethan doesn't take issue with her like he did with my curse word. I'm close enough to hear him whisper, "Yeah, but you're *my* bad girl."

I hold back a gag. Barely.

When Cody lodges a cheesy noodle up his nose, I decide I'd rather deal with that than watch the ongoing foreplay between brother and future sister-in-law.

As I'm dislodging the offending pasta, Joey clears her throat. "Guys, can I ask a favor? I hate imposing, but I was wondering if I could stay here for a few days. I only found out about Silas selling the house this afternoon, and I'm too furious to track him down to stay with him. I need some time to cool off, since our great state of Texas takes things like murder seriously."

My mother pipes up before the words are barely out of Joey's mouth. "Certainly, dear. It's no imposition."

Joey smiles gratefully but then looks to Ethan and Tori. You know, since they're the ones who live here. My mother technically lives with me, but she likes to hop between my house and Ethan's.

"Of course." My brother doesn't hesitate. "If you don't mind squeezing in with Tori's family."

Cody tugs on my T-shirt and I lean toward him.

"I hafta poop."

Chuckling, I motion for him to go. "Thanks for the news alert, but I think you can manage."

His little lips twist in concern. "I can't weach my booty to wipe."

Ah, the joys of being an uncle. But the kid is almost four, and I'm thinking we need to take this to the next level.

I whisper, "How 'bout you go do your thing, and I'll wait outside the door. If you need any help, I'll lend a hand."

Or maybe I'll just ball up some toilet paper and nudge it in his direction because I'm really tired of wiping kids' asses. And their noses and vomit too, if I'm being honest.

Nodding, he hops out of his chair, and we excuse ourselves.

When he's done doing his business, I make sure he washes his hands with soap this time. As we head back to the dining room, I'm feeling better about things.

I'll get a little space tonight and clear my head. Kick back with a beer and ESPN. Get a good night's sleep. And maybe jerk it a few times before I see Joey again. Then I won't have these crazy ideas messing with my head.

I'm helping Cody climb into his seat again when my mom claps her hands. "Then it's settled. Joey will stay with Logan so I can help Ethan with the kids and Tori can spend more time with her parents when they get here." Then little Miss Beverly June Carter, matchmaker extraordinaire, winks at me. "Son, isn't this perfect?"

Internally I groan. Perfectly torturous.

I'm scrambling to think of a reason why this won't work when Patrick decides to get in on the action.

"Joey can always stay with me. I have a big bed."

This time, four words crystallize in my head: *Over my dead body.*

6

JOEY

By the time we drop off Patrick at his place and drive back to Logan's, the sun has set.

Logan's been quiet the *entire* drive. His silence is getting on my nerves because something obviously crawled up his butt at dinner.

"You could've left me at Patrick's if me staying here bothers you."

"It's fine. I don't mind you staying with me."

It's too dark to see his face, so I have no way of knowing whether he's lying. For the record, he lies a lot. Another excellent reason I should get over this infatuation with him. A smart girl wouldn't waste her time loving a man who lies. But I'm what you'd call book smart. Hand me a test, and I know how to study for it. Give me a book, and I can devour it in a day. But drop me off in a five-mile radius of Logan Carter, and I fold faster than my brother when there's a bill to pay.

What I notice, though, is how Logan doesn't say he *wants* me to stay at his place. He said *he doesn't mind*. Big difference.

Why do I torture myself like this? It's not like I can throw myself at him and make him love me. And that's so desperate.

Someday, I promise myself, I'll get to a place in my life where I don't feel like a fool.

When we pull up to his farmhouse, all of the lights are out except one that shines from the kitchen. It brings a host of memories of us enjoying movie marathons and hanging out with friends.

It's weird that I've been here a million times over the years, but I've never stayed the night.

Logan moved here shortly after he graduated from high school. Since Ethan was getting married, the main Carter house was too small for Bev, Logan, Ethan, Allison—Ethan's ex—and baby Mila. So Logan got this bachelor pad to himself until Allison and Bev came to loggerheads, and Allison kicked Bev out of the family home. Nobody's missing Allison these days.

I turn toward the mountain of firewood along the side of the house. Once, when I was fifteen and too young to do anything fun, I sat there on a Saturday night with my girlfriend Misty and listened to a party Logan threw and wished I was older. Wished that he'd come out or I had the courage to go in.

I was worried about him. He'd been so distant after his father died. He didn't want to talk about what happened. Didn't call me anymore. Didn't want to hang out. I couldn't blame him. He'd graduated from high school. Why would he want to spend time with a sophomore?

But I wanted to talk to him so bad that I snuck out of the house, determined to make it happen.

Except I got here and couldn't take those last few steps.

From that sad pile of firewood in the shadows, we watched pretty girls with short skirts and loud guys stumble in and out for hours.

I heard the music blasting and the laughter.

The beer bottles clanging as they hit the trash bin.

The moans once it got late.

My face flushes with embarrassment at the thought.

I was insanely jealous and hurt and a thousand different emotions, though I didn't have the right to any of them seeing how I was basically a peeping tom.

I realized that was creepy, hanging out next to Logan's house during a party, even if we were friends, albeit somewhat estranged at the time.

I never told him I did that. I'd be mortified if he knew, though I only did it once. Trust me, I learned my lesson.

Even when I got older, I mostly avoided his parties. I could go my whole life without seeing another girl wrap herself around him.

Since high school, his fandom has only grown. Now Logan can't go anywhere without getting hit on. Once he started competing with his brother at cutting horse competitions a few years ago, his popularity among the female persuasion exploded. I'll be the first to admit he looks pretty dang fine in his Wranglers, but it's embarrassing to watch women trip all over themselves to hang out with him.

I must've cramped his style. And staying here with him certainly won't help matters, but it's not like I have other options.

When he presses his hand to the small of my back as we stroll up the front steps, I almost stumble. He might put me in headlocks, but he rarely puts his hands on me otherwise.

So far today, he's hugged me so hard he lifted me off the ground, he threaded our fingers together as we held hands, and he's ushered me along with his hand on my back.

But who's counting? Not me.

Because I'd have to be a teeny bit crazy if one minute I'm debating whether he even wants me here, and the next, counting the number of times he's touched me.

"Wanna order a pizza?" he asks as he unlocks the door.

I sigh into the air-conditioned living room, and he sets my small suitcase on the ground. "How can you be hungry? You ate not two hours ago."

"By the time the pizza arrives, another hour will have passed, and by then I'll definitely need more food." He pats his trim stomach. "I'm a growing boy."

He gives me a sweet, almost silly smile, the one I love so much because it's just for me. None of his buddies are here to impress. None of his fangirls or buckle bunnies. Not even his family. Just me. Ignoring my racing heart, I reach up to cover his face with my hand and gently shove him out of the way.

"Your pretty little smiles won't work on me, Logan Carter." Now I'm the liar. "If you're growing it's because your head's so big you can't get it through the door. You really should get that condition checked by a doctor."

He laughs and turns on a few lights. "Missed you and your sass, Jojo. Order us an extra large. You know the drill."

The drill: I order and he pays.

He claims he likes when I order because I'm so nice on the phone that the pizza people would never spit in my food. It works for me because I never have any money to pay for takeout. Win-win.

By the time I'm done ordering, he's shucking off his boots and grabbing *a freaking puppy* from behind a child gate blocking off the kitchen.

I squeal. "When did you get a dog?" Oh, Lordy, I'm in love. "What's his name?"

A smile pulls at Logan's lips as he watches his puppy arf-arf in my face and try to lick my nose.

Logan pauses and tucks his hands in his back pocket. "I got Rambo last month at one of those side-of-the-road setups. He was the runt."

"Let me guess. You felt bad for him." He rolls his eyes

because it's true. Logan might act all big and tough, but he's got the biggest heart. "And you named the little guy Rambo. Aww." I talk in a baby voice to the dog. "That'll give you courage, huh, handsome?"

I probably sound like a freak, but I don't care because the dog likes my baby voice. He's a big ball of brown and white fur with an adorable face like he's a shih tzu or bichon. Like the kind of puppy I've always wanted, but we were too poor, and pets cost money. We never could've afforded vet bills, so I understood, although it didn't make me want one any less.

"It's hard to believe, but he was even smaller when I got him."

"He looks like a baby Ewok." I can let my inner Star Wars freak flag fly around Logan. We've watched the first six movies together in chronological order *and* in the order they were released. For the record, both of us prefer the original three movies.

His smile widens. "I knew you'd love him."

"Can I kiss him and name him George?" I butcher the reference, but I'm too high on puppy love to care.

Logan gives me a quizzical look, and I chuckle. "I forget you didn't like *Of Mice and Men*. I guess the end was sad." I read the classic out loud to him his freshman year. Yes, I was eleven, but he told me he wasn't going to do the assignment because he couldn't get into the book, so I sat his bratty little butt down behind the barn and read it to him. He Googled any words on his phone we didn't recognize. Between that and his study guide from class, we managed okay.

All I knew was I didn't want him to get in trouble with his teacher because then Mr. Carter wouldn't let Logan hang out with me. We spent the entire week eating Twizzlers and talking about Steinbeck.

Being young, poor, and stranded in the country isn't so bad if you like to read. Thank goodness there's a decent library nearby.

"You're the only reason I got a good grade that semester. You and your enormous brain." He taps on my forehead like a pest, and I swat him away.

"I like big books and I cannot lie."

I thought that week was a grand way to spend my afternoons even if I didn't understand everything about the story. Like why Curly kept his hand in a glove of Vaseline for his wife. I didn't get it at the time, and if Logan did, he didn't explain it to me.

One day at the market a few weeks ago, I was squeezing an avocado to check the ripeness when it dawned on me that Curly wanted to use that soft hand for sex. *Duh.*

Logan's phone buzzes in his back pocket, and when he checks it, he stills and glances at me, a guilty expression all over his face. "Need to take this. Make yourself at home."

My heart deflates as I watch him head toward his bedroom.

He's probably making plans with some hookup. And while he won't go about it in front of me—he makes a point never to do that—I'll hear about it from our friends. Because in a small town like this, someone always makes sure to tell me. Like they're honor-bound to feed me the gossip so I'll know the boy I've been pining over since I was a kid is a skirt-chaser.

Life is too short.

My thoughts wander to the bus ride here. Mrs. Reynolds is right. I need to rip off this Band-Aid and tell him how I feel. Maybe it won't make any difference. But before I leave for Florida, I'm going to tell Logan Carter I've been in love with him my whole life. Then my conscience will be clear, and maybe, *maybe* I'll finally be able to move on.

Because he obviously doesn't see me as anything but his friend.

Not if he's still making after-hours plans.

A sad sense of resolve settles over me.

Not wanting to overhear Logan making arrangements with another woman, I reach for the remote and click on the flatscreen, flipping channels until I land on *You've Got Mail*. Heck, yes, I could definitely use some Meg Ryan and Tom Hanks magic. A girl can never see that movie too many times.

I take a minute to call my cousin Dawn and let her know I'm alive.

She squeals in my ear. "Joey, the salon looks amazing! We just have to paint next weekend and hire two more stylists, and we'll be all set."

"I'm so sorry you're having to do all this work without me. I swear I'll make it up to you when I get back." The thought of leaving so soon feels like a leaden boulder on my chest, but I can't wait around here for Logan to get a clue.

Dawn and I catch up for a few minutes, and then she sighs. "How's the dickhead treating you?"

"He's been great, actually. Not a dickhead at all."

"Yet."

"Yet," I reluctantly admit.

In the background, I hear her mother mumbling something.

"My mom says not to let that boy bamboozle your heart again."

I chuckle and agree to be strong. After we get off the phone, I kick off my flip-flops and curl up on the couch and tuck Rambo under my arm.

It's a comfort to see that everything in the living room is the same. From the hand-me-down couch to the horse magazines on the coffee table and the worn recliner, it's tidy and clean. Logan's a neat guy and takes care of his things for the most part. And despite the money the farm is raking in these days, he lives a modest life.

Reaching behind me, I grab the blanket that's draped over

the back. Logan loves to keep the house chilly at night, probably because he works in a sweltering barn.

The long day catches up to me, though. Meg Ryan hasn't even met Tom Hanks yet when I pass out. I'm pretty sure I'm drooling on the puppy when a knock on the front door jars me awake.

"Keep the change."

Hearing Logan's voice makes me smile. I've missed him so much.

His footsteps draw near before the pizza box hits the coffee table. "Whatcha smiling about, Bitsy?"

My throat is scratchy and dry, but the words tumble out anyway. "Just like being here with you." It's an honest moment. Maybe too honest.

I crack open one eyelid to see how he's taken what I said, but he's grinning. Of course, food might be the reason for his joy. The couch dips with his weight.

"I like having you home too." He stuffs a slice in his mouth like he's been starved for a week.

Rambo nestles closer to my neck, and I take a big whiff of his sweet puppy fur.

Logan lifts an eyebrow. "Did you just sniff the dog?"

"Maybe." I scratch under his ear, and he pants in my face. "Though I have to say I never had you pegged for this kind of pet. I thought you'd get a rottie or a boxer."

Logan's eyes shift to me. "You saying Rambo isn't manly enough?"

I snort and shake my head. "No, I'm saying this fuzzball is more my speed than yours." Quietly, I add, "I always wanted a puppy, but my parents never let me get one." We didn't have the money for food and clothes, so a dog was out of the question. By the time it was just Silas and Gran, I had too much going on to take care of a pet.

"I remember." He returns his attention to ESPN. "You should have some pizza." Before I have a chance to respond, Logan tosses two slices on a paper plate and hands it to me. "Eat up, buttercup."

With a groan, I set Rambo on the ground and try to sit up, but every muscle in my body protests. I'm tangled in the blanket and too tired to deal. I flop back in defeat.

"You okay?" Logan unwinds the fabric from my body and helps me swing my legs to the floor.

"Just sore. Twenty-seven hours on a bus will do that to you." When he doesn't say anything, I glance over at him. His shoulders are tense, and his brows are tight. "Why are you ticked off?"

He runs a hand through his messy blond hair, an exasperated sound coming from his mouth. "Because you took a bus, by yourself, across the country, when you could've told me you were coming, and I would've gladly paid for your airline ticket. I saw the shady characters who came off the bus today. How many of them hit on you?"

"No need to get your panties in a twist, Sherlock. Did you happen to see the granny who sat next to me for most of the ride? I'll have you know she threatened the guy who made a pass at me, and I didn't have any problems after that."

That was the wrong thing to say because he looks angrier. "And what if Granny Do-Gooder hadn't been around? I'm grateful she was, but after I heard you were taking the bus, I Googled 'bus-related crimes,' and I read things that would light your hair on fire. Did you know a girl was beaten up at a rest stop in the bathroom? If you insist on going back to Florida, I'm buying your airline ticket, so don't sass me about it."

I open my mouth—to say what, I don't even know—but I close it again and stare at the boy I've loved nearly my whole life, gratitude filling my heart. "You don't need to worry about me, but thank you for caring."

He nods and grumbles, "We'll run you a bath tonight. That'll help your sore muscles."

He may only love me as a friend, but that's more than what I got from most of my family growing up. And maybe that's part of his allure. My parents were strict and narrow-minded and never affectionate. Would it have been so hard to give me a hug every once in a while?

In contrast, Logan's family never ran short on affection. His mother hugged me nearly every time she saw me. Logan used to hug me all the time too until I sprouted boobs, and then he migrated into these funny side hugs. I used to think he was afraid of my tits, but I knew his reputation, so I figured it was just *my* body that somehow freaked him out. Puberty *is* weird, so I couldn't blame him.

We eat in silence, side by side, the room dark except for the side table lamp, the light from the kitchen, and the TV.

"What's on the agenda this week?" My teeth sink into a slice of pepperoni. Heaven. "Tori said you would help me coordinate, Mr. Wedding Planner."

"Ha, ha. I only helped her get the flowers because I have a friend." He gives me a good-natured shove and pulls out his phone. "Let me text Tori for the schedule."

A minute later, his phone vibrates, and he swipes it open, and he frowns.

"What's wrong?"

He hands it to me. "Nothing. Just a lot going on."

Tori sent a detailed spreadsheet with the wedding party itinerary. Wednesday the girls have a dress fitting. On Thursday, we're having a family lunch with Tori's parents. And on Friday, the weekend before the wedding...

My eyes dart to Logan. "We're going to the coast?"

"Guess so." He sighs.

It's a joint bachelor-bachelorette weekend. It looks like most of the wedding party and a few friends are going.

"There's a link to the condo." Oh, wow. "This looks like fun. What a cool idea." I'm so excited, I almost forget I can't afford it. "But... how much is this going to cost?" I saved up for my bus ticket and dress and a few nights eating out, but this will blow my budget. Plus, I still have to buy some clothes since who knows what Silas did with my stuff. I didn't pack a ton because I figured I had a few outfits at my grandmother's house. Which the mother-effer sold.

Logan reaches for a napkin. "I got you covered, home slice. You're good to go."

This. He's always doing things like this, which makes it hard to keep those walls erected around my heart.

I swallow past the lump in my throat. "I'll pay you back. I promise." Even if it means I skip lunch every day for a month, I'll pay him back.

Sure, I used to feel like he took me for granted sometimes, but he still looked out for me.

"Jo." He waits until I look at him. "You don't owe me anything. This is what friends do for each other. You've always had my back, and I got yours. It ain't a big deal."

Friends. Right.

I can pretend all I want this is enough, but when he says that word, it feels like a neon DO NOT ENTER sign above his heart.

I nod and force a smile on my face. "Well, thank you. I'm grateful." I truly am.

But if I'm going to get through the next two weeks, this is a good reminder of where I stand with him. Even if I make my big declaration about how I feel, I won't get my hopes up because chances are slim to none that he feels the same way.

7

LOGAN

Rambo trots after me, his tiny paws clicking on the hardwood floor down the hall.

Joey's bedroom door is ajar, and I peek in, smiling when I see her flopped like a starfish on my mom's bed, the blankets and sheets a heap around her. I close the door quietly so I don't wake her up when I rummage through the kitchen.

It's barely five am, and I'm not expected at the ranch for a few hours, but I need to run some errands first. The wedding activities are throwing a wrench in my schedule. I'd completely forgotten about Ethan and Tori's plans for the weekend, which is not like me, but I've been running on fumes.

I feed the pooch and scratch his head. He's damn cute for a puffball. "Be fierce, my man. Look after Jo."

Grabbing my keys, I head for the door. I'm not sure I told Joey I had to work today, but I'll send her a text later so I don't wake her up. I hate when my phone buzzes on the night table and wakes me. Sleep is a precious commodity, and that girl is exhausted.

After our late-night pizza, I ran her a bath, and she was so sore, I could hear her moaning and groaning through the door as she changed her clothes.

That sent my filthy mind into overtime.

And I might've had a weak moment.

Once we both went to bed, I locked myself in my room and sought out my favorite porn on my phone, but nothing did the trick. I threw it on my bed, closed my eyes, and everything I'd tried to ignore yesterday came rushing back to me. Like Jojo's incredible body in that tank top and how she'd felt when I'd hugged her at the bus station. The way her thick golden hair tumbled over her shoulders and her voice when we talked on the couch, low and sweet and soft.

I popped off like a firecracker on the Fourth of July.

Now I'm feeling the guilt. I've always managed to avoid jerking it to thoughts of my best friend, and I need to get this shit on lockdown if I want to survive living with her for the next two weeks. No more naked thoughts of Joey.

I stop at the gas station to fill the tank and grab a crappy cup of coffee, and then I'm on the road again. When I get to the Stock Yard, I'm the first one here, but that's nothing new.

The Stock Yard is a mom-and-pop store two towns over that sells everything a rancher could need. I've worked in the back, restocking their supplies and taking inventory a few times a week for the past two years, usually in the middle of the night. But since Ethan's wedding and honeymoon take precedence, I need to rearrange my schedule.

An hour later, I've shelved the incoming feeds and reordered everything on my list when Hank, my boss, arrives.

"Well, I'll be damned." He gives me a wide smile. "I could've sworn you were a vampire. I don't think I've ever seen you here during the day."

I let out a laugh. "Thanks for calling me back so late last

night. This wedding stuff is more high-maintenance than I thought. Won't be able to do any late-night shifts until the end of the month."

"You do what you got to do for family. I understand." He wipes his sweaty forehead. "You gonna take some time off for yourself after that? Been burning the midnight oil for a long time now, son."

I know he wants to ask me why I do this when I run a successful business with my brother, but Hank's good people and knows when something's private, so he never pushes.

"Nah. I couldn't bear it if everything went to hell while I was away." I give him an easy smile and reach for my keys. "I'll be back tomorrow to take care of the rest here, but then I'm headed out of town for the weekend with my brother and the wedding party. I'll hopefully get a chance to work Monday night. But I'll keep you updated."

He nods thoughtfully. "If you need more time, just let me know."

More time off means not getting paid, which means I can't do it. "Thanks again, sir."

I don't have to call him 'sir,' but he works himself to the bone for his family, for his lovely wife and kids and grandkids, and has nothing but my respect. Fidelity and loyalty are tough things for some guys to grasp, but he's a shining example of what a man can have if he keeps it in his pants.

As I'm crossing the parking lot, my phone rings. Only three people call me this early, and since I'm about to see Ethan and my mother, I'm guessing it's not them.

The name flashes on my phone, and I let it go to voice mail.

Speaking of fidelity...

I'm running late, and if I pick up now, there's no telling how long this call will take.

A text comes through as I'm starting the truck.

Stop avoiding me.

I roll my eyes and reluctantly respond. *I'm not avoiding you. I need to get to work. Texting while driving is illegal, remember?*

Are you trying to be charming? I'm in no mood for your games.

I laugh out loud. *I'm* the one playing games? Jesus Christ, the balls on this woman.

Samantha used to be laid back, but in the last several months she's become super clingy. I make a mental note to encourage her to go back to school where she can make more friends, and then I try to redirect this conversation.

I promised Zach I'd take him to the movies to see the new Marvel flick.

Is Zach all you care about?

Pretty much. Yeah. But she already knows the score. *Can we talk later? I promise I'll call you tonight.*

My phone is blissfully silent after that last message. I already know what she wants, and it ain't happening.

When I eventually pull up to the ranch, I have a headache that might split my brain in two, but I plaster on a smile as I stroll into the kitchen.

"You're late." Ethan glares at me over his breakfast. He looks like he's already put in a good two or three hours in the barn judging by the sweat soaking his T-shirt.

"Dad always said, 'Better late than never.' Sorry, I needed my beauty sleep." I hate quoting my father, but this headache is taking its toll on my ability to bullshit.

Tori hands me a plate heaping with pancakes, and I press my hand over my heart. "Swear to God, if Ethan wasn't marrying you, I would."

Ethan grunts his annoyance, and I chuckle under my breath. I love to get under his skin. Call it the little brother syndrome, but I take great pleasure in yanking his balls. Tori's hot, sure, but she and Ethan have always had eyes for each other, and they know I respect that.

Tori smiles and sinks into Ethan's lap as she waves at me. "You're a little scrawny for my taste."

My brother gives her one of those googly-eyed smiles, and just like that, they're off in their own little world, and he's talking in that gentle voice he only uses with her or the kids. "I'm sweaty, baby."

"S'okay. I don't mind." She gazes at Ethan for a second before she plants a kiss on his cheek.

I cough and get back to her diss. "Scrawny? Ouch. And here I was planning to get y'all something nice for your wedding." Damn. I need to get them a gift. I'd forgotten about that.

She slides the syrup to me. "You know you don't need to buy us anything. We love having you around. In fact, you're the brutha I always wanted." She makes a goofy face at me. My brother is so damn lucky.

"Shucks, Tor. Now I *really* need to get y'all something nice." I make a mental note to pick Joey's brain. She'll know what I should get. "Unless I can just go with that homemade coupon book with free babysitting that I saw on Pinterest?"

Tori's head jerks up. "If you think for a moment I won't jump on that and suck up your Saturday nights, think again, stud." She picks a piece of turkey bacon off Ethan's plate and takes a nibble. "And since when do you use Pinterest?"

"I'm a man of many talents."

"Clearly."

I shovel in a few bites of breakfast. "Where're the kids? It's too quiet."

Ethan points over his shoulder. "With Mom. She's playing Legos with them."

With my fork halfway to my mouth, I pause. "Don't let her overdo it. She'll tell you she's not tired when she is."

"You do know our mother is an adult, right? She tells me when she's had enough."

This bonehead. "Don't you know anything about women? She only tells you when she's at her breaking point, which is well beyond what she should do."

Ethan shakes his head at me. "That's really good advice. Maybe you should think on that a little longer."

Tori elbows him.

"What?" I look between the two of them. "What aren't you saying?"

But two tiny demons stomp down the hall and interrupt the conversation.

"I'm starving!" Cody announces as he swipes his arm across his nose.

Tori reaches over to wipe his face with a napkin. "You two eat more than hobbits. Come on. Time for second breakfast." She pulls out a big bowl of sliced fruit and settles the kids at the table.

When I'm done eating, I rinse my plate and tuck it away in the dishwasher. "What time do you need Joey for the dress fitting tomorrow?"

"Can you bring her here at three?" Tori reaches for a napkin to clean a glop of something that flew off Cody. "The fitting isn't until the evening, but I want to take her shopping."

"I can take her shopping. What does she need?"

"Oh, I don't know. Everything?" I stare at Tori, confused, and she sighs like I'm a dunderhead. "She was planning to pick up more clothes at her grandmother's..."

She pauses while I piece together the clues.

"But Silas probably threw out her stuff when he sold the house." God, I'm a moron. "Of course she needs more clothes."

Tori gives me a patient smile. "So three o'clock?"

"Let me take her shopping tomorrow."

She folds her lips between her teeth for a second. "Sounds good. But be sure you make suggestions because you know she won't tell you she needs anything."

"Okay. Yeah. Like what?"

I get out my phone to take notes.

"I don't know. Shirts, shorts, bras, underwear, a swimsuit, tampons..."

"Whoa. *Whoa.* That seems awfully personal. You want me to say, 'Hey, do you need tampons?' She'll curl up and hide behind a giant bin of Cheerios."

Mila waves in my face from her seat next to me. "What are tampons?"

I blink slowly. "Nose plugs. For when you get a nose bleed."

"Don't tell her that." Tori laughs. "Honey, they're for females. We can talk about it tonight, okay?" She glances at Ethan and he nods.

I swipe an apple slice from the platter. "They *are* good for nose bleeds. I speak from experience. When Kimmy Schumacher's brother punched me in the face for kissing his sister, she gave me a tampon for the bleeding. Worked really well."

Ethan chugs down the last of his coffee. "It's amazing you're as pretty as you are considering how many people have taken a swing at you over the years."

"Aww, bro. I'm touched." I pretend to cry and the kids crack up. "Okay, so I'll take Joey shopping, and I'll be sure to ask if she needs feminine products." God help me.

I'm not squeamish about things like that, but Bitsy gets embarrassed easily, especially around me for some reason.

And fine, I'll admit addressing things that go in particular parts of her body I try not to think about might make me uncomfortable.

"You sure she can wait 'till tomorrow? I got too many things to do today or I'd run her into town this evening."

Tori nods. "I grilled her last night, and she said she just needed to do some laundry, and she'd be fine. I think that'll get her by for a little while, but definitely not for her whole visit."

I down the rest of my coffee, mentally tallying the tasks I can get done today to clear up my schedule for Joey's shopping trip tomorrow.

"How'd she like her puppy?" my brother asks as he get up.

"Um." I scratch the scruff on my chin. "Didn't tell her."

Wide-eyed, Tori gasps. "Why not?" She starts muttering to herself, something about serving it up on a silver platter, but then trails off.

"Did you miss the part about her going back to Florida? Can she have pets at her place? If I had known she wasn't staying, I would've thought this through better." Staying here means I could've helped her with the pup while she settled in.

I was so excited to give her the gift, but now I feel like a dumbass for not being smarter.

A darkness settles over me when I try to imagine what it'll be like if she leaves permanently. There'll be a Joey-sized crater in my life, and I'm not sure I'm ready for it.

Tori taps on the table. "You overthink everything. Just give her the dog already. Who knows, maybe that will help persuade her to stay? Trust me—she'll be ecstatic about the gift."

It's funny how most people think I'm impulsive, but Tori's been here a few years and she knows me better than that. Well, maybe my younger self was impulsive, but the grown version of me has a mortgage, bills, and too many responsibilities to count, so I have to be smarter.

My mother waltzes in, looking no worse for wear after playing with the kids this morning. "Who'll be ecstatic?"

I can't handle any more talk about Joey, so I thank Tori for breakfast, kiss my mom on the top of her head, and leave the peanut gallery while I make my way to the barn behind the house.

At least the horses won't ask me what I'll do with myself if Joey leaves for good.

8

JOEY

With a pained groan, I roll over and blink at the clock on the bedside table. I can't believe it's almost noon. Beverly's bed is ten times more comfortable than mine in Florida.

That bus ride wore me out, and I nearly slept myself into a coma last night.

Rambo's wet nose peeks over the bed.

"Hey, handsome."

He wags his tail happily, unaware of the knot in the pit of my stomach. While I'm still pissed as hell at my brother for selling Gran's house, this is the longest I've gone without talking to him. He could be partying in Vegas or lying in a ditch for all I know.

Reaching for my cell phone, I speed-dial my brother and get the same outgoing message: "Leave a message or don't. Nobody cares."

Charming, isn't he?

"Silas, hey. It's me. You're starting to freak me out a little. Call me so I know you're alive." I don't bring up the house because if I nag him over the phone, he'll never call back. "I'm leaving again for Florida soon, so I hope to hear from you."

When I hang up, I scoop up Rambo and snuggle him. His

furry face makes me smile even though I don't much feel like smiling.

Hunger gets the best of me, so I shuffle into the kitchen, pour some coffee, and pop two slices of bread in the toaster. Plopping down at the kitchen table, I tuck my bare legs under my shirt—Logan's T-shirt—and get comfy.

Pulling the neck of the material to my nose, I breathe in his yummy scent. He tossed it to me last night as we were getting ready for bed. I hadn't even asked him for it, but he seemed to know I could use something to sleep in. It's a shirt I got him for his birthday last year that has a keg on the front and says "I'd tap that."

Once I'm done eating, I decide to attack that pile of dirty clothes in my suitcase. I pause when I walk by Logan's room, wondering if I should do his laundry too as thanks for letting me stay here. But handling someone's dirty clothes seems too personal. He might not want me touching his stuff. I have a brother. I know boys are disgusting. My brother went through more socks his senior year of high school than I went through my entire childhood.

Silas used to tackle me to the ground to rub his dirty socks in my face. He thought he was hysterical.

It was probably a blessing that I never understood why they were hard and crusty until I was older. I shudder at the memory.

There are worse things than crusty socks, though. I eye Logan's laundry basket in the corner of his room. What if I stumble across another woman's clothes? Or condoms?

I blink back the sudden rush of heat in my eyes and scold myself for feeling hurt when I have no claim whatsoever to Logan. But this is my pattern. I know enough about what he does when I'm not around to get crushed.

Nope. Definitely not touching his laundry.

By the time the washer buzzes, I'm over my emotional crisis.

I just need to keep reminding myself that I'll be back in Florida soon and I can survive whatever happens here in the meanwhile.

I'm dangling over the ledge of the washer, reaching for my shorts that are plastered to the bottom, when a cough behind me makes me lose my balance and I nearly knock my head against the agitator. A second later, two large hands settle over my hips, and I'm lifted out of the enormous Whirlpool machine.

My face is ten shades of red when I make eye contact with Logan, who's laughing so hard, he can barely breathe. "You fell in."

I yank my T-shirt down over my butt. "Shut up. I'm tiny. How the heck does your mom do laundry with this thing anyway? She's not that much bigger than I am."

He reaches behind a cabinet and pulls out a step stool.

"Oh." I cover one bare foot with the other, wondering how much of my rear he just saw. "What are you doing home? Didn't you say you were working late today?"

Shrugging, he runs his hands through his damp hair. He smells like clean sweat and the sun. I'm guessing he changed his T-shirt before he came home, though, because it's not soaked like he just walked out of a sweltering barn. "Thought you might want some company for lunch. Wasn't sure how much food I had in the fridge, and I didn't want you to starve. Brought home a few basics. Eggs. Lunch meat. Some frozen pizzas."

It doesn't matter that we ordered pizza last night. He'd eat that for every meal if left to his own devices. "Red Baron?"

"Of course." He grins at me, and for a second, I'm swept up in those blue eyes.

Smiling back, because I can't help but be pleased I know things about him other women don't, I motion toward the kitchen. "I could make some sandwiches. You probably want something quick so you can get back to work. Or would you like some eggs and tots?"

He nods comically, and my smile widens because I know how much he loves eggs and tots. We discovered this combo the summer before I started high school. If you brown tater tots and crumble them up as you stir in the eggs, you get a delicious treat. "I would fucking love that."

His exuberance makes me laugh. "Do you have any tots?"

"Oh, I have tots, baby, and I've been saving them for you."

We both freeze, like we've tripped an invisible wire.

Awareness prickles my skin.

Logan has ten million nicknames for me, but he's never, and I mean, *never* called me "baby."

And call me crazy, but that sounded an awful lot like flirting.

Something warm stirs in my chest, and it battles with the cynical voice in the back of my head that says he's so used to calling his hookups that name, it slipped out.

Rambo busts in and jumps between us, breaking the spell. Logan disappears but returns a minute later to toss me a pair of sweats. "Till your clothes dry." He clutches his T-shirt at the neckline and pitches his voice up an octave. "So you don't try to take advantage of my virtue."

"You wish." Giggling, I shove his handsome mug away from me.

But yeah, maybe I do wish.

9

LOGAN

Joey's been in my kitchen before, probably dozens of times, but today, for some reason, I can't take my eyes off her.

Her hair's piled in a knot on top of her head, and my giant T-shirt slips off her slender shoulder. My sweats, which she rolled three times around her waist, hang loose from her hips.

If I ask her, I know she'll say she's a hot mess.

But to me? I've never seen her look more beautiful.

No makeup. No designer clothes. Just Jojo. The girl I've always known.

I reach down to adjust the goods.

Chill the fuck out, man. First you flirt with her in the utility room, now you're watching her like a perv.

I wipe my palm over my face, needing to stamp out whatever's going on in my head.

When she was bent over the washer, and I got an eyeful of her tight round ass in those little cheeky panties, the only thought registering in my pea-sized brain was how much I'd like to take a bite out of that. And then fuck it.

See? Pea-sized brain. Because nothing good will come from these urges.

Hitting on Joey is the worst idea I've ever had. Joey's built for happily-ever-afters and white knights and shit, and I'm a Friday night fuck against my Ford and a few good laughs.

I force my eyes off my best friend and grab my phone to distract myself.

"Why is there so much ice on these?" Joey asks, shaking the bag of taters in the freezer.

"Probably 'cause they've been there since winter." As I scroll through my feed, my eyes glaze over the images. "What?" I can feel Joey staring at me.

"Haven't you had eggs and tots since then?"

"Who's gonna make them for me, Jo? You know I can't cook for shit." I burn them every time. "My mom won't eat frozen potatoes to save her life, my brother thinks it's a sacrilege, and Tori mixes in chilis and vegetables." Tori's don't taste bad, but it's not the same as Joey's. I shrug. "Anyway, it's weird eating that without you. Maybe next time don't leave so damn long so I don't starve."

Now I'm just being a cock, because she doesn't need to cook for me, and I know this, but I'm still sorta pissed she left in the first place.

Her shoulders droop, and that smile she's been sporting this afternoon fades.

Nice job, dick. No wonder she wants to move halfway across the country.

"Hey. I'm kidding. I don't mean to give you a hard time."

The sound of the chair pulling away from the table makes me look up. Joey sits and fidgets with her hands. "I'm s-sorry I didn't call you from Florida. I guess... I needed to get some perspective."

Reaching over, I grab her hand. "I know you're not ready to talk about it, and I respect that. I just need to ask you one question."

She nods slowly, but I can see the hesitation in her eyes.

"Did I do something or say something that hurt your feelings? Is that why you left? Because, Jo, I swear I'm making myself mental trying to figure out if I did. If that's why you ghosted me. Because I'm a cock and you finally realized it."

Her eyes fill with tears, and it's a knife to my stony, black heart.

But she doesn't say anything.

There's my answer.

Fuck. *Fuck.*

"Whatever it was, Bitsy, I'm so sorry. You know I'd never hurt you on purpose. You're my best friend. I don't know what to do with myself without you." I squeeze her hand, my soul shredding with every tear that streams down her face. "Let me make it up to you. I know I get all up in my own shit and take you for granted, but I promise I'll be a better friend. From here on, I swear."

She wipes her eyes, and I can't stand it anymore. I pull her out of her chair and into my lap where I squeeze her to me. She cries softly, and I kiss her head and rub my hand down her back.

"You're important to me, Jo," I say softly. "Don't leave me like that again, okay? I know I might not always have you here by my side, but stay in touch. I get worried about you. And no matter where you go, you're always gonna be my best friend. You have to know that."

She nods, and I squeeze her tighter.

I've had a few good friends in my life. Once upon a time Silas, then Joey and my buddy Isaiah, who doesn't get home much anymore. I know better than to think Patrick is a good friend. He might hang around a lot, but only 'cause it's convenient. Of all my friends, Jojo is my ride-or-die. She'd bury a body in my back yard if I asked her to.

I chuckle, and she sniffles and looks up. "Why are you laughing?"

"You, squirt." I kiss her forehead and smack her on the ass. "So we gonna eat or what? I'm hungry enough to try cooking for us, but I know it'll suck."

"No, you're banned from cooking. I got you."

I smile at my favorite girl. "I know you do."

10

JOEY

BRIDESMAIDS DRESSES MAY BE NOTORIOUSLY UGLY, BUT I'M stunned silent by the silky-smooth material cascading around me as I twirl in front of a three-way mirror. "This is the prettiest dress I've ever worn. I feel like a princess."

Tori claps behind me. "You look like a princess. That rosy color looks amazing on you, and the cut is so flattering. Maybe I should make you wear something uglier so you don't upstage me," she teases.

Olga, our seamstress, prods my side. "I take in here. You skinnier than before."

Back in Florida, my aunt took me to a dressmaker to get my measurements so I could send them to Tori. I can't imagine creating something like this simply by knowing a few numbers. This woman has some crazy skills.

I shake my head. "It leaves room for me to enjoy a few tacos. This is such a beautiful dress, Olga. Thank you so much."

Once I'm back in a pair of jeans and a T-shirt, I wait for Olga and Tori at the front of the cozy shop, next to an old-fashioned cash register. With my debit card in hand, I brace myself for the final amount.

"Everything is paid," Olga calls to me as she ambles closer.

That's not right. "I only sent you the down payment, remember? I'm pretty sure there's a balance."

"Bride has discount for big party. You all set."

Tori joins me and gives me a bright smile. "Let's hit the road. Logan looks antsy." My eyes dart outside to Logan, who's leaning against the window, scrolling through his phone.

"But—"

She grabs my arm and yanks me forward while I call out to Olga, "If it's a mistake and I owe you money, please let me know."

"Thanks, Olga! You're the best!" Tori calls behind us as the door swings closed and practically pushes me toward Logan. "You guys really should get going before it's too late."

"Too late for what? I thought we were hanging out tonight."

"Nope. You're going with Logan. Have fun, and don't forget to get sunscreen." Tori wraps me in a hug and then hops in her truck and zooms off.

I watch her speed away. "Did Tori just ditch me? That girl is part tornado, I swear." I turn to Logan. "What am I missing?"

Laughing, he puts his big hand on my shoulder and maneuvers me to the passenger side of his truck. "We got errands to run, home slice."

He's freshly showered after working all day, and the ends of his dirty blond hair are damp and curl against his baseball cap. He smells so good, I could lick him. "Wedding errands? Cool. I've been wanting to do more to help."

I'd hoped to wake up early and have breakfast with Logan, except he was long gone by the time I got up, but at least we get to hang out now.

I'm still dying a little from what he told me yesterday. Because Logan is not big on apologies. He's more likely to do something nice for you than apologize.

Once I'm loaded in the truck, Logan closes my door, and I watch him as he strolls to the other side.

A breathless sigh rushes out of me as I study the broad set of his shoulders and the way those worn jeans hug his muscular thighs. He hasn't shaved, and his jaw is covered in a golden scruff I want to rub against. And that smile he shoots me, the one that crinkles the corners of his eyes and looks a bit mischievous? I feel it all the way down to my toes.

When he starts the truck, I flip on the radio and search for a good song. "Sorry that took so long. I wanted to see Tori's dress, and we had to do my fitting too."

"It's fine. I didn't mind."

"She is going to be the most beautiful bride. I'm so excited for her and Ethan. They deserve to be happy after... everything." He nods. If anyone knows what Ethan and Tori went through, it's Logan. "I hope their big day is perfect."

I tap the dash twice with my fist, and Logan rolls his eyes because he thinks I'm ridiculous for using plastic to 'knock on wood.'

When we pull into Target, I sigh with delight. I might not have much money right now, but wandering through the aisles of this store always puts me in a good mood.

We grab a cart, and I put on my no-nonsense hat. "Okay, what do we need? Did Tori give you a list?"

"Sorta." He pulls out his phone, stares at what I'm assuming is the list, and then back at me. He opens his mouth but closes it again.

"Lay it on me. If we split it up, we can get this done quickly and be home for the end of the Astros game." I know he wants to watch it even if he hasn't mentioned it.

And if I'm tickled pink by saying 'home' as though we live together, I'll never admit it.

You're only here for two weeks, Crazy Daisy. Don't get carried away.

When he doesn't say anything, I snatch his phone and study the list. My eyebrows go higher and higher with each item. "Tori wants us to get her tampons? Really? I mean, I don't mind, but there's light flow, medium, or heavy. Applicator or non-applicator. Scented or un—"

With a pained groan, he holds up his hand. "Hold up there, Bitsy. That's, um, that's not for Tori." He winces. "Those are things she wanted me to get you."

"Because I need tampons? Because she's worried about my flow?" I'm laughing as his face turns redder and redder. "Wow, there is a first time for everything. I don't think I've ever seen you blush before."

"I'm not blushing. Men don't blush."

"Whatever. Your face is overheating, and it's hysterical." I glance around at the store, biting my lower lip to stop smiling. I'm almost too shocked by the list to be embarrassed. "Can you please explain what's going on?"

He takes off his baseball cap and thrusts his hand into his hair, making it stand up on top. It's adorable. "Tori thought that since you couldn't get your stuff from your grandmother's house you might need some essentials. Toiletries. Underwear. You know, since you probably haven't heard from Silas."

My smile drops. "Oh." I drop my head and stare at my flip-flops, a rush of emotion hitting me. "No, I haven't heard from my brother."

How pathetic is that? The only member of my immediate family in the state of Texas has completely deserted me. Even if Silas is a turd on most days, the little girl in me who always looked up to him is crushed.

This is bad karma. I blew off Logan. Now Silas is blowing me off. My heart hurts over both.

Things with my brother are probably a lost cause. Silas does what he wants, and that's that. He's just like our father, who never gave a damn about anyone but himself.

As for Logan, after what he said yesterday, I'm even more confused in some ways. Did I misunderstand that conversation I overheard last winter?

"Hey." Logan lifts my chin. "Let's unpack the 'Silas is a shithead' issue later. Tori said girls like shopping and that retail therapy is supposed to make you fart rainbows or something."

I don't expect to laugh, especially when I'm feeling this low, but that's the effect he has on me.

"I do like shopping, and I could use a few things, but you don't have to do this with me. If you'd prefer to drop me off and come back in an hour, that's fine. I could meet you out front when I'm done. I'm sure you have more important errands to run."

"Nope. My only goal tonight is to make sure you have everything you need for three days at the beach."

I'm way too excited about what that could mean.

Spending time with Logan during my visit is the worst idea ever, because when sweet, thoughtful Logan comes out to play, I melt into a puddle of goo.

It's moments like this over the years that endeared him to me even when I knew I shouldn't get too attached. Because the second I hear about him sneaking off with some random girl, my heart will get pulverized.

Because Logan will eventually get that itch, and he has several women sniffing around who would be more than happy to scratch it.

I school my features and force that treacherous thought out of my mind. For now, for tonight, I want to enjoy hanging out with my best friend. Before everything blows up in my face. Because it will.

"Plus," he says, tugging on a strand of my hair, "this is my treat, so go crazy. Buy the whole store. Make me regret that time I shoved mud down your shirt when you were a kid."

Laughing, I nudge him out of the way and push the cart. "No way you're paying. I can afford to get myself some toiletries, for Pete's sake." I think. "Although that was a mean thing to do. The mud was cold. Why'd you do it anyway?" He never would give me a straight answer.

I stop the cart in front of a wall of swimsuits. Lordy, I hate squeezing my body into shiny strips of spandex.

His footsteps stop right behind me. "You asked me what a boner was in front of Jessica Holliday."

I spin around. "I did no such thing."

"Did too, you little perv."

Suddenly, the memory is crystal clear. Cringing, I shrug. "I might have, but honestly, I didn't even know what a boner was then."

His eyebrows lift. "Exactly. You didn't know it was embarrassing for a thirteen-year-old boy in front of his crush."

"Aww." I reach up and pat his chest. "Young love thwarted before it began."

He endures my teasing with a droll expression on his face, and I laugh harder. Returning my attention to the swimsuits, I toss three in the cart to try on, not really caring what they look like since I'll wear a T-shirt over them anyway.

As we meander down the store, I call out behind me. "Didn't you hook up with Jessica a few years later anyway? You can't complain if you still got laid."

He doesn't respond right away.

I hold up a pair of shorts. Cute.

He coughs. "How'd you know about Jessica?"

Psshh. "I know about all of your women. You forget we live in a small town that thrives on gossip. For some reason, people always feel the need to tell me about your lady-killer ways." I pause to count on one hand. "Jessica Holliday, Emily Sanchez, Renee Caruso, that exchange student with the freckles. The chicks you screwed in the barn. I'd need more time to remember them all."

But never me. Even when I was old enough.

That sobering thought plunks me right back in the friend zone. I may be enthralled by the attention Logan's been giving me since I got home, but I can't let my head float away with grandiose ideas.

When he doesn't respond, I turn around and am caught off guard by his stormy expression. Why is he pissed? I decide to backtrack, not wanting to ruin the evening. We've been having fun, and I want to get back to that. Despite his history with girls, it's a topic we rarely discuss.

I open my mouth with the craziest thing I can think of.

"Did you know your mom explained to me what a boner was?" I make the goofiest face I can and then cover my face, because when I think back to what happened, I can't believe I was so clueless.

It takes a few seconds for that to sink in, and then he shakes his head, amused. "Jesus. I knew you and Bev were close, but I really had no idea. I'm afraid to ask how that came about."

He only calls his mom by her first name when he's being extra cheeky, and I smile to myself.

We resume our stroll through the store, and I reach for some new flip-flops. "Well, my mother never had the birds and bees convo with me, and I got my period for the first time when I was really young, a few days after that mud incident, actually." It's all coming back to me now. "So when Bev found me crying outside of the school because I legit thought I was dying, she took me to the ranch, cleaned me up, explained pads and tampons and how to use them, and answered my questions. Of course, since that boner conversation with you was fresh in my mind, I had to ask."

I brave a glance at him, and the soft look in his eyes makes my heart race.

"You never told me that."

I shrug. "I was embarrassed. That's not something you tell —" *The boy you've always loved.*

"I get it."

His eyes are so blue, so exquisite, I have to look away, so I don't see the hug coming.

When I'm wrapped in his arms, I melt against him. "What's this for?" My arms automatically wrap around his waist.

"You've never had it easy. Ever. But you'd never know it because life never knocks you down. I admire that about you, Jo." His voice in my ear sends chills down my arms. "And the whole time, I was a spoiled brat. It's amazing you wanted to be friends with me."

When he lets me go, I realize how much I needed that hug. "I don't remember it that way. I seem to recall needing someone to look out for me and you wanting the job for some reason." Because even before Silas started treating me like I was poo on his shoe, he never had my back. Not like Logan.

There I go again with intense conversations. Wanting to lighten the mood, I tell him the rest of the story.

"You know, your mom handled my female issues like a champ. I'm not sure if I could've kept a straight face while explaining that a 'penis gets engorged when aroused.'" I chuckle into my hand.

"Christ. She said that?"

We're both laughing as I nod.

Since we're near the changing room, I grab the swimsuits and other clothes out of my cart. "I'll just be a sec."

"You gonna let me see what you get this time?"

"Did you really want to see my bridesmaid dress?" Tori kicked him out of the shop before I tried it on.

"Yes, ma'am. And now I wanna see what I'm buying."

"Shut up. You're not paying."

"We'll see." He swirls his finger in the air. "Get to it. And if you don't show me the choices, I'm buying everything."

I roll my eyes and take the changing room closest to the entrance, so we can keep talking. "Which color?" Staring at the swimsuits, I realize I should've put more thought into this when I was standing in front of a huge rack of choices. "Hot pink, baby blue, or orange?" Ugh, I hate orange. Why did I grab this monstrosity? "Ixnay on the orange. It's hideous. I'm not even going to try it on."

"Then why'd you grab it?" he yells back.

"Because you were distracting me. I couldn't focus." I can never focus on anything around him.

"My vote is for hot pink."

I change into it, leaving my undies on, because trying on swimsuits is kinda gross. Thankfully, I'm wearing one of those seamless thongs.

"Any day now," he calls out.

Like he cares what I get. I'm laughing when I pull my T-shirt over the two-piece. I turn around to make sure my booty isn't hanging out. My cousin Dawn says my head is messed up because my father was so strict about my clothes when I was growing up. I tend to cover myself up.

"The pink is fine. I'm gonna get it."

"Josephine. Get out here."

I peek out of the dressing room and smile at the nice attendant folding a mountain of clothes at a long counter who's been listening to us yammer back and forth. "Can I show him my outfit before he gets any more temperamental?"

She smiles. "Sure."

Hesitantly, I shuffle out toward Logan. Thank goodness I shaved the important bits today.

He glances up from his phone. "I can't see the suit, which means I'm buying all of them, even the orange one."

"You are such a pain." I strip off my shirt before I overthink it.

I stare at my feet. At Logan's work boots. At the rack over his shoulder. Finally, I get the courage to look him in the eyes.

But he's still busy checking me out.

My nipples pebble under his stare.

Coughing, I motion behind me. "I'll go try the other one."

When he doesn't say anything, I figure he doesn't like the pink suit. Once I get into the blue two-piece, I don't bother to put on the T-shirt. I don't want to prolong this. He'll just make me strip it off anyway. The thought makes my stomach flip.

While I'd love nothing more than for him to fall at my feet in love with how I look, I have a better shot of getting struck in the head by a meteor.

This time, I throw caution to the wind and pull my hair out of the ponytail as I strut out the dressing room because I'm so tired of being haunted by ghosts. My dad and his strict rules can take a flying leap.

Using an über-deep voice, I purr, "What do you think?" How do those Instagram girls do this? I'm laughing and tossing my hair with my mock model moves as the attendant gives me a thumbs up.

When Logan doesn't say anything, I stop joking around. "So... Not the blue?"

I can't read his expression, but he stares another long minute and then returns to his phone. "Get them both."

"I don't need two swimsuits. That's wasteful." Tucking my

hands behind me, I add, "I'm leaning toward the pink one. The rear on this one is a little indecent."

He makes a face like he doesn't believe me. "Turn around."

"What? No." I was planning to shuffle backward toward the dressing room while he was glued to his phone. Ugh, why did I bring it up?

"How am I supposed to make an informed decision, Josephine?"

When did this man become so difficult? I turn around slowly. Wait. Did he just groan? Now I'm hearing things.

"See. Indecent." Nobody needs to see that much butt cheek. I spin the other way and try not to fidget under his stare.

He licks his bottom lip. "What if you got the pink top and those bottoms to match?"

"You like these bottoms?"

"I think all of mankind will like those bottoms."

My face burns because I have some junk in my trunk. "I do like donuts."

"Ain't no shame in having a great ass, Jo. I'll have to beat away the assholes at the beach, but whatever." He frowns before he shakes his head and points over his shoulder. "Why don't I meet you in the electronics in half an hour?"

I nod slowly and watch him walk away, wondering what just happened. Didn't he want to see what I pick out? I'll never understand this boy, plain and simple.

Twenty minutes later when I give the attendant the clothes I'm not getting, she fans herself with her hand. "Your boyfriend is so hot."

With a deep sigh, I pile up the rest of the outfits on my arm. "Logan's not my boyfriend. We're just friends." Words I've said a million times. I wish my heart would believe them.

Her eyebrows spike up. "Are you sure? Because the way he was looking at you..."

My heart beat spikes. "Really?" I've been wrong about Logan so often I'm afraid to read into anything he says or does anymore.

"Oh, yeah, girl. Get on that."

I want to be brave enough to find out if that's true.

11

LOGAN

For a three-day weekend at the beach, our caravan is bringing way too much crap, and it's spread across my brother's front lawn like his house vomited.

I have a duffle bag in one hand and a cat-sized dog in the other. Years of traveling to cutting horse competitions have taught me I only need the bare essentials.

Speaking of essentials...

Joey grins up at me and takes Rambo from my arms. She's the bright spot right now.

I've enjoyed having her at my house the last few days, even if I am spontaneously sporting wood whenever she wanders around in those tiny sleep shorts. Seeing her in that damn swimsuit was like squirting toothpaste out of the tube—now that I've seen her like that, I can't forget.

At this point, I'm not sure I want to.

Coming home to her after work and spending time together —uninterrupted by my niece and nephew or mother or brother or friends—it's been giving me ideas, thoughts I shouldn't be having.

When I got home last night after shoveling horse shit all

afternoon, Jo had dinner on the table, a smile on her face, and a cold beer in her hand for me. After I showered, she sat me down to eat, and we talked and laughed and then kicked back with a movie, and for a second, it hit me. This could be us. Late-night dinners. Horseback rides in the meadow. Old eighties movies in the dark.

Having her in my house feels right. I don't know shit about domestic bliss or serious girlfriends, but if I ever attempt anything that crazy, I have to admit I'd want it with Joey. This girl gets me, and she *knows* I'm an idiot and do dumbass things often, but she still cares for me.

And it's obvious to me now that I care more about her than I've ever let myself believe.

Would it be so bad if she and I happened?

I'd need to tell her so many things. Too many goddamn secrets to count. Would she be hurt I've kept them from her?

As if on cue, a text from Samantha vibrates my phone.

Our internet went out. Can you come over and fix it?

I swipe it away. I can't deal with her right now. I feel like I'm always dealing with her. She knows I'm leaving town for the weekend, and yet she texts me anyway as though I'm at her beck and call.

The thought of getting this shit off my chest, of telling Joey everything, is such a temptation.

But how do I start that kind of conversation? *Sorry, Joey, I've been lying to you.* For how long? *Years.*

Yeah, that'll go over well.

Even if she understands why I've done what I've done, I know this will hurt her.

My cell buzzes in my back pocket, and I roll my eyes.

I'm sure the last thing I should be doing is getting serious with Jo when I have Sam's bullshit to deal with, but every day we get closer to my brother's wedding reminds me that I don't have much time left with Bitsy. She could up and leave and go back to Florida.

Without her here... I sigh. The only thing I'd have are my old habits, and I'm not sure I can do that anymore.

None of my baggage is worth losing Joey. I just need to find a way to tell her. To explain.

"We're never leaving," I grumble quietly, venting about the only thing I can at the moment.

Somehow, a family affair has become family plus friends after Patrick overheard the itinerary for the week and invited himself. Tori's too nice and told him 'the more the merrier!' Which meant Patrick took it upon himself to tell some of our buddies, who loved having an excuse to head to Port Aransas and rented the condo next to ours.

I scratch our overgrown squirrel, who's snuggled in Joey's arms. "Rambo, what do you say we blow this popsicle stand and head home for a nap while these clowns figure out the world's biggest game of Tetris?"

Joey holds the puppy in front of her face and talks in a baby voice. "Play nice with the other kids."

When she lowers Rambo and looks up at me with those big gray eyes and that beautiful smile, the urge to kiss her is so strong, it nearly topples me over.

I'm in over my head with her. How much longer can I fight this?

I lick my lips, mesmerized by the shape of her mouth, but a peal of laughter interrupts our moment.

"Oh, my gawd. That dog is *sooooo* cute!"

It takes me a second to put a name to that annoying voice.

No.

Please tell me he didn't.

Only one woman in this town laughs like that, and when her

head pops up into my field of vision, I want to strangle Patrick for inviting her.

Renee Caruso.

Yup, a chick I hooked up with in high school. The one Joey knows about and mentioned the other day when we went shopping.

Renee seemed like a cool girl when we were growing up, but after attending a fancy college out East, she came back with the world's most annoying laugh.

And she's headed straight for us.

Fucccck.

I glance at Joey, who's now staring at her feet even though I'm willing her to look at me.

It's okay. I'll talk to her on the drive down to the coast and make sure she knows Renee is Patrick's doing. I have Jo's favorite songs on my phone that I can blast through the speakers in my truck, because I want our first real road trip to be special, and I won't let anyone ruin it.

Renee's shrill voice makes me grit my teeth. "Why, Logan Carter, you're better looking every time I see you."

As I hold back a groan, my eyes dart around for Patrick. He invited her, so he should be her welcoming committee.

When I can't find him, I force myself to talk. "Hey, Renee. It's nice to see you." I might not be excited she's coming, but my mother raised me to not be a dick, though it's hard some days. No pun intended.

Joey takes a step back to make room for Renee, who throws her arms around my neck. *Okay. Guess we're doing hugs.*

I pat her awkwardly on the shoulder and wait for her to dislodge herself.

When she does, she's still standing so close to me I shuffle back to create more space.

"Thanks for inviting me! I feel so special!"

What the hell? "I didn't in—"

A loud whistle brings everyone to a standstill. My brother and Tori are standing on the front porch, and Tori looks like a cruise director with a sunhat, clipboard, and pen. She hooks one arm in Ethan's and waves her clipboard at us.

"We want to thank everyone for coming to our pre-wedding weekend bash. Weddings are too crazy a time to catch up with our friends, and we weren't really feeling the bachelor-bachelorette party thing, so we thought we'd try something else. We'll be meeting up with a few more buds at the coast, but since y'all are the ones making the long drive, you deserve extra love. I want to get the cell numbers of everyone driving. I'll make a few quick copies for you so if you have to stop to get gas, you should let someone in the caravan know. We don't want anyone to get lost or stranded."

Tori explains who's going in which cars, and I'm surprised when I realize my mother isn't coming. I lean over to Joey and tell her I'll be right back before I jog over to discuss this with my mom, who's sitting on the new porch swing with Cody and Mila.

"Please tell me you're not babysitting this weekend." We've talked about this, how she shouldn't be running after the kids. Glancing around to make sure no one can hear us, I lower my voice. "You know what the doctor said."

"Cool your jets, son. I'm not babysitting. Two of Tori's cousins are doing that. I'll just be here to keep an eye on things."

I don't know who she thinks she's fooling.

Running my hand over my face, I sigh. Sometimes I feel like all I do is plug up holes in the dam only to have three more gush.

She leans forward to pat my arm. "Tori's parents are helping with her sister's kids, and I have their number. If I need anything, they'll be nearby. Now, please go have fun and stop worrying. You're gonna get gray hair before you're thirty at this rate."

I recognize the firm set of her jaw. Ain't no talking Beverly Carter out of something she wants.

Relenting, I decide I'd better get more info. "Who are the cousins? How old are they?" It's rare when we let someone new into the inner sanctum of our babysitting circle. Cody and Mila mean the whole world to the Carter clan.

"They're honors students at UT, worrywart. We met them last Christmas. We'll be fine."

No wonder she wanted to stay with Ethan while Joey's in town. She needed to plot her shenanigans.

"You'd better not set foot in the barn." The ranch hands can take care of the horses while we're gone, but if Mom goes in there for any reason, she's bound to start helping there too. "And you're grounded when I get back," I tease, leaning over to give her a hug. "Call me if you need anything. I can be home in three hours flat."

"No speeding! You know as well as I do that the drive takes longer than three hours."

"Then stay outta trouble." I kiss the kids on the top of their heads. "Don't run your grandmother into the ground, you hear me? Or no birthday presents."

The little brats giggle. They know I'm full of shit.

It's not quite ten in the morning, and I'm already dragging my feet. The three hours I put in at the Stock Yard before dawn are kicking my ass. I've helped Tori pack up the cars belonging to two of her friends, along with ice chests stocked with enough food for the next apocalypse.

When I reach my truck, I yawn. Through the tinted

windows, I count four bodies, which means we're ready to go. I hop in the driver's seat as the engines around me start and the caravan gets moving.

It's about time. If I have to repack another truck, I'm gonna lose my shit.

Rambo barks next to me, and I look over and freeze when I see Renee in the passenger seat holding Joey's puppy.

Oh, fuck no.

But it gets worse because a quick look in my rear view mirror tells me Jo's not in my truck.

I smack the steering wheel. "Where's Josephine?"

Twisting in my seat, I glare at Patrick, who shrugs. "She was here, and then, I don't know."

Sometimes I wonder how we're friends.

Patrick's seated behind Renee, who's cooing at Rambo. I cringe when I think about what happened in the last half hour that resulted in this seating arrangement.

In the back of the cab, wedged between Patrick and our buddy Cash, is a curvy brunette who smiles at me and starts talking, but I'm too pissed to exchange pleasantries.

How did this happen? There was one fucking person I wanted to spend time with, and she's not even in my truck.

I turn my head, noticing we're the last vehicle in the driveway.

Goddamn it.

She's gone. Again.

12

JOEY

THE FLAT SOUTH TEXAS COUNTRYSIDE ZIPS BY MY WINDOW, AND the desolate landscape calls to the deep sense of sadness that's been building in me since Renee Caruso crashed the fantasy I'd built up for this weekend.

I chat with Tori's older sister Kat and her husband Brady from the back seat. I'm huddled between an inflatable raft and several duffle bags.

Brady and Kat are the sweetest couple. I've come to know them well since they moved here several years ago. Even though I adore them, I'm having a hard time focusing on the conversation.

Because my head is a mess.

For a hot minute at Target two days ago, I thought I'd seen a spark of interest in Logan's eyes, a sensation that's grown the more time we spend together.

This morning shot that balloon out of the sky.

Now, the only thing I can hear is Renee Caruso thanking Logan for inviting her.

Like I want to spend four hours trapped on a road trip with Logan and one of his former—current?—hookups.

While Logan was talking to his mom, Patrick teased Renee about this "being like old times" and how he bet she was "dying to reconnect with Logan." But the nail in the coffin was how he joked she "can't leave scratch marks like last time."

I wanted to crawl into a hole and die.

Instead, I handed Patrick the dog and ran off to find another ride.

I'm not proud that conversation sent me into a tailspin. You'd think after years of running into girls who'd banged Logan, I'd be used to it, but this week has messed with my heart. We'd been having so much fun together since I got home. Like we were in our own little bubble.

And that's the problem.

This, my time visiting, is a façade. It's not real. I don't live with Logan, and I'm not his girlfriend, as much as I'd like to be, and no amount of wishing for that is going to transform him into my Prince Charming. The sooner I come to terms with that, the better off I'll be.

Easier said than done.

Brady catches my eye in the rear view mirror. "We heard you're heading back to Florida after the wedding. Is that permanent?"

Why torture myself anymore? Especially since Logan will likely hook up with Renee this weekend. The thought makes me want to turn around and skip the beach altogether.

"Probably. I need a change in scenery." Or maybe open-heart surgery to remove the boy next door.

Kat turns in her seat and reaches back for my hand. "We're going to miss you, and our girls are going to be so sad if you go."

I've babysat their two daughters countless times over the years. Thinking about this being one of my last days here to see my friends breaks me in a whole new way. My voice comes out quivery. "I'm going to miss them too. Maybe we can video chat sometimes."

She nods. "We'd love that. And if you ever need something, you let us know. You're just as much family to us as my sister and Ethan."

I give her a watery smile. She has no idea what that means to me.

Brady clears his throat. "My wife has a way of getting her friends to confess their deepest, darkest secrets until they're curled up in a ball crying. I'm going to break this up before you need therapy."

I chuckle at Kat's annoyed gasp.

About an hour later, my phone pings with a text. Anger and nervous energy whip through me when I see Logan's name.

Whose car are you in?

He hasn't texted me much since I've been back in Texas. I scroll back and see his messages from earlier in the year that I didn't respond to, and guilt washes over me.

Even though I'm still upset, I know I can't do that again. It's childish. No matter what he did or how hurt I was last winter, that's no excuse. I won't stoop to behaving like my brother, who can't seem to be bothered with my existence.

I'm riding with Brady and Kat. And because I don't want him to die, I add, *Don't text and drive.*

We stopped for gas. I assure you I'm a law-abiding citizen. Most of the time.

I fight a smile because he's too dang charming for his own good. But I'm still feeling sideswiped by what happened at the ranch, and I'm not ready to let go of that yet.

Two minutes later, he pings again. *Why'd you leave? I thought you were riding with me.*

I think long and hard about how to respond. Part of me wants to lie and say Kat invited me or that I figured Logan wanted to hang out with his friends, but that's not fair to either of us.

It's time I got brave.

I was upset.

There. It's a start.

What happened?

My heart flutters like a hummingbird in my chest as I consider telling him the truth. I hold my breath as I type.

I started to wonder why you wanted me around if you're just planning to hook up with Renee. I'd rather not have a front seat to that show.

Send.

The second it's gone, I want to delete the message. It reeks of jealousy, but there's nothing I can do about it now.

The message bubble that indicates he's typing pops open and disappears. Opens. Disappears.

Anxious minutes pass as I stare at the screen.

Brady taps on the steering wheel. "There's a lot of groaning back there. You okay?"

I sigh. "Why are men so difficult?"

"This about Logan?" He glances at Kat, and she smiles and turns away.

I answer as honestly as I ever have. "When is it not about Logan?"

They both chuckle.

When my phone pings, I almost drop it.

I didn't know she was coming, I swear. I'd planned to spend the entire weekend with you, not the guys. Patrick invited these people, not me.

I guess I believe that. Patrick is a bit clueless.

It buzzes again, and this message sends a wave of butterflies soaring through my stomach.

When we get there, don't disappear again. Stay with me in my condo this weekend so we can hang. Okay? I miss you, Bitsy.

Splat goes my heart.

Grinning at the nickname he gave me when I was six, I agree. God, he makes me insane.

Now that we've cleared the air a little, I keep an eye out for his truck, but we never spot his Ford, even when we get on the ferry. Disappointment keeps building in me, ramping up my desire to see him until I'm crawling out of my skin.

When we eventually pull into the condo complex at Port A, I scan the parking lot, looking for his truck.

"Your boy's over there," Brady says and gives me a wink in his rear view mirror.

If *Brady's* teasing me, everyone must know I've got it bad for Logan.

I feel a flush burning up my neck, and then I'm embarrassed for being embarrassed, but I've never really done this before. I've never had a boyfriend or even come that close to having one. Taking care of my grandmother sucked up most of my energy and time, and the little I had left, I wanted to spend with Logan.

Hanging out with Trent in Florida didn't make me feel like this, half crazed out of my mind if I didn't see him, which is why the friends-with-benefits thing we did sort of worked because my heart wasn't invested.

Well, it would have worked had I not started crying.

Staring hard at my phone, I re-read Logan's messages. *I miss you, Bitsy.*

It's not like he hasn't told me he's missed me since I've been back, but for some reason, this feels different. Like we're crossing some invisible forcefield we've always stood behind.

Unless I'm totally misreading him.

It wouldn't be the first time.

Kat twists in her seat. "*Amiga*, I've been Team LoJo for ages. You boot those girls outta his truck and take what's yours."

God, she's observant.

She holds out her fist, and I laugh and bump it with mine.

We're a few parking spots over, but there aren't any cars between ours and his. All this talk about me and Logan has made me nervous, and I'm not sure what I should do when I hop out of the truck. Suddenly, I feel like I'm fifteen all over again when I liked, well, Logan.

I take a few deep breaths, the ocean air calming me. We're so close to the beach, which is on the other side of the dunes, I can hear the waves crash along the shore.

But when Logan slides out of the driver's seat, I don't have to guess what I should do because he heads straight for Brady's truck, and the moment he reaches me, he wraps me in a hug and kisses the top of my head.

"Sorry about that misunderstanding," he murmurs against me.

I swallow past the lump in my throat and nod. "Sorry I got upset. I should've told you I was going with Kat." Tentatively, I rest my hands on his hips.

"Wrong answer." I lean back to look up at him, confused. "You should've kicked Renee's ass out of your seat and come with me."

A bark behind him makes us turn, and Renee is standing there, looking irritated, holding Rambo against her hip like he's a fashion accessory. Yikes. I wonder if she heard what he said.

But Logan doesn't seem worried. He shifts, keeping an arm around my shoulders. "Hey Renee. Can you give Joey her dog?"

Her frown deepens, her eyes darting between us and narrowing on Logan. "I thought this was your puppy."

"Nope. I bought it for Jo as a welcome home gift because I missed her so damn much while she was in Florida."

Dead. For real this time, I'm dead.

I only hope there's at least a kernel of truth in his words.

13

LOGAN

AFTER BEING TRAPPED IN MY TRUCK FOR HOURS WITH RENEE AND her yappy friend Wendy, I'm grateful for the comfortable silence between me and Joey as we unload her truck and then mine. Rambo trots happily at her feet, his black leash occasionally jerking one direction and then the next when he gets excited by the commotion.

Our party has commandeered the lawn in front of the condos, which consist of five houses on enormous stilts. We'll be occupying three this weekend. Tori's friends are in one, Ethan's in another, and mine in a third.

Tori is handing out room assignments and keys to the houses when Jo and I finally get a chance to talk to her and figure out where we'll be staying.

"Okay, guys, I have two options for you." Tori taps her chin as she studies her clipboard. "Jo can have the couch at my house and Logan can have a twin bed at Ethan's, or you can share a room at Patrick's. He just told me there was space." She winces at me. "I know I said I'd get you both rooms, but one of Ethan's college buddies showed up out of the blue with his girlfriend, and I'd feel weird making them sleep in the living room. So I had to shuffle everyone around. I'm so sorry. Don't be mad."

Joey shrugs. "No big deal. I'll take anything. You know you don't have to stress about me. This weekend is about you and Ethan. Don't worry on my account."

I'm not entirely sure what I paid for when I gave Tori a check earlier this week. While I don't want to make any trouble since she's busting her ass to make this fun for everyone when it's her own damn wedding party, I'm not excited about Jo sleeping on a couch.

Before I let myself think too hard about it, I opt for the easiest solution. "I'm not mad, Tor. You're doing your best, and this place is awesome. We'll share the room at Patrick's." She gives me a grateful smile. I turn to Joey. "You okay with that, Bitsy? I promise not to steal the covers."

A pretty pink rushes across Joey's cheeks. "Yeah. That's fine."

Rambo jumps between us, and Tori bends over to pet him.

When she stands, she grabs Joey's arm. "Please tell me Logan finally confessed he bought this puppy for you."

Jo's blush deepens. "He might've mentioned it a few minutes ago." She bites her lower lip to hide her smile.

But I see it and smile back.

Time seems to stand still as tendrils of her hair flutter around her. She licks her lips, and I watch her tongue swipe her skin, leaving it slick.

Tori looks between us and laughs. "My work here is done."

The minute Joey and I are alone, I pull her close to me and whisper in her ear. "I meant what I said about why I bought him for you. Missed you, Jo."

She's warm and curvy in the right places, and after that car ride from hell, I'm dying to figure out what's going on between us.

Her arms wrap around my waist, and I rest my chin on her head, loving her sweet floral scent.

"Missed you too, Logan. Thank you for the puppy. I love him so much." Her words get muffled against my chest, but I don't care because she's exactly where I want her to be.

Now more than ever, I wanna know why she left last December. What did I do? Because the other day she basically confessed I hurt her somehow, and that fucking wrecks me. I've tried to put it out of my mind since she's been back because I didn't want to pressure her. She might act like she can handle anything, but I know she's been through a tough time with her grandmother passing. And we've been getting along so well this week I didn't want to rock the boat.

But maybe now's the time. Maybe tonight, once we've had time to relax and unwind, we can finally clear the air.

After one more squeeze, I let her go. "Let's drop off our stuff in the room and head for the beach. We have two hours before the barbecue."

She agrees, and we grab our duffle bags and head up to Patrick's condo. Except when we reach the front porch, she tugs on my shirt and brings me to a stop.

"Is this going to be weird?" She lifts her chin, motioning to the voices coming from the living room.

"Why would it be weird? You know everyone as well as I do."

She gives me a look that says *really*?

I stare back at her until it sinks in. Renee.

Fuck.

All I was thinking was Joey and I could share a room together. Not that we'd be staying in a condo with Renee. This is what happens when I don't think things through.

"Babe, that was a long time ago. It happened once when I was in a bad place, and I swear to God it didn't mean anything."

With her lips pressed together, she nods but still doesn't look convinced, and it's suddenly imperative that she believe me.

Feeling like she's too far away, I grab her by her slender hips and pull her against me and graze my lips across the shell of her ear. "Jo." She shivers. It's not cold. It's a breezy eighty-five-degree day. I'm doing this to her. "Are you jealous?"

Silence stretches between us until she finally asks, "Would it bother you if I was?"

Smiling against her neck, I shake my head. "For some reason, it's sexy as hell." She laughs, and I pull her tighter until I'm sporting wood against her stomach. "Well, we've never done this before."

I cough, wondering if I should let her go, but she winds her arms around my neck, pushing those perfect tits against my chest. With a growl, I kiss her neck and breathe in the sweet warmth of her skin. She gasps, and that sound rocks me.

Now that I've started touching her, I can't stop. I run my palm over her back, wishing we didn't have so many clothes between us.

She whispers, "Guess there's a first time for everything, huh?"

Fuck, yes.

Only...

"Babe, we have to stop before I'm walking hunched over from this chub." Her shoulders shake with laughter, and reluctantly, I pull back. Her fingers fly to her neck, absentmindedly touching where I just kissed her. "Tell me something not sexy."

She thinks for a second. "Remember when you taught me how to farmer snot? I was eight, and I went home with boogers running down my face."

My lips tilt up in a grin. She was this pocket-sized blonde sprite with a tangled mess of hair, enormous gray eyes, and ratty overalls. About the cutest thing I'd ever seen in my life. "Who needs tissue, right?"

Shaking her head, she gives me a playful nudge. "My mother marched me straight into the bathroom and hosed me down."

I don't know what's come over me, but I wanna stare at her all day, except I'd rather get her in that swimsuit. "Come on. We're not gonna let anyone ruin this weekend for us." She smiles as I thread my fingers through hers and tug her toward the condo.

When we walk in, everyone stops talking, but this is my brother's wedding celebration, and fuck them if they pull anything on me. I'll just find us another place to stay if *my friends* give us any attitude. We'll probably spend most of our time with Ethan and Tori anyway. We just need a place to sleep.

I nod at Patrick and he nods back. "Hey, man. Heard we could stay here. That okay?"

His attention is drilled on our linked hands. He swallows. "Of course. But there's only one room left."

I give him the biggest shit-eating grin, since I'm pretty sure he wanted to tank things with me and Joey before they started because he wants her for himself. "That's okay. We only need one room."

14

JOEY

THE BATHROOM DOOR CLOSES BEHIND ME WITH A QUIET SNICK. I'M freezing with the air conditioner, but it'll be warm once we hit the beach in a few minutes.

Taking a page from Tori's playbook, I grabbed some old cutoffs to ease myself into wearing a two-piece in front of my friends. I tug down my bikini top to make sure it's covering the vital parts.

I'm still putting my hair into a messy ponytail when I stop in front of the queen-sized bed where Rambo wags his tail. Logan stares at me from the other side of the small room.

Slender board shorts hang off his trim hips, and he smiles, looking like my teenage dream, the one I spent way too many nights fantasizing about. His hair is disheveled, messy from pulling off his T-shirt, and there's nothing more I want to do than run my fingers through it.

Sweet blue blazes, I'm really rooming with Logan.

All of his tan muscles are on display. Those shoulders I want to lick. Those arms I've been lusting over since forever. And holy guacamole, those abs.

My mouth goes dry as I'm slammed with the possibility of what's happening between us.

I think... I think he wants me. That's what's going on here, right? Because he's never put his hands on me like he did today.

I didn't imagine that erection he pressed against my stomach fifteen minutes ago on the porch or the way he dragged his lips across my neck. Elation and terror spiral through me. Taking things further with Logan will either be the smartest thing I've ever done or the dumbest.

Everything in me heats with desire, but I can't deny this might be lunacy. We could obliterate a *lifetime* of friendship.

One of the reasons I left for Florida was because I was done chasing after him, hoping for whatever scraps of time he had for me. Too often, I felt like he didn't see me. That I was this fixture in his life he was so used to, I was almost invisible.

I don't feel invisible now.

His eyes travel down my body, and chills break out on my skin.

"Thought that swimsuit was hot, but damn, Jo. Now you got the whole farm girl vibe going, and it's kinda killing me."

My whole body buzzes when his words settle over me.

"I got the swimsuit you liked." He wasn't looking at what I had in my cart when we wrapped up my shopping trip because he was too busy arguing with me over who was going to pay for it. I won, eventually. I'm glad, especially now that I know he bought me Rambo, the sweetest puppy on the planet.

Logan eyes my top like he has x-ray vision, and an ache takes residence between my thighs.

"Ready to go?" If we don't get away from this bed, I'm likely to fling him down on it. And yeah, I'm nervous about that too. It's not like I have much experience in that area.

Rambo runs circles on the bed, and Logan grabs his leash. We load up with a few provisions and head out. The living room is empty, which is a relief. I don't want to have problems with anyone this weekend. Renee looked like she wanted to claw out my eyeballs earlier.

As Logan and I step outside, we wave to Ethan and one of his buddies, who have fired up the grill and are kicking back with a few beers.

"We'll be back soon to help you with the barbecue," Logan calls out.

"We got this. Go have fun." His brother returns to his conversation.

My flip-flops slap against the wooden path between the condos and over the sand dunes until we reach the beach.

"I feel bad Ethan and Tori are doing so much. Shouldn't they be the ones who relax?"

Logan shrugs. "I think they're excited to have their friends here. Besides, they'll be leaving for their honeymoon soon."

"Where are they headed?"

"Cancún for five days. They don't want to leave the kids or the ranch for too long."

"Who's gonna watch Cody and Mila while they're gone?"

"Who else? Me."

If I had been in town when Ethan was planning his trip, he probably would've asked me to pitch in so Logan didn't have to do everything by himself.

"But your mom will help, right?"

"Uh…" He shoves his hair out of his eyes. "No. She's going out of town."

That's odd. Bev's usually glued to the kids if their dad has to go away on business. "Where's she going?"

He pauses to point at Kat, who's relaxing on a beach chair with a few of her friends. "Come on. Let's see if they'll watch Rambo for a few minutes while we check out the waves."

We set up a dog bowl with water and hand Kat the leash.

Rambo hops in circles, excited to have more people to charm. While Logan chats with them, I prop my beach bag on a towel and debate sliding off my shorts.

A dozen women on the beach are wearing bikinis. No biggie. I can do this.

After a quick look around to make sure no one is paying attention to me, I slide off my cutoffs.

I shuffle back to Kat's group of friends and am about to thank her for watching Rambo when I'm in the air.

"What the—"

The earth flips upside down, and I'm dangling over Logan's shoulder and staring at his muscular backside.

"Time to hit the water, Bitsy."

"Oh, my God, you lunatic." Laughing, I wrap my arms around his waist as he goes bounding down the beach. When water laps at his ankles, I beg him to put me down.

Several strides later, he yells, "Take a deep breath!" as I go airborne.

I scream and clench my eyes shut, and then I'm underwater. With a sputter, I swim to the top and wipe my face. The water is warm and feels amazing, but I need to get even before I can appreciate the awesomeness of Port A.

"You turd." I choke on laughter as I charge him and try to take him down with a dunk, but he's too fast, and he flips me into the water again. He may be bigger than I am, but I can't let him act with impunity.

Staying under, I swim up behind him and leap onto his back, catching him off balance, and he falls over, taking me with him.

We roll under the water, and he wraps his arms around me as he rises to the top. I don't know how we got out so deep, but I can't reach the bottom anymore.

"You got lucky," he chides, hoisting me higher. Instinctively, I wrap my legs around his waist as I cling to his broad shoulders.

"Lucky? You call that luck? That was some badassery if I do say so myself. You weigh, what, like seventy-five pounds more than I do? And you let a little girl take you down?"

His cinnamon breath fans my face, and I smile up at him. He's still the most handsome man I've ever seen, and right now, with water glistening on his body and that unfettered smile on his face, I'm one hundred percent sure no matter what happens this weekend, I will always love him.

Lowering his voice, he whispers, "I wouldn't say you're a little girl anymore, Jo."

I swallow, my heart hammering in my chest. "No?"

He licks his bottom lip, his hands settling on my rear. "You're all grown up now, aren't you?"

Staring into his bright blue eyes, I nod as we lean closer. His nose dips to mine, and I can feel it, the way we both recognize how this changes everything.

When his lips gently skate against my skin, I'm breathless. I've waited a lifetime for this kiss, a lifetime to love the boy who's grown into this stunning man.

A lifetime for him to see me, the girl next door, as something more than his sidekick.

The kiss is everything I could've wished for.

Sweet and soft but electric.

Sublime.

Gentle kisses turn harder as my mouth opens to him and his tongue slides against mine. I shiver in his arms, overwhelmed by the sensations ricocheting through me. Overwhelmed by how much I want him. Confounded by the need to be as close to him as possible.

The guttural moan that rumbles in his chest sends another spark of pure pleasure through me. "Fuck, Jo. Why haven't we done this before?"

I run my fingers through his hair, and our heads shift,

turning the other way like an intricate dance we've choreographed before our lips connect again.

I mutter the answers to his question.

"Because I was too young."

Kiss.

"Because you were too stubborn."

Kiss.

"Because we weren't ready."

Kiss.

With a growl, he parts my lips again and delves deeper. "Well, I'm ready now."

Between my legs, he grows hard, and I gyrate my hips, thankful we're in deep enough that no one can see what our bottom halves are doing.

Those rough fingers skate along my bikini bottoms, and my pulse races. Yes. All the yeses.

Someone shouts on the beach, and abruptly we pull back, panting and out of breath.

He smiles and cups my face.

When he speaks, his voice is rough. "We'd better stop before things go too far." A chuckle escapes him as he leans closer to kiss me one more time. "Tonight, though, we need to talk."

He moves us closer to shore. I slide down his body and take a step back.

Is he merely putting off telling me something terrible? The heart-pounding elation zipping through my body comes to a screeching halt. "That sounds ominous."

"Nothing bad, Bitsy. I promise. Just..." He squints in the sun and studies my face. "I wanna make sure we're in the same place. That we want the same things."

I nod, ignoring that twinge of fear whispering that we *don't* want the same things. That maybe he's looking for something casual, his usual.

But he did say he's ready now.

I nod, knowing that if he wants to be friends with benefits, I won't do it. I won't do casual. Not with him. Because my heart can't handle being disposable to him.

Although... when was the last time Logan Carter had a girlfriend?

My stomach twists as I consider the answer, the one I don't want to hear.

Because the answer is never. Logan has never had any kind of significant relationship with a woman that lasted beyond a fling or hookup.

Wanting to be brave, I return the smile. "Of course. We'll talk." I have some things I need to say as well.

Needing a break from the intensity of his stare, I glance at the beach, where our friends play volleyball in the sand and hunt for seashells. Two of Tori's bridesmaids splash in the water closer to shore.

No one pays any attention to us, fortunately.

Everyone's having fun, which is what we should be doing too.

Determined to shake off my somber mood, I tug on his arm. "Race you to the beach?"

And I take off running.

15

LOGAN

AFTER A FIERCE VOLLEYBALL COMPETITION WHERE WE LET ETHAN and Tori's team win—'cause I'd be a shitty brother if I rained on that parade—I collapse in the sand. Lying back, I toss my arm over my face to shield it from the sun. The moment my eyes close, all I see is Joey. The way her lips felt so soft. That silky hair through my fingertips. Her luscious body against mine.

Needing to hide how she affects me, I flip over onto my stomach, adjust my junk, and turn my head, which gives me the perfect view of Josephine, who's laughing with Tori and Kat.

That kiss has my head in a place it's never been before, thinking about shit I've never considered with any other woman.

But Joey's different. I've always known this. I've always known she's special.

She was right. I wasn't ready for this. For her. I've been too damn stubborn about crossing a line with her.

I wasn't always so opposed to it, but it's been a long time since I've seriously considered anything with Jo.

Patrick drops down next to me. "Corona?"

I nod and sit up. "This your way of apologizing for being a cock?"

He laughs and chokes on his beer. "Cutting right to the chase, huh?"

"What's the point in beating 'round the bush? I know you have a thing for Joey, but she's off limits." I point at his overheated face. "And you brought Renee to piss off Joey."

Anger radiates off him as his mouth tightens. "See, you've been saying Joey's off limits for a while, but I don't see you making a claim there."

I look him straight in the eyes. "Things have changed. I'm gonna try to figure this out."

Patrick shakes his head, the anger fading from his expression. "You suck." He shoves me, and we both crack a smile.

It's hard to stay mad at him. After Silas went rogue and our buddy Isaiah took off to some hellhole to be an extreme sports guide, Patrick's the only one who stayed around after high school. We stayed friends 'cause it was either that or hang out with the old men and listen to them complain about their balls sagging.

After another drag of his beer, he sighs. "I like Joey. I have for a while. Nothing like that unrequited, star-crossed lovers crap you two have going on, but I'd be an asshole for trying to come between you." Another sigh. "The Renee thing wasn't malicious. I figured one of the guys would be into her. She's hot as fuck." He gives me a long look. "You're not looking to piss a circle around Renee too, right?"

A hot surge of disgust rises up in my chest. "You really think I'd be trying to get serious with Joey while making the moves on Renee?"

He shrugs, and that has my heart sinking.

That's not the first time I've been told I'm too much of a player for the likes of Joey. It pisses me the hell off. It always has.

Although, if I'm being honest, until Joey up and left for Florida, I doubt I was ready to get serious with one woman.

Turning to Patrick, I level him with the truth. "If I ever fuck over Joey, you have my full permission to kick my ass down Main Street."

He smirks. "Don't think I won't take you up on that."

I sure as hell hope he won't have to.

16

JOEY

LAUGHTER BELTS FROM TORI AS ETHAN WHIPS HER INTO HIS ARMS. They're standing in the middle of the pool with their friends nearby, but as they look into each other's eyes, they might as well be alone. Their love is palpable, the thing of fairytales. It swells my heart to see how blissfully happy they are together.

They're some serious couple goals.

I sigh, wondering if this burgeoning tryst with Logan will blossom into anything meaningful.

Of course it's meaningful for me, but will it be for him? I know his reputation. I don't want some flash-in-the-pan vacation fling. But I'm not sure I can avoid it with him.

He sits on the other side of the pool, talking to Patrick. They seem to have mended whatever drama that had come between them. In other words, Renee.

Patrick has his arm over her shoulders as he talks to Logan on the other side of him, and although Renee seems aloof, she appears to have switched her objective for the weekend just fine.

If I weren't so nervous about tonight with Logan, I'd have a Cheshire cat grin that she backed off.

Tori jumps out of the pool and dries off next to me. She

follows my line of sight and snorts. "I bet that's not how she expected to spend her weekend."

I give her a crazy, wide-eyed smile that I know will make her laugh. "Tough shit, huh?"

We both cackle.

I don't really curse, thanks to my father who would tan my hide if I so much as gave a dirty look, but Tori has the mouth of a sailor, and any time I let a foul word slip, it delights her to no end.

Her sister Kat saunters over to us. "You two are up to mischief, aren't ya?"

Tori holds her fist up to me. "Hell yes, we are." I bump her back and chuckle.

"Have I thanked you yet for agreeing to do our hair next weekend?" Kat wraps a towel around her waist. "I feel bad making you work at the wedding."

"I'm honored to be asked. Seriously! It's no hardship to work on y'all's hair." If I'm being honest, I'm kinda glad the person they scheduled had to bail. "We need to talk about styles and do a practice session this week to make sure I know exactly what you want for Saturday."

"You're such a lifesaver." Tori squeezes me in a python hug. "I can write you a check for everything when we get home."

I gasp. "You are *not* paying me."

"Oh, yes, I am. I didn't ask you so you could do it for free. You do great hair. I'm lucky to have you. I didn't ask initially because I wanted you to relax and enjoy the festivities with us, but I'm in a pinch. I fully expect to pay you, though."

"How about a discount?" Like a super-huge discount. I love this girl too much to make her pay full price. I've only known Tori two years, but she and Kat totally adopted me as one of their own. The fact that these two are now part of the Carter clan is one of the best things to ever happened to me. I love

Logan and Ethan, but it's amazing to have a few more girls around. "It can be my wedding gift to you."

She growls, and I laugh. "We'll see."

Kat nudges me. "How's the new salon coming?"

"Great. My cousin is painting the new location now." I feel bad ditching her with so much work, but Dawn can't be too upset I'm not there to help. I gave her nearly every penny I'd saved living with her to invest in the new business.

"We were kinda wondering about the salon and how that would work with..." Tori tilts her head toward Logan and widens her eyes meaningfully.

That's a really good question. One that makes me ill if I think about it too long.

I swallow. "You mean starting a new business in Florida while—"

Tori does a hip thrust. "Knocking boots with that farm boy in Texas."

Heat sears up my neck. "Let's not get ahead of ourselves. No one's 'knocking boots.'"

"Yet." She starts humming that Luke Bryan song, and I hide my face because I'm too embarrassed to look at my friends.

"Ladies."

My heart skips at the sound of Logan's deep voice.

Before I can turn around, he drapes a tan, muscular arm over my collarbone and draws me to him.

Tori sighs and gives me a conspicuous wink.

"Mind if I steal Jojo for a bit?" Logan's chest rumbles against my back, and every cell, every molecule in my body surges to life.

"Let me grab Rambo."

Tori waves me off. "I'll watch him tonight. Go have fun."

She and her sister give us enormous grins as Logan tugs me

out to the beach. The sun has almost set, and he threads his fingers through mine as we walk along the damp sand.

I keep stealing glances at our hands.

And those kisses earlier today in the ocean? Holy Hogwarts, that was hot.

We walk for a while, the sound of seagulls and lapping waves the backdrop to our leisurely stroll. The entire time I try to control my breathing so I don't hyperventilate.

It was different when we were on the beach this afternoon surrounded by our friends, but walking alone with him along the shore at dusk, hand in hand, is another thing altogether.

The butterflies in my stomach go kamikaze when his thumb rubs over my wrist.

This is Logan, I remind myself. I've known him my whole life. More than anything, he's my friend first. We'll figure out the rest.

Finally, my heart gets under control as I accept that there's nothing to be nervous about.

Except that we might get naked.

There goes my calm.

Chill the eff out, Joey.

"I can't believe we've never been here together," he says, pausing to toss a stranded starfish back out to sea.

"I was always so jealous I couldn't tag along." My father never would've allowed me to stay anywhere overnight with the Carter clan even if Bev promised I'd get my own room.

By the time he abandoned us, my grandmother was too sick for me to take any kind of vacation. Watching my mother waste away from cancer was horrific, but the unpredictability of Gran's Alzheimer's wrecked me in whole new ways.

Pushing those grim thoughts out of my mind, I pick up a shell and study the striations. "I'd hear about the walks on the jetty and you guys fishing with your dad, and I would've given anything to go. Silas always made sure to tell me every little detail. Those must have been some of the best memories of your father."

When he doesn't say anything, I reach for his hand again. It must be bittersweet to remember his dad. Daniel Carter was the most amazing man. Always caring. Always involved. Patient. And so friendly, he could charm the bark off a tree. Basically the opposite of my father, whose mercurial moods would swing so intensely, I couldn't keep up.

"My dad... yeah." He clears his throat.

I lean my head on Logan's shoulder as we stare out at the water. My heart aches when I think back to how he found his father in the barn when Mr. Carter suffered a fatal heart attack. Everyone was devastated, but Logan worst of all.

He turns to face me. The expression on his face is so serious, so solemn.

Shoot. I didn't mean to bring up his dad. This topic always makes him somber. I can understand. I don't want to reminisce about tragic events in my life either.

Before I can say anything, he asks, "Can we talk about what happened at Christmas?"

I still.

My heart starts racing again, but for a completely different reason.

Of course he wants to talk about what happened over the holidays.

How can I explain it without sounding needy?

My eyes dart away, a flush of embarrassment staining my cheeks. I try to tug my hand out of his, but he holds on tighter.

Moving me closer until I'm pressed up against him, he whispers into my ear, "Joey, please. Tell me what happened. Whatever it is, I need to know. It's making me crazy, wondering what I did to you."

Nodding, I tilt my head down and close my eyes.

I can do this. I can tell him. He's right.

Stepping back, I look out into the darkness, where the crests of waves are highlighted by the moon.

"It was the culmination of things that week." I kick a shell at my feet deciding to get this off my chest. "Remember when we went to the River Walk to take photos with your family?"

Out of my peripheral vision, I see him nod.

"I didn't want to talk about it before since everyone was in a good mood that night and Ethan was going to propose to Tori, but that was the worst week ever. First my car—well, Gran's Buick—was vandalized, and the next day, the day y'all took those photos, I lost my job."

"Seriously? What happened?"

I explain how someone smashed my window and trashed the interior while I was at work. Fortunately, one of my coworkers helped me fix my window, but that was just a prelude to getting fired.

Recalling that afternoon has me seeing red all over again.

"This client hated how I cut her hair. She screamed at me when I was done and made a huge scene." My lips twist as I remember how embarrassed I was to be called out in a salon full of people. "It was so strange since she had specifically requested me. Called. Made an appointment. Asked for me. I swear I gave her the exact cut she asked for, but she made such a stink, and since I had been late a few times, Shelly fired me."

"Bitsy, I'm sorry. Wish you had told me."

"I wanted to." Just thinking about that night upsets me, which is why I've tried not to since I've been home. "But I didn't get a chance."

"Because you left for Florida?" he asks hesitantly.

"No, because *you* left."

He's silent, and I know he's probably trying to remember what happened that night.

I cross my arms over my chest, hating how vulnerable this makes me feel, but I promised myself on the bus home that I'd be honest about what happened. That I'd be brave. "We were supposed to take photos. You said you wanted a pic of the two of us, so I tagged along." Like always.

I held everyone's coats while they took photos. At the time, I didn't mind. I love the Carters, and it's not like I'm officially part of their family. I didn't expect to be asked to take a photo with the whole clan, but I thought Logan wanted one of the two of us.

"The whole night you were texting someone, and then you disappeared, wandered down from where we were to make a call." Pausing to take a breath, I turn to look him in the eye. "The photographer left while you were gone. We never took our photo. And then I heard what you said."

Sad, pathetic Joey was heartbroken Logan hadn't bothered to remember the photo.

The space between his eyebrows tightens, but I can't tell if he's still clueless.

"On the phone. I heard your conversation. I hadn't been trying to eavesdrop, but your mom asked me to get you, and I heard."

His expression doesn't change, and I groan, upset I have to say the rest out loud and annoyed I didn't push him in the river at the time. "I *heard* you say I needed to get a life. That you were tired of dealing with me. That I exhausted you."

"What are you talking about, Josephine?" He looks completely perplexed, like I'm speaking a foreign language. "I've never, not once, thought that, much less said that. Even when you were this tall and needed piggy back rides across waist-high grass because you were afraid of the snakes. How many summers did I carry you across Mr. Johnson's field?"

A reluctant smile tugs across my lips even though Logan does not look amused. "You did carry me."

"Damn straight, I did. Every fucking time, Jojo. Every time." He grips my shoulders. "And I've never complained or felt the need to. Do you know why?"

I shake my head.

"Because I love having you around."

At first, I don't say anything. I can't. Emotion chokes my throat, and I have to blink back the crazy fountain that wants to erupt from my eyeballs.

"So you weren't talking about me?"

"No, dummy." He hugs me so tightly, I laugh.

"So... I misunderstood?"

"Yes." He tilts my head up and stares back at me with such intensity, my heart catapults itself into the sand dunes. "And I hate that you thought I said that about you."

Tears stream down my face despite my best attempt to keep them back. His rough thumbs wipe them away.

"Aww, Bitsy. You had such a shitty week and then you thought I said that? And I flaked on our holiday photos?" His eyes squeeze shut, like it's coming back to him. "Wait. We were supposed to hang out after, but I took off... Fuck. I *am* an asshole."

I'm in his arms again, grateful I've said my piece and feeling foolish I misunderstood on such a huge scale, even though he was being a self-absorbed douchecanoe that night, but one thing still doesn't make sense.

Sniffing, I tilt my head. "Who were you talking about?"

"Uh... What?"

"If you weren't talking about me, who were you talking about?"

"Oh, um." He lets go of me to rub the side of his neck.

Awkward silence stretches between us. "Just some female drama."

My eyes narrow.

Last fall, I thought he and I had gotten closer. I thought *maybe* he was seeing me as something more than his sidekick, but I was obviously hallucinating if he was having "female drama."

I nod and take another step away.

See, this is why I can't trust myself around him. I'm always misreading him when it comes to our relationship. I can read him like a book when it comes to his interests or emotions, but I can't figure out what I mean to him or how he feels about me.

But I do know one thing for certain—Logan goes through women like my brother devours a bag of Oreos.

Fast.

Without much discernment.

And with no remorse for gluttony.

If we do this, I know the outcome. I'll have a big, fat broken heart, and he'll be on to the next flavor of the month.

"This is a bad idea," I say to myself and start back for the condo.

"Wait. Jojo. Come on." He grabs my hand and pulls me to a stop. "I'm sorry for the misunderstanding. I hate that I hurt you."

I give him a tight smile and keep going. "It's fine. We're good."

Behind me, I hear him swear under his breath, and I walk faster.

How humiliating. I was thinking he was into me last fall, and I was wrong. Again. How many times am I going to be off base?

"Joey, don't go."

I don't pause. What's there to say? I'm tired of chasing after this boy. I'm not going to wear my heart on my sleeve for him anymore.

"What did I say? Why are you upset?"

When he jogs out in front of me to block my path, I skid to a stop.

"What do you *feel* for me, Logan? Am I just your former friend's kid sister? Am I your zany BFF with the crazy hair? Am I just a hookup this weekend because I'll be going back to Florida soon?" I fling my arms, feeling like I'm losing my mind, but I've kept my feelings for him locked away for so long, the words spew out of me. "I mean, why now? I've known you my whole life, and you've never kissed me before. Why today? What's different? How are we different now than, say, *last Christmas* when I thought we were moving toward something more than being friends? But we obviously weren't if you were dealing with other girls and 'female drama.'"

I'm out of breath from ranting, every muscle tense. Because if the past has taught me anything, it's that I'm going to get hurt. Logan has that power. As much as I hate to admit it, he has always held my heart in the palm of his hand. Even though I ran away last winter. Ran as far as I could go. And I'm so scared he's going to obliterate me.

Part of me hates how much I just divulged, but I'm so freaking tired of this. Either he tells me what I need to hear, or we hammer the nail in this coffin before my heart is irreparably damaged. If that means I have to make a fool of myself in the meanwhile, so be it.

I need the truth. For once.

He pulls me into his arms so fast, I nearly trip. "Of course you're not a fucking hookup, Joey. We're doing this now because I missed you like crazy when you were gone. I thought... I thought I had lost you, but you're back. And I feel like I'm getting a second chance to do what I should've done a long time ago."

When his lips sweep across mine, he groans and tightens his arms around me, promising to never take me for granted.

Just like that, my heart squeezes in my chest, the muscle memory of being in love with him for so many years overpowering good sense.

And I give in.

17

LOGAN

THE CONDO IS DARK WHEN JOEY AND I BUST THROUGH THE DOOR, which I promptly pin her against as I kiss her.

I don't know what happened out there on the beach. I can't begin to untangle my feelings for Jojo except I know they're big and unwieldy.

I'm a fucking asshole. I see that now. I've taken Joey for granted and hurt her and there's no way around how much I need to come clean and tell her what's been going on, but right now, I need to touch her more than I need my next breath.

Her legs wrap around me when I take her tight little ass in my hands. "Fuck, you feel amazing."

She smells like sunshine and flowers and that fruity lip balm she loves.

And I can't get enough. Kissing her has uncorked something in me. Something I buried deep during a dark time in my life. Back when I was too stupid and she was too young.

She's not too young anymore.

No, the Josephine in my arms is one hundred percent woman.

My fingers toy with the tie on her bikini top and test the limits of my restraint.

Over the years, I've tried my damnedest to not think of her this way. To not notice the way she's filled out. To not notice the way her ass looks amazing in jeans or that her tits are so round and perky.

Now that we're doing this, it's like I've been smacked by a tidal wave of lust.

And all I can think is *fuck yes.*

Those plump lips skate across mine before she opens to me again and our tongues slide against each other. She's slick and wet and so fucking sweet. It makes me want to taste the rest of her. My cock throbs at the thought.

I could have her cutoffs on the floor in a heartbeat and be inside her in ten seconds.

Pulling back, I rest my forehead on her shoulder and try to catch my breath.

This is too fast.

I'm definitely screwing this up.

Because the last thing I want her to think is she's a hookup, and if we continue at this warp speed, that's exactly how I'll make her feel.

She's not a quick fuck. This is Jojo, my best friend. She deserves more than me groping her where any of our friends could walk in and see us.

"What's wrong?" Her fingers delve gently into my hair to push it off my face.

I hate the uncertainty in her voice.

How have I not understood? Not seen the want in her eyes? Not admitted my own need for her?

"Nothing, baby. For the first time, nothing is wrong." I let her feet drop to the floor before I place a kiss on her forehead. "Let's get cleaned up. We're gonna get sand everywhere if we don't."

I adjust my hard-on before I flip on a small lamp so the rest of our condo mates don't kill themselves when they return. Darting into the kitchen, I grab a couple of bottles of water and a bag of cookies and then reach for her hand.

"We're gonna need a snack later to keep up our strength. Trust me." I wink and drag her down the hall to our room, loving the sound of her laughter.

"What about Rambo? Should we go get him?"

"I'll stop by my brother's to get him before we turn in. Ethan gave me a spare key."

Because if Joey and I do go farther tonight, I don't want Rambo interrupting.

Once we're in our room, I hand her a towel and direct her toward the shower. "You first. After my turn, we'll meet back here." I kiss her. "We'll pick up where we left off. Just not somewhere Patrick or Renee or whoever can walk in on us with our goodies hanging out."

She snorts, and I laugh with her. "Good thinking."

She sashays into the bathroom and closes the door. The water turns on. I imagine her untying that tiny bikini top and the shiny fabric sliding to the floor. I've slowly been going insane today watching her in that swimsuit. Seeing her nipples pebble in the breeze and wishing I could warm them. With my mouth.

Jesus knows I'd give my left nut to join her in the shower, but taking a little breather might be for the best. I don't want our first time to be memorable because we had half of Port A up our cracks and seaweed in our hair. We spent the whole day at the beach or in the pool, and tonight will be much more pleasant if I wash the sand off my dick first.

Anyway, I need to slow this down. Make tonight special. Maybe jerk off in the shower so I don't blow my wad in two minutes. I'm usually proud of my stamina, but being with Joey makes me feel like a teenage boy touching his first tit.

Can my sweet little best friend handle all the ways I want to corrupt her? God forgive me, but I plan to find out.

Fifteen minutes later the water shuts off and the door opens. A cloud of steam billows out as Jojo emerges, a vision in a white t-shirt and panties, smelling so good I want to tackle her to the ground and taste her.

Fuck me sideways, she's hot. I can see her tiny nipples on her perfectly plump breasts poking through the thin material.

"This is gonna be the fastest shower in history." I smack her ass as I bolt for the shower and wash the goods in record time.

18

JOEY

Calm down.

Taking a deep breath, I try to get my heart to stop racing, but after a few minutes, I realize I'd have better luck attempting to fly home by flapping my arms than trying to relax.

I lean back on the bed, reclining on my elbows before I tuck my damp hair over my shoulder and try to *seem* relaxed.

Does this look dumb?

Should I put on some sleep shorts?

Am I trampy for just sporting undies underneath this top? Logan saw me today in a bikini, and I'm technically wearing more clothing now.

Frowning, I twist my legs sideways and pull my t-shirt this way and that.

For Pete's sake, I feel like a moron lying here, trying to look sexy. With a groan, I flop back and cover my face with my arm.

Of course this is the moment Logan steps out of the bathroom.

"Babe, you okay?"

My lips pull up. Not sure I'll ever get used to him calling me that. *Am I your baby? Yes, please.*

I open my eyes and take in the raw masculine beauty standing before me.

Holy half-nekkid hottie. Someone call the fire department for the nine alarm.

Logan gives me that sexy smirk I feel *everywhere.*

Those long dark eyelashes intensify his crystal-blue eyes, and drops of water glisten over tan, taut muscles. Light brown hair, now dark from the shower, hangs rebelliously in his face. Never mind the small towel barely clinging to his narrow hips...

Jesus, Mary, and all the saints, I don't know how I'm going to survive this.

While I've hoped for years that Logan and I would get to this point, I guess I thought I'd be more sexually experienced by now. More confident in my sexual abilities.

I've only done this once.

And it wasn't a great experience.

Okay, it was a terrible experience. I cried. Like, a lot.

Earlier today, I didn't have time to think. I was in the moment and just reacted. We kissed and groped, and I was running on pure animal instinct and a lifelong crush.

But now my brain has caught up to the reality that my Logan fantasy has a good chance of coming true.

If I had any clue what to do right now.

With a panicked groan, I toss my arm over my face again.

He chuckles. "I know. I'm freaking out too. Let's just hang out, okay?"

I mumble back in agreement.

I can handle hanging out. I think.

But you're in your underwear, you little freak!

I'm in a full-on panic until I hear clothing shuffling around. Oh, my heavens. Is he taking off that towel? I owe it to the female population to witness this.

I peek out from under my arm in time to catch him pull dark gray boxer briefs over his taut backside.

I was so caught up in him when we made out earlier I didn't fully appreciate what was happening, or I would've made an effort to feel those buns. I feel a little deprived for not thinking quicker on my toes.

My attention is drilled to that vicinity when he turns around and I get an eyeful of man bulge.

And I hold my breath.

Because there's no way that monster's gonna fit.

I didn't think Trent, my summer friend with bennies, was that big, and sex still hurt. Logan's Titan-sized dong can barely be contained by his briefs.

Shaking my head, I squeeze my eyes shut again, my brain flooding with the negative thoughts I've racked up over the years about my relationship, or lack thereof, with Logan.

I have no clue what I'm doing.

Logan's too experienced.

Logan loves experienced women.

Trying to learn how to have sex while watching PornHub has to be one of my dumber ideas. Nobody gets that excited being pounded. I mean, I can't imagine that to be the case.

I flinch when the bed dips next to me and look up to see the gorgeous face that's starred in most of my fantasies since I was young.

"Hey." He runs his thumb over my bottom lip. "Let's do what we always do."

Um.

"We've never been in the same bed half-clothed."

When he laughs, the brightness in his eyes does something to me. How long has it been since I've seen him smile like that? It makes me wonder what's been going on in his life that's dimmed his light.

"What I mean is let's have fun." Leaning down to press a feather-light kiss on my mouth, he whispers, "Let's relax and enjoy our weekend. Nothing too serious. Nothing more than you feel comfortable doing." His eyebrows pull together. "Nothing too fast that we can't handle. This goes at our speed, okay? And we can continue figuring this out when we get home."

I'm nodding at how sensible this sounds. Loving how this feels like more than a weekend fling. How this seems like a bridge to something more significant.

Because do I want to have sex with Logan? Heck yes.

Am I terrified of going that far? Abso-freaking-lutely.

I'm like a Pee Wee player who got called up to the big leagues and is still figuring out how to wear a jock strap, much less hit the ball.

Warmth spreads through my body as he shoots me another megawatt smile and kisses my forehead. Reaching for his jeans, he points to the bedside table.

"Pick out a movie on my phone. I already connected to the WiFi so we can watch Netflix. I might as well swing by Ethan's next door to get Rambo."

My trigger-sensitive butterflies take flight when he covers me with a blanket. With a wink, he heads out.

Logan Carter.

If my heartbeat had a sound beyond the thump in my chest, it would be his name.

I sigh like a lovesick teenager.

Smiling to myself, I flop back on the bed. I'm pretty sure Logan has never told any of his fangirls things would continue when they got home.

Common sense battles with my emotions, warning me that I am more invested in this emotionally than I have any right to be when the only thing we've done is kiss. I shut down that train of thought before I sabotage my mood and reach for his phone, which lights up with notifications.

I chuckle at his drunk dudebro texts.

Patrick: Cant find my wallllllet. Got a condum?
Cash: This chick puked on my shoe. Im gonna be sick from the smell.
Sam: Youre suck an asshole. Why cant you come over?
Jordy: I just pissed on a cat. Wuuups

How those knuckleheads survive is beyond me.

I'm still scrolling through Netflix when Logan returns and our puppy gives me a happy little ARF!

"Hey, cuteness." I lean over the bed to pick up Rambo.

"Careful. He's still damp. I washed his feet before I brought him inside so he wouldn't track in sand."

"Good thinking." I jump up and grab some towels to make a nook for Rambo on the floor next to me. He must be wiped out from a day at the beach because he promptly curls up.

I'm sitting on the edge of the bed when a big arm wraps around my waist and pulls me back.

Giggling like an idiot, I settle back against Logan's bare chest.

"You're so warm." He nuzzles his face against my neck, and I squirm from the shock of his cold extremities.

"You're an icicle." With concerted effort, I sit up and yank the covers over us before we lean against the headboard and a few pillows.

With only the side lamp on and *Back to the Future* glowing from his phone, we settle in to watch something we've seen a million times together.

But I can't focus on the movie. My attention is too drawn to the way his arm drapes over my shoulder and his thumb slides up and down my bare arm. I'm too cognizant of the rise and fall of his chest against my side and his scruffy chin at my temple. Too aware of the roughness of his jeans against my bare legs.

Half of the movie is over, but all I can think about is how his other hand is now resting on my hip, his fingers toying with my T-shirt that's drawn up over my stomach.

A hot, heady beat drums between my legs.

He smells amazing. Like the ocean scent of his body wash and the faint smell of leather. Like a man. Not the kid who taught me how to farmer snot or the teenager who didn't always shower after he got sweaty.

By the time the movie is over, I'm slick and hot and so turned on, my eyes are crossing.

He leans over to click off the lamp, leaving the moonlight streaming through the window, and like we already know the drill, we reach for each other in the dark. Rough hands pull me over his body. My legs straddle his hips. My hands land in his hair.

His are on my rear.

Sweet, drugging kisses make me writhe on top of him where his jeans scrape my thighs and his bulge bumps up against the most sensitive part of me.

"I'm not..." I gasp for breath. "I don't really know how to do this."

The embarrassing confession bursts out of me, words I can't take back. Words I wish I could.

So stupid, Joey. Why can't you deal like an adult?

He stills beneath me, his chest rising and falling just as quickly as mine. "So it's... been a while? Or are you saying..."

"I'm not a virgin. I mean. Yeah, no."

The guilt of that night a few months ago slams into me again, and I freeze. Granted, my head tells me I shouldn't feel guilty about it, but my heart has other ideas.

Twisting to the side, he tucks me beside him so that we're

facing each other, our faces inches apart, our legs twined together. With a tender touch, he threads his fingers through mine. "Jo, baby. I'm not sure what that means."

I swallow, hating, *hating* that I have to explain it.

After I left for Florida this winter, I never imagined having any kind of intimate conversation with Logan, so having this one fills me with dread. Rationally, I know it shouldn't. It's not like we were together. We've never been together. And it's not like he was saving himself for me.

The idea of that, of him, waiting for me, is so preposterous I laugh awkwardly. Logan is the king of hookups. The thought propels me to answer his question.

"I, uh, did try to have sex." Here comes the awkward part. "Once."

A pause.

"That guy you dated in high school? That Mason kid?"

I shake my head. "We never really dated. Not seriously. I didn't lose my virginity in high school."

Now that my eyes have adjusted to the dark, I see his confused expression.

Sighing, I decide to let it out. "I had a friends-with-benefits situation in Florida, but it didn't go well."

A low growl has me looking up, startled to hear it coming from Logan. "He *hurt* you?"

"No. No. Nothing like that. Well, not on purpose."

He scrubs his face with his palm with a pained groan. "Joey, what does that mean?"

Frustration surges through me, but I want him to know the truth. My parents' relationship crashed and burned because of their lies, and I want to start this on the right foot. With honesty.

"It means I *tried* to have sex. It means it didn't feel good. I didn't enjoy it, so I made him stop." How freaking horrifying. I hide my face in the pillow. "It means, I'm not a virgin.

Technically. Because it went in. For, you know, like a minute or two."

Kill me now. Throw me in a barrel of piranhas. It would be less painful than this moment.

A long, strained silence fills the dark room before he pulls me back to his chest and tugs my thigh over his hips. "I'm not sure where to start with all of that." His hand comes up to cup my jaw gently. "I hate that your first time wasn't with someone who meant something to you." I can feel his heart thundering in his chest. "I hate how I wanna find that shithead and kick his ass for not making it good for you. Which is dumb as fuck because the last thing I want is to think about you being with anyone but me." He clears his throat.

I'm too overcome to speak. To go so far as to tell him the reason I made myself sleep with Trent. That I was trying to get over him.

"Come here." Scooping me up, he lifts me until I'm resting on top of him. My head on his warm chest. My arms nestled between us. Our legs twisted together.

With a kiss to my forehead, he smooths his hands up and down my back. For the longest time, we lie there in our own little world for two, until the heartache from this past year starts to settle. And I realize what I want.

In Florida, I thought I needed to move on and get past Logan.

But what I want is to move on *with* him.

My voice is hoarse when I look up and whisper the words. "Will you show me what to do? How to enjoy it?" I sniffle.

"Enjoy what, baby?"

"Sex."

19

LOGAN

ALTHOUGH MY HEAD STRUGGLES TO MAKE SENSE OF HER WORDS, my body's ramped up and ready for duty, all my blood heading south toward that raging hard-on already pressed against her hip.

Bottom line: Jojo's killing me with one heartbreaking confession after the next.

I trace her bottom lip with my thumb and think back to her words on the beach. She wasn't wrong about last fall, about us getting closer. I didn't really think about it too hard because keeping Joey at arm's length always seemed like the best way to protect her from me and my own stupidity, but yeah. Maybe I started to get a glimmer of something more with her until the "female drama" ramped up to nuclear proportions and redirected my attention, reminding me I had a lot of shit on my plate.

Then Joey left.

And had sex with a friends-with-benefits. Probably with some random dude. Fuck.

I did that. Deep down, I know I pushed her away like I always did, and she ended up with someone else. I deserve every ounce of pain for making her resort to something casual. She'd never be casual to me.

The worst part is how she knows about the women I've been with in the past despite my best attempts to keep them away from her.

It makes me wonder what else she knows.

Realizing I haven't answered her question, I lean up to kiss her and repeat the words I'd said to her earlier. "There's no rush, Bitsy."

The furrow in her brow says otherwise. "Except... I'm leaving after the wedding."

She says the words so quietly, I almost think I'm imagining them. "So you're serious about that?"

"Yes. I invested in my cousin's salon. In Florida." She tries to scoot off me, but I wrap my arms around her.

"You're not going anywhere, so get comfortable." I kiss her again, because I can, and struggle to find the right words to say. It's not as though I didn't know about the salon, but I didn't realize it was a done deal.

My gut tells me we need to find another solution. My pride demands it. I feel like she and I have been dancing around this chemistry between us for too long for her to go traipsing back to Florida in a little over a week.

"Can we play it by ear? Figure out what we're doing and what's happening between us before you move across the country?" And because I'm a cocksucker, I add in something I know she can't resist. "Just think of Mila and Cody. They'll flip the fuck out if you move away forever."

I'll flip the fuck out if she leaves forever, but I'm not ready to beg. Yet. Although that's likely in my future. But everyone knows you don't break out your Hail Mary pass in the first quarter, so I'll bide my time while I try to figure out how to make her dreams come true here. With me.

Her lower lip juts out, and I lean up to taste it. "Until then, yeah, I'll show you how to have sex. And it'll be so good, you'll never wanna leave my bed."

An unrestrained laugh leaves her. "Those are big words."

"That's not the only big thing I have for you, Bitsy." I wink at her like an asshole and slide her to the bed so I can tug off my jeans and rearrange my junk in my boxer briefs. I'm wishing like hell I'd tugged one out in the shower like I planned, but something about that felt wrong with Joey waiting for me in bed.

I pounce on her, making her squeal with laughter. It's so easy to make this girl happy. She's always been like this. Easy laughs. Gentle smiles. Genuine talks.

No wonder I never wanted to take it farther with any of my hookups. Why would I want to when I've had the real deal this whole time waiting for me to get my head out of my ass?

Sweet kisses turn urgent as I slide her T-shirt off her. She helps, her shy smile hidden under the material as it whips off her head. And then there's that beautiful expanse of skin that makes me so hard, I groan.

I'm on her like a fucking animal marking his territory. Licking her pink nipple while squeezing the other perky breast.

Her hips buck against me, and I reach down, elation spreading through me when my fingers reach her wet panties. I slow my movements, my caress gentle.

"What do you like? How do you touch yourself, baby?" Screw my hard-on. The only thing that matters tonight is making my girl come like she's never come before.

"I, uh..." Cue awkward pause. "I have a hard time without using something. I can't go old school and just use my fingers."

My vivid imagination goes crazy filling in the blanks of what that *something* could mean.

"So you use a dildo? Or a vibrator?" Her eyes dart away from me. Even in the dark with only the moonlight to witness what we do, she's embarrassed to be talking about these things. "It's okay." I kiss her and stroke her again through the damp fabric between her legs. "It's nothing to be embarrassed about. Everyone gets off. In fact, I'm gonna be getting off to memories of this night with my hand wrapped around my cock whenever we're not together, so seriously, you can say anything."

She laughs and then nods. "I use something on my clit. It's small and it vibrates."

Good girl. She's starting to relax.

"Well, I don't have anything that vibrates, but I have a pretty good idea you'll like this."

I don't wait for her response as I glide down her body, kissing and licking as I go until I get to that scrap of light-colored lace over her hips. Running my nose over her dainty mound, I inhale her earthy, sweet scent, a mixture of lotion and lust that smells so good, I have to palm my erection hard so I don't embarrass myself.

Once her panties are tossed over my shoulder, I kiss down one leg. Holy shit. She's bare. Smooth as silk. It's like I can hear angels singing over her pretty pussy. I lick my lips and open her with my thumbs.

She squeaks, and before I can lick her, her hand is in my face. "Oh, my God, Logan."

There's my bashful girl. I'm surprised she held out this long before freaking out about me going down on her.

"You're supposed to wait until you're coming to yell that, babe. Hang tight. I gotcha." I push her hand out of the way and give her a stern look. "I'm gonna lick you until you're riding my face, and we're both gonna love every minute of it."

She swallows, the tension rolling off her in waves, but I wait patiently. I've got the whole night to show her how this is done, and I'm happy to bide my time. My girl is going to fly so high she forgets what planet she's on. After a moment, she nods slowly, and I give her a wicked grin before I resume the coveted position between her thighs.

Spreading her apart, I draw my thumb through her wetness. Over her soft outer lips that glisten. Around her entrance that's gonna feel like heaven. Over her back door I might need to finger. Over and over I go. Up and down.

But the one thing I don't touch is that bundle of nerves. Even though her hips start writhing.

When I finally run my tongue over her, our matching groans nearly break me. I wanna tell her how amazing she tastes, but I'm too busy shoving my face in her pussy and lapping her up. I know she's into it because she yanks on my hair as her hips lift to my mouth.

"Yeah, baby. That's right. Fuck my face."

I lick her again, but this time, I ease my finger into her tight channel and am rewarded with her panting moans.

Once. Twice. Three times I thrust before I add another finger. And then I circle her clit with my tongue around and around.

And then she's flying and pulsing on my hand, screaming so loud, I reach up to cover her mouth.

I'm laughing, and she is too, even though I can still feel her contracting on my fingers.

Rambo barks from the other side of the room, and we laugh harder.

When her limbs fall to the bed in exhaustion, I slowly pull out of her and lick my fingers clean. "That was the hottest damn thing I've ever seen in my life."

I flop on the bed next to her and cuddle her to me. She tosses her leg over my thigh and wraps her arm around me.

I'm hard as steel, but right now, the most important thing is holding her.

After a few hard deep breaths, she leans up to kiss me. She

pulls back suddenly, her nose wrinkled. "I can taste myself on you."

"Hot as hell, right? If I let myself think about eating you out, I could probably come without even touching myself."

"Jesus, Logan." She hides her face in my chest, and I laugh.

"You're so fun to tease."

She raises her head, a glint of challenge in her eyes. "Maybe I want to tease you too."

And then she's straddling my hips and riding my cock through my briefs.

My eyes clench shut. "Feels. Too. Good."

"Bet this will feel better." She slides off me to pull down my underwear and then sits back down, her bare pussy snug up against the length of me.

I glance down and groan at the sight of my swollen cock peeking out between her bare thighs.

Her damp core glides across me, and my balls tighten.

"Oh, fuck."

She whispers, "I saw a clip of a porn once like this and thought it was hot. Can you... can you get off like this?"

Can I get off like this? I almost laugh, but I'm too busy obsessing over Joey watching porn to answer with words.

I yank her to me and kiss her, and we're instantly all grunts and groans as we rub our wet parts together.

"Need you to come again." I know she can because every time my swollen head thumps against her clit, she shivers in my arms. "Come on, baby. Make yourself feel good. Ride me."

Hesitantly, she changes her angle and sits up.

Her head tilts away, and I gently grab her chin. "Don't be shy. I wanna look at you. You're fucking glorious."

And she is. Joey takes my breath away. Her tangled hair is in total disarray, hanging down over her shoulders and giving me peeks of her tight nipples. So fucking gorgeous.

As she stares into my eyes, she starts to move again. It's intense looking at someone while you get off, but I'm entranced. She's cast some voodoo spell on me, and I can't turn away.

Her breasts bounce every time her hips thrust. Those slender thighs tighten as she works me over. Her bare lips hug my length like we were made to fit together.

But then the little vixen who's been hiding in Jojo reaches down and massages my crown every time it peeks out, and I almost go over the edge. Except I can't blow before she does.

Licking my finger, I reach behind her and swirl it over her tight little hole until she gasps.

She has to know by now that I'm a dirty bastard.

Her eyes widen and then go molten. Fuck yeah.

Her hips pick up speed when I push my finger into her, and she comes on my cock with a strained moan. Nirvana takes me over the edge with her, the sensation so intense, I almost black out.

Minutes later, I'm still unable to talk, my ability to speak overridden by how hard I came.

As we're lying wrapped around each other panting, I make myself a promise to figure out how to keep Joey in Texas.

Because there's no way I'm letting this girl go in a week.

20

JOEY

I touch my lips as I indulge in the fantasy of what happened last night.

My evening with Logan was amazing, better than I ever thought possible. He put me at ease and helped me enjoy what we did. I never felt pressured to do anything beyond that nudge to let him go down on me. And I'm really glad I gave in because he blew my mind. As far as sexual experiences go, Logan gets two enthusiastic thumbs up.

Here's where it gets awkward.

I've known him my whole life. Yet now I also know he muff-dives like a champ and has an erection the size of a Louisville slugger. And he now knows what I look like when I'm coming on his face.

Insert a full-body blush here.

But what I still haven't figured out is how his baseball bat will fit in any part of me.

So am I freaking out that I got so intimate with Logan? Absolutely.

Am I pretending to be a mature adult who has this under control? Definitely.

Am I fooling anyone? Ask again later.

But Tori is taking my news in stride, so maybe I appear calmer than I am in reality.

"It's not weird that I'm telling you?" I whisper, my eyes darting around to make sure no one can hear us.

Tori and I sit on the beach, enjoying the sun and sea breeze while our friends play volleyball or frolic in the water.

Of course, I beelined it to Tori as soon as I made it to the beach this morning, desperate to get her input about what's happening between me and Logan. But talking about me and Logan hooking up might be more than Tori wants to hear considering he'll be her brother-in-law soon.

Tori, latching onto my paranoia, somehow responds without moving her lips. "I'm sure. Not weird. Not weird at all. As long as we aren't discussing dick size."

I blush ten shades of red.

"But judging by your expression"—she pauses to lift an eyebrow—"it's significant."

Laughter busts out of me. I'm too distracted by her talking like she's a secret agent handing off a dossier to be mortified that my face is giving away personal details about Logan's privates. Like he'd even care. He'd probably strut around like a proud peacock to know I think his manhood is enormous.

"How do you do that?" I motion toward her mouth.

"It's cool, right? I saw some ventriloquist on PBS once when I was a kid and got obsessed."

"It's somehow both cool and bizarre. If you paired it with that weird eye thing you do, you might give me nightmares."

She snorts. "You mean this?" Her eyes open dramatically and shift left, then right, back and forth while she recites the national anthem without moving her lips.

"Whoa."

We both crack up.

After slathering on a healthy amount of sunscreen, I hand it back to her and take a swig of my Corona while I moon over Logan, who dives after the volleyball like some kind of sun god, all bulging muscles and devilish smirk.

So while I'm definitely freaking out over what happened last night, I liked it. A lot.

Almost as much as I enjoyed waking up to his hard body wrapped around mine.

When I woke up tangled in him this morning, he threaded his fingers through my hair and was about to kiss me when Patrick pounded on our door and asked if we wanted breakfast.

I tried not to watch Logan get up and stretch—buck-ass naked—but it was a losing effort. We took quick showers, separately, because even though he offered to wash my back, with the light of day shining in the room, I felt my shyness swallowing me whole again. But we walked out of the condo holding hands, and while it's a bit unnerving to be around our friends and his family like a couple after so many years of just being friends, I'm really freaking ecstatic.

And more than a little tortured.

I bump Tori with my elbow. "Do you really think it's smart to start something now when I'm supposed to go home in a week to work with my cousin?" I lower my voice again. "Even if I've had a thing for Logan for my whole life, I promised Dawn. Plus, I gave her my entire savings."

She chugs some water and rolls her eyes. "*This* is home. They're just borrowing you for a stretch. Don't confuse things."

I shake my head, smiling. "Be serious. I need your advice."

"The pressure!" She shoves me with a smirk. "Fine. I'll be serious. Take things slow, like Logan suggested, and we'll figure out the rest. And for the record, I'm proud of that boy for sounding so mature."

"Right?"

"Totally. Who knew that inside that sweet, albeit misguided, manchild was a guy ready to settle down and make a commitment?"

I pause. "Is that what we're doing?"

Like she's Susan B. Anthony giving a speech, she narrows her eyes and peers out across the sand where the guys are chatting, and waves her arm. "You, Joey Grayson, have accomplished what women across South Texas have only dreamed of doing. You have wrangled the elusive Logan Carter into a relationship."

When she sees my face, she shrugs. "What? It's not like he's seeing anyone else. Just you. And you're not seeing anyone. What do we call that, when two people are exclusively seeing each other?"

There goes her eyebrow again.

"Holy shit."

"That's right, mama. Holy shit." She holds up her fist, and I giggle and jab her back. "Because I will tell you he has *never* brought a hookup to a family weekend or had some rando stay one night, much less two weeks, in his house. You, my little biscuit, are special."

The words hit me so hard, my eyes sting. Between my dad leaving us after Mom died and my brother treating me like dirt, the idea that Logan actually sees me as something special is almost more than I can handle.

"That makes me strangely emotional." I wave my hand across my eyes so I don't start bawling.

Like the good friend she is, she wraps her arm around me and squeezes tight.

I sniffle, eager to change the subject. "Are you and Ethan having fun this weekend?"

"So much fun." She finally releases her python grip on me. "It's great to see Ethan kick back and relax. He works his ass off, even when I nag him to take a break. This wedding stuff forces him to take a breather."

Concern rifles through me. "But the farm is doing better financially, right?"

"It definitely is, but Ethan's eager to finish paying Allison's settlement from the divorce so she can get out of our hair. Trying to expand our operation has a lot of overhead, though, but that's what we need to do to compete at a high level. Once we're done with that settlement, we should be golden."

Ethan's ex was a holy terror back when Tori first came to work on the ranch. Allison never cared about the horses they raised or even her kids that much, if I'm being honest, until Tori came on the scene.

"You and Ethan make such a great team. Allison was never that for him. And she's always been such a biotch to you and Bev. But I do love her kids."

Tori smiles. "I love her kids too. They're the only reason I haven't decked Allison in her snooty face a time or two."

"Mila and Cody are going to be so lucky to have you as their mom."

It's her turn to get misty. She blinks quickly. "I'm really excited to be their mom." Clearing her throat, she wipes her eyes. "I'm not looking to replace Allison in their lives, but I hope they know, in my heart, they're mine. That I'll always love them like my own."

I sniffle. "We really shouldn't cry about this."

After swiping another tear, she laughs. "I know. I've just... been feeling more emotional lately... with all of this wedding excitement." She grabs my hand. "Since we're having this big heart-to-heart, I really have to tell you I hope you and Logan work out and get married and have babies, and *eeep*! Then you'll be my sister!"

We look at each other, eyes wide, mouths open. "Ohhhh. I really want to be your sister."

Like *so*, so much.

A deep voice interrupts. "What are you two gossiping about?"

I squint into the sun to smile at Ethan. "Nothin'."

"Uh-huh." He grabs a drink of water and leans down to kiss Tori on the forehead before turning to me. "You having fun, squirt?"

"So much fun. Thanks for inviting me."

"Are you kidding? The first thing Tori said when we decided to take a trip down here was that you were coming even if she had to fly to Florida and pick you up herself."

Kat plops down next to me. "Did I ever tell you about the time Tori hosted my bachelorette party and had a little mixeroo with the party favors?"

Tori laughs and shakes her head. "This again? I thought you said you were over it."

"I'm over it, but that's why I got you this gift."

A minute later, Tori is holding up a candy necklace with...

My eyes narrow as I try to make out the details. "Are those tiny penises?" Peni? What's the plural of penis?

Tori howls with laughter and wraps it around her neck. "Aww. Now my dreams are coming true."

I smile as Logan walks up, his eyes brightening when he sees me.

Speaking of dreams coming true, maybe mine aren't so out of reach.

21

JOEY

"JUST BE BACK IN TIME FOR THE BONFIRE!" TORI YELLS ACROSS THE beach while Logan and I head for his truck. She makes a naughty gesture with her hand, and I laugh.

Logan turns around to see what she's doing, and she waves sweetly with Rambo in her arms like she wasn't just insinuating we were sneaking off to do something dirty.

I glance up at him. Are we sneaking away to do something dirty?

My nipples tighten at the thought, and I shiver.

"Cold?" He tosses his arm over my shoulder, and I slide mine behind his back, loving the feeling of his solid body against me.

"I shouldn't be cold. It's warm and sunny." I'm only wearing a bikini top and cutoffs over my bottoms, but this is standard beach wear.

He pauses to look me over, his eyebrows pulling tight. "Yeah, but sometimes you can get too much sun." One big palm lands gently on my forehead. "You drinking enough water?"

I nod, secretly eating up how much attention he's giving me.

Is this pathetic? Am I totally swooning over a guy? Probably yes on both accounts, but I've waited too long for Logan to see me as more than his friend to care.

After a quick peck to my lips, we're back in motion. When we reach his truck at the back of the parking lot, he grabs my hips from behind to help me jump in.

But when we end up at the gas station, I'll admit I'm disappointed. Which is silly. *What? Did you expect him to pull over behind the sand dunes for a quickie?*

As we walk through the narrow aisles, pausing to grab chips and ice and lighter fluid, I wonder why we're not running off to do something crazy. Logan is renowned for crazy. He mooned the minister of our small town when he was in high school, for Pete's sake. Then he slept with the guy's daughter.

Ugh, I know too much about his sex life. So much more than I want to know.

"I'm gonna grab a Big Red. Want anything?" I point toward the cooler with my favorite soda.

"Nah. I'm good. Meet me at the register." With a wink, he's strolling to the front of the store.

Judging by my erratic heartbeat, I'm pretty sure that wink will be the death of me.

Smiling to myself, I grab a couple sodas and am headed toward the register when a girly squeal makes me stop.

"Logan Carter! Well, I'll be damned. It's so good to see you, handsome!" A brunette in a teeny-tiny bikini goes bounding up to him and throws her arms around his neck.

I stop, mid-stride, to watch.

Two blondes join her and fawn.

Blah, blah, blah. I've missed you! Blah freaking blah.

Hard. Eye. Roll.

I wish I could say they're trolls, but the three women are gorgeous. Big smiles and bigger boobs. Flashing shiny jewelry and batting their salon-enhanced lashes.

They're all aflutter. Hands on his arms. Cooing and flitting about like he's better than chocolate.

You should see my new cutter. He's such a beaut. Maybe you could take a look at another one I'm thinking about buying. He's great in the saddle, but I'd love to get your opinion.

She rattles off the horse's pedigree, and my heart sinks.

It's worse that they're into horses and talk Logan's language.

The brunette twirls her hair with one finger while she gushes, "I haven't seen you since Dallas. When are you gonna let me lope your horse again, sugar?"

I snort, and Logan turns to me like he just remembered I'm standing here.

I avert my eyes. I can't look at him. Because I don't want to see what's there. Lust over these girls? Regret he's with me this weekend instead of partying it up? Disappointment that I don't fawn over him like his fan club?

He holds out his hand and says my name, but I ignore him and move toward the register. "I'll meet you at the truck." My stupid voice is quiet, barely a squeak. So different than the confidence his fangirls ooze.

My head is racing. One side of my brain tries to remind me that girls do actually lope riders' horses—warm them up in the ring—before a competition, but the other side screams that this girl wants to ride Logan. If she hasn't ridden him already.

When I reach his truck, I take a few calming breaths.

Talking to him last night about how he feels about me was somehow easier than this. Easier than dealing with his past.

Maybe it's because I can't compete with these kind of girls, confident women who go after what they want. Women who can afford twenty-thousand-dollar horses when I can barely afford flip-flops at Target.

What would it be like to get what I want? My whole life I've been scrambling to make ends meet and never quite achieving this goal. It's exhausting.

Almost as exhausting as the idea that this run-in won't be the last. How many more times will we run into girls Logan knows in the biblical sense?

I get that it's not fair to hold his past against him, but I can't help how much it hurts to think of him with other women.

It's not as though this is the first time I've witnessed such a reunion. He had one yesterday with Renee. Except this feels different.

Because now I know what it's like to have his hands on me. To melt under his kisses. To wake up to his warm body and gentle touches.

To feel like he's mine.

But he's not mine. And he probably never will be.

The Logan entourage exists the gas station, and I turn my back to them so I can blink away the sting in my eyes.

Will it always be like this? Will I always feel second best?

I need a distraction in the worst way, so I pull out my phone and notice I've missed a call from Dawn. I dial her up before I give in to my homicidal rage and murder someone.

"Joey, I'm glad you called! Do you remember that contractor..."

I try to listen to my cousin, I do, but I glance over my shoulder as the brunette says her "friend can join them for some fun if he wants" and my hearing cuts out like my circuit breaker overloaded.

I take deep breaths to keep the tears at bay, but this blow to my heart is an arrow to the bullseye, and the hope that had been building this week bursts. Suddenly I feel like that pathetic kid who tagged along behind Logan, following him wherever he went.

When my vision clears, the women have gone, and Logan is

standing in front of me frowning, but I can't speak. I'm too busy wondering if he's envisioning a ménage with that girl and her friend.

It's almost comical. I've barely lost my virginity, and Logan has women in different parts of the state who want to sex him up. It makes me embarrassed about the things I admitted to him last night, to only having done it once and learning moves from PornHub.

A tinny voice catches my attention, and I lift my phone back to my ear to find my cousin talking away. I let her yammer on as Logan quietly unlocks my door and I get in the truck.

Logan gets behind the wheel, and I feel him watching me, but I stare out the window. A whirlwind of colorful houses on stilts whiz by, and I try to make sounds like I'm listening to what my cousin is saying, but I don't because I'm having an out-of-body experience.

We pull up to the condo, and I get off the phone still not having a clue what Dawn explained. I'll have to call her back. She'll think I'm a nutcase for not absorbing one moment of the conversation we just had.

When Logan parks, I reach for the door handle, but he puts his hand on my thigh.

A knot of emotion wells in my chest.

"Bitsy, I'm sorry about what happened back there." I swallow, and he lets out a long sigh. "You know"—he coughs—"you know my history, better than I'd like, so I'm sure none of that shit comes as a surprise, but just to be clear, I've never been with those chicks, and I have no plans to search them out."

At a loss for words, he pauses, so I fill it in. "So you haven't had a ménage?" I don't know why I ask. Maybe to torture myself with how our experiences are so vastly different.

When he cringes, my heart sinks.

"Fuck." Dropping his head into his hands, he pushes his hair out of his face and turns to me. "This might be hard to believe because I know I have a terrible reputation, and I can only imagine what you're thinking right now, but I haven't been like that for a while."

I want to believe him, more than I want my next breath, but there've been too many times where I've seen him sneak off, presumably to get laid, to give those words much credence.

Logan must see my reluctance because he grabs my hand and looks in my eyes. "I swear, Joey, I'm not sleeping around and partying anymore. I'm not that guy."

He doesn't shift or hedge or hesitate, and that lightens something in my chest.

I suppose it's possible he's cleaned up his act since I left for Florida.

Or you're so strung out on him, like a drug addict, you want to believe him to get your next hit.

A rough palm smooths over my neck, and he tilts my head up to face him. "Jojo, let me prove it to you. Let me prove you can trust me."

He's saying the right words, and I want to believe the guy I've known my whole life, but I'm worried we're too different. That he needs wild and willing strippers who can contort their bodies into exotic sex positions instead of the girl next door.

Uneasy, my pride still smarting, I lift a shoulder and offer him the same words he spoke last night. "How about we play it by ear? See where things take us?"

Because I have one week left to figure out if Logan and I stand a chance or if we're too different after all.

22

LOGAN

THE RICH SMELL OF DARK CHOCOLATE WAFTS FROM THE PAN AS I pour it into a thermos.

"Yum!" Renee leans over my shoulder, making me cringe.

"Careful. This is hot." I move away from her, annoyed that she's in my space when I'm pretty sure she spent the night with Patrick.

But her being with my buddy is not why I bolt across the kitchen.

I didn't need Joey to spell out how she was feeling this afternoon after running into those women at the gas station. The hurt and embarrassment was stamped on her face. It gutted me.

When I realized Joey was standing a few feet away, listening to Tanya and her friends blather on, I reached for her. I wanted to throw my arm over her so Tanya knew I was with someone, but JoJo either ignored me or didn't hear me when she stalked up to the register.

Tanya's family spends a shitload of money on horses, and I didn't want to risk offending her. Our ranch is too small to afford making enemies. I was cordial, but I didn't hug her back or flirt like I usually would. Not that I wanted to. The only person on my mind since she stepped off that bus is Joey.

Sitting in my truck while she struggled to look at me made me think back to the other times this has happened, to the times before she left for Florida. Did it bother her, and she just hid it? Was I too dense to notice?

Surely she hasn't had feelings for me since her freshman year of high school. That would be crazy. I almost laugh out loud. *Take your ego down a notch, asshole. Not every woman is in love with you.*

I won't deny I'm uneasy going down this road with Joey because we could screw up our friendship, but the alternative— potentially losing her forever—terrifies me. So if I have to test out having a relationship to keep her here, I'll do it. Our dynamic is changing so quickly, I'm scrambling to catch up, but I can't deny the magnitude of what's happening between us.

We didn't even have sex last night, and I'm already losing my head for her, something that's never happened to me before. I've never had the kind of connection to a woman the way I do with Jojo. And I can count the number of times I've slept in the same bed with a woman after getting intimate—that number would be zero.

Snuggling up after the deed is not something I do. Ever. But I didn't want to let go of Joey last night, and I certainly didn't want to leave our bed this morning. Although I'll admit I'm a little unnerved to find out how much this girl might unravel me when we finally do have sex.

Renee moves in front of me as I reach for my backpack, interrupting my thoughts.

"Can I have some of that? I'm really in the mood to get warmed up." Renee bats her eyelashes at me. Are we talking about hot chocolate right now?

"I made this for Joey, but there's the container. You can make more." I screw on the lid to the thermos and pack the rest of the snacks I brought for the bonfire.

"She doesn't have to know," she sing-songs softly.

What the fuck?

"It's spoken for. Make your own." I toss her the container and laugh when she nearly drops it.

"God, you're a dick."

"Never said I wasn't."

With my backpack on my shoulder, a small ice chest in one hand, and the thermos in the other, I stroll out of the condo and down the wooden boardwalk toward the bonfire on the beach.

Even with the distance I'm putting between me and Renee, I'm still brimming with irritation. Like my clothes don't fit anymore. Like who I am and what I want don't match anymore.

Things with Joey could go south because of dumb shit I've done, and I have enough issues to deal with at the moment to consider how many ways my past might fuck me.

I'm still in a funk when I reach the party on the beach, but seeing everyone enjoying themselves dulls my pissy mood.

I drop the cooler between my truck and Ethan's.

"The tailgating idea was genius," I muse. "Did I come up with it?" Between three other trucks are lawn chairs and blankets. Coolers everywhere. Loud but mellow music plays in the background. Some of the guys tend to the giant bonfire in the middle, lighting up the night sky.

Ethan slaps me on the back with a smirk. "No, dumbass. Your girlfriend suggested it. She said you used to tailgate in the back field before games in high school. And it's better than just having the chairs."

Girlfriend.

Hearing that word gives me pause. I've always been the one to tease Ethan about the chicks he dated. Of the two of us, he was the one who did long-term relationships.

I give him a big-ass smile. "*My girlfriend* is awesome."

Joey is chatting with Kat on the other side of the bonfire. Even though we spent most of the day together, not to mention the past week, there's nothing more I want than to hang out with her alone, especially after what happened at the gas station.

Ethan studies me a second before he leans closer. "I wasn't kidding when I told you to take care of her or I'd kick your ass. You'd better treat her with respect."

Annoyance flares again, and I ask under my breath, "Does everyone think I'm a giant heathen? Like I'm going to fling off my clothes for an orgy? What the hell, man?"

He places a hand on my shoulder to turn us away from our friends. "Logan, she's not like the other women you date. Just... she's been sheltered. She might not know how to guard her heart."

What does that even mean? Guard her heart? "I'm not gonna hurt her. She's my best friend, for fuck's sake." This whole conversation sounds too familiar, and my stomach knots. When my brother brought it up yesterday, he and Brady were ribbing me, giving me shit like they always do. This, though, this is different.

Ethan's eyes narrow. "You ready to cut out those extracurricular activities?"

Anger heats my blood, but I remind myself I can't be mad at him. Not when he's why I've busted my ass all this time to keep shit on lockdown.

But the idea of Ethan doling out the same advice as our father, albeit less heavy-handed, still feels like a punch to my gut.

Tori strolls over and wraps her arms around my brother, smiling at him like he's a king. Grinding my teeth together, I force myself to keep it together a little longer.

Wait until after the wedding and they get back from their honey-moon. They're so happy right now. Do not fuck this up.

I cough. "I promise I only have the best intentions. I won't mess this up." Any of it.

Ethan nods slowly and focuses his attention on Tori.

Needing some space, I head over to my truck, lower the tail-gate, and hop on. I stare into the fire, not really seeing anything.

A sensation I know too well seeps into me. Hollowness. The kind that makes me want to claw at my skin to see if there's a heart still beating in my chest.

After my father died, my mother dragged me to a shrink. She said I needed to talk to someone because finding him face down in his own vomit was traumatic.

I much preferred getting shitfaced and fucking to those sessions with Dr. Pritley.

Fortunately those therapy sessions only lasted about a month. By then Ethan was back from A&M with his pregnant fiancée, and money was tight. I gladly bowed out, reassuring my mom I was okay with a you-can-take-me-seriously sorta smile and a few jokes. She probably figured you can't joke around if you're depressed as fuck.

My vision sharpens, and Joey gives me a hesitant smile from the other side of the bonfire.

Tilting my head, I hope she gets my meaning.

She hugs Rambo to her chest and looks down, and for a second, I wonder if she's gonna ignore me—she might after what happened this afternoon—but she trots over.

I slide off the bed of my truck and motion toward one of the lawn chairs sprawled in front of the fire. "It's warmer down here."

"But there's only one chair left."

Silly girl. I scoop her into my arms, relishing the laughter that peals out of her, and plunk us down in a chair.

Rambo tries to lick my face off.

"Dude," I sputter and wipe my chin with my arm.

Before long, we're roasting marshmallows while Midland plays angsty ballads from someone's stereo. Rambo nestles at our feet, and Joey's in my lap. Ethan and Tori shoot the shit with their friends, and that blanket of fog lifts off my shoulders. For a few minutes, under these stars, by the warmth of the fire, everything is right in the world.

After I pull a blanket around us, I drag my lips against the shell of her ear. "I'm really glad you're home," I whisper. "I missed you."

I sound like a broken record, but half of me is afraid I'm gonna wake up tomorrow and find that she's hightailed it out of town without knowing what she means to me.

She continues to stare at the fire, but her lips tug up in a shy smile, so I keep going. Because I know this afternoon was rough, and I want to reassure her. I *need* to reassure her. "Last night was incredible. I can't wait to do it again." She can probably feel my lengthening dick against her ass. "But, Jo"—I wait for her to look at me—"I can't change my past or my mistakes. God knows I've made a ton, and I need you to believe that I want a fresh start. Something's gotta give because I can't keep fucking up. And maybe... maybe you can help me with that."

I realize she doesn't know anything about the hole I've dug for myself, but if there's anyone I want on my side, it's Joey.

She frowns and glances around. Then she looks up at me with those soulful gray eyes and whispers, "Logan, are you in trouble? Did something happen while I was away?"

I swallow, wishing I could unload everything right now. It would be such a relief.

It's on the tip of my tongue, but my brother laughs from the other side of the fire, reminding me why I can't, and I reluctantly shake my head.

"No, I'm not in trouble. Exactly." I debate how to say it since I haven't confided in anyone except my buddy Isaiah, and that was an accident. He's biking in Bolivia or some shit, so he can't go blabbing his mouth. "Just bit off more than I can chew."

Jo waits patiently for me to tell her more, but when she realizes I'm not going to, she nods. "Okay. Well, when you're ready to tell me."

Hitching her closer to me, I hug her tight. I knew she'd understand on some level. She's always been there for me, even when I was an asshole. "Thanks, Bitsy. I will." Which reminds me. "Have you heard from your brother?"

She stills. I hate bringing him up and seeing that miserable look in her eyes, but I need to know. "No, and as much as I hate to admit it, I'm worried."

"I'm sure he's fine." And living high on the hog with the money from the sale of their grandmother's house. I hesitate. "He doesn't hack your phone anymore, does he?" I try to look casual despite the fact that Silas is the reason I haven't confided in her about the mess I'm in. But if he's not in her life—creeping around to listen to her messages and read her texts—then I'll feel better about sharing the shit that's been going down after the wedding.

"No, he hasn't done that in a while. Not since the last time you threatened to kick his ass."

Silas has never been a friendly guy, but since he got wrapped up in drugs, he's unpredictable, not to mention meaner, and I made it clear to him that I don't want his mistakes to hurt his sister.

Soon, Silas is in our rear view mirror as we reminisce about when we were kids. Jo and I talk softly over the crackle of the fire for the next few hours. By the time we get back to our room, it's late.

The condo is an ice box, and I beeline it to our bathroom where I turn on the shower and crank the hot water.

"Come here, baby. Take your shower and warm up. I'll find us a movie to watch."

Joey grabs fresh towels and smiles up at me in the doorway to the bathroom. I kiss her forehead and move to let her in, but she grabs my hand, so I pause.

Her head tilts down, and she looks up at me through those lashes, a hesitant expression on her beautiful face. She shifts awkwardly. "Wanna join me? You know... maybe scrub my back?"

Oh, fuck.

A million emotions race through me, and I try to stamp out the lust that jets to the top so I can think straight. Mostly, I don't wanna rush her.

"Are you sure?" I run my hands along her bare shoulders and try hard not to notice her pebbled nipples through her bikini top. "We can take our time. We don't have to do anything else this weekend if you're not comfortable."

I'm not the kind of guy who pushes a girl into doing something she doesn't want to do. A real man respects a woman's boundaries.

She looks away, a pretty pink hue tinting her cheeks, and I realize how hard that was for her to ask.

Does she think I don't want to do this with her? Of course I want to watch rivulets of water course over her lush body while steam billows in the background.

"Hey." I tilt her chin up and kiss her. "Fuck, yes, I wanna take a shower with you. If you're comfortable with that."

I don't have to wonder how she's feeling because she's in my arms, and I'm breathing her in as we kiss and stumble into the shower.

Hot water sluices over her, and I lean back for the visual,

because holy shit, she's a dime. Tangled blonde hair, honey-tanned skin from our weekend in the sun, and perfect, rounded curves I wanna get lost in.

"Fuck, you're beautiful, Jo. What the hell is wrong with me? Am I blind?" I kiss her again because I'm not expecting a response. I'm too busy wondering why I haven't appreciated how amazing my best friend is. How kind and supportive and funny. And how fucking gorgeous.

I've never been a lucky guy. Never been the one to come out ahead, but right now, with Jojo in my arms, I hope for once my luck holds out.

23

JOEY

BEING WITH LOGAN LIKE THIS IS ALMOST TOO MUCH TO HANDLE. Emotions surge in my chest, like happiness and want and love are going to explode out of me in a bouquet of color.

His hands are in my hair and on my rear, and mine are on his broad shoulders. I can't tell what's hotter, the water rushing over us or the electricity sizzling between our bodies.

We meld together, his tongue thrusting against mine as we slam into the shower wall and laugh.

"Are you okay?" Concern and affection shine through his eyes as he runs his thumb over my bottom lip.

I nod, wanting to tell him I've never been so happy before. That I don't know what's swirling in my heart, but it's too big for me to name.

I know it's too early to say such things, so I don't, but being with him like this tonight will be enough.

Maybe it was seeing him handle Renee in the kitchen earlier this evening that has me ready to set aside my fears and push ahead. I'd come back from the beach to grab another towel and I saw her hit on him, shamelessly suggesting they could screw around behind my back.

Nothing could've kept the smile off my face when he blew her off.

It made me realize that I'd overreacted this afternoon. Neither of us can control our past, but Logan seems serious about giving us a try, and he'd never deliberately hurt me. I don't want to be the jealous girl who goes off the deep end anytime another woman talks to her guy. I saw how that green-eyed monster tanked my parents' relationship. That's the fastest way to strangle something good.

And then he scooped me into his lap at the beach and spoke softly to me all night, whispering in my ear, holding me close. By the time we reached our room and he suggested a shower, I couldn't help but ask him to join me. Another first. One I only want with him.

I always imagined this moment would make me feel vulnerable. Getting naked under harsh bathroom lights sounds like something I'd want to hide under a rock to avoid. But in this moment, standing before Logan and seeing how much he wants me makes me feel powerful and desired. It makes me want to shed my reserved exterior and be brave like I was last night.

I step away and take a deep breath. Reaching back to the strings on my bikini top, I slowly pull the fabric.

My bikini top falls to the floor with a wet plop, and time stretches out as I unsnap my cutoffs and slide them off with the rest of my swimsuit. A groan rumbles from Logan's chest as he studies me from head to toe. "Damn."

I resist the urge to hide myself and let him take his fill while water beats across my skin. I don't want to be the girl who's afraid of her shadow anymore.

The next moment, I'm in his arms, skin to skin against his hard chest. The sensation is so intimate, everything in me flares to life.

Shamelessly, I rub against him as we kiss. I need to feel him. Need to prove that this is real. That I'm not going to wake up in the morning and find tonight was a dream.

Feeling bold, I let my hands roam. Over his strong shoulders and chest. Down his sexy eight-pack. Through the trail of hair leading down. Until my fingers reach his trunks.

Remembering what we did last night, I rub him over the fabric and try to ignore the mounting fear when I consider his size. Because seriously, how is that behemoth going to fit?

Like he can read my mind, he pulls me close and whispers, "We'll go slow, Jojo. Only what you want to do. You're in control."

I nod, relief settling over me enough to relax again. "I want this. Show me what to do."

He starts to pull me closer, and I shake my head. "Show me."

For a second, I can't believe what I'm about to attempt, but I'm tired of hiding what I really want when it comes to this man.

Slipping my hands into the waistband of his trunks, I slide them down over his slender hips and muscular thighs as I fall to my knees. Until his hard length bobs in front of me.

Through the droplets clinging to my lashes, I look up and take him in my hand. My heart pounds like I've run a marathon as I say the words, "Tell me what you like. How to make you feel good." He made me have an out-of-body experience last night. I want to return the favor.

"Fuck, I love this side of you, baby," he groans, thickening in my palm.

His eyes hood as I take a tiny lick across his swollen head, tasting the salty bead of fluid at the tip. Gently, I tug up and down as I marvel at how he can be velvety smooth and yet so hard.

His palm wraps around mine to grip himself tighter, and I encourage him with a nod. With his other hand, he fists my hair, and the intensity makes me catch my breath. A devilish smile spreads on his face. "Open up. Wanna feed you my cock, gorgeous girl."

Dang. That's hot. But I'm not surprised Logan is a dirty talker. *Bring it, big boy. I like this side of you too.*

I rub him over my lips before I comply and slide him against my tongue.

He lets go of my hand once I get the rhythm he likes. We watch each other, his eyes glued to my mouth where I'm stretched wide. I can't go too deep, but he doesn't seem to care. Whenever I do something he likes, his hold on my hair tightens, which sends a zing through my body.

What's crazy is how turned on I am from doing this. I'm slick and swollen between my legs, the pulse beating there growing with every suck and swipe of my tongue on his body.

Finally, I can't stand it any longer and reach down there to give myself some relief.

"Fuck, yes. You look so hot doing that. Touch your pretty pussy for me."

I'm on fire from his words. From the way he's looking at me. From the way he responds in my hand.

I want to make him unravel, so I pick up the pace, eventually relaxing enough to take him to the back of my throat.

His gravelly moan is the only encouragement I need to do it again and again until he tugs my mouth away in warning.

Warm cum shoots on my neck and breasts and chin. I work him over with my hands until he yanks me off the floor and kisses me until I'm breathless. His hand snakes down between us, his fingers working their magic.

"You're so wet. Did my dirty girl get off on blowing me?"

"Yes," I admit as I writhe against him, my eyes clenched tight. I come in record time.

As amazing as the orgasm feels, I'm not sure it beats the tenderness that fills me when he holds me afterward.

We stand under the warm water, breathing hard, my nose pressed against his neck, his in my hair, a lifetime of things unspoken between us.

Maybe that's enough for now.

24

JOEY

THE RIDE HOME IS QUIET, SAVE FOR THE CLASSIC ROCK LOGAN plays softly in the background. Three of the guys sleep in the back seat. Renee drove back with someone else, thank goodness.

I'm drowsy too, but I'm enjoying holding Logan's hand too much to nap. Every now and then, he shoots me a smile, and I grin back, feeling like I'm a balloon barely tethered to the ground. Whatever this is between us feels almost too good to be true, but for once in my life, I'm getting what I want and I refuse to question it.

When we pull into a gas station with the rest of our caravan, everyone gets out to stretch their legs, and Logan motions me toward the side of the truck.

"What's wrong?"

He's frowning and rocking back on his heels.

"Nothing. Nothing's wrong. Just..." He looks around. No one is around, but he tugs me closer. "I, uh, wanted to apologize for last night. For—" He waves at my chest.

I lift my eyebrows. "For?" An uncomfortable silence stretches between us. "Wait. Do you regret what we did?"

"No. God, no." He kisses me soundly and then rests his arms

on my shoulder and lowers his voice. "I just... I didn't... I didn't mean to come all over you. I don't want you to feel disrespected or anything."

An adorable flush darkens his cheeks.

"Logan Carter, I do declare that you're blushing," I announce like Scarlett O'Hara. "First the tampons at Target and now this."

He rolls his eyes with an awkward laugh.

Pushing up on my tiptoes, I kiss him and whisper, "Maybe I liked that part of our shower and maybe I'd be okay if you did it again." His eyes heat, and now it's my turn to laugh when he yanks me against his truck and sticks his tongue in my mouth. We make out like the world might end tomorrow until someone clears his throat.

"All right, love birds. Break it up." Ethan smirks at us, and Logan shrugs and kisses me again, not giving a flip that his brother is standing five feet away.

Logan points at Ethan. "This is payback for that time I found you and Tori in the flatbed of your truck, *in our back yard*, on a Sunday morning." He clicks his tongue. "Doing the dirty on the Lord's day."

I slap a hand over my mouth to mask my giggle, but it still squeaks out.

"Laugh it up, chuckles," Ethan chides. "Your turn will come."

Logan pulls me closer. "We've been totally respectable. Well, mostly." He scratches his jaw. "In public at least." His eyes meet mine. "Right, babe? Except for the last little smooch-fest."

"Totally respectable." I nod dutifully.

A smile resides on my face for the rest of the drive. We're almost back to the farm when I figure out why I'm so giddy.

It feels good to be claimed by someone. And not just by anyone. By my best friend. After feeling left behind by my family, the sense of belonging settles over me like rain after a long drought. I never want it to end.

I'm drowsy but so content when we pull up to Ethan's driveway.

Bev greets us at the door, the weariness on her face making me pause. "Did y'all have fun? Please tell me no one got arrested." She seems to pick up speed as she doles out hugs to everyone, and I shake off my concern. Bev's a powerhouse. Nothing gets her down.

It's not like things with Mama, I chide myself. My mother had dark circles under her eyes for months before my father thought to ask her if something was wrong—and it was only when his dinner was late to the table. He'd ask out of his own inconvenience and not genuine concern for his wife.

When Bev reaches me, looking as spry as ever, she squeezes me tight and whispers, "Glad you finally got to go to the coast with our family, sweetheart."

That she remembers how I begged my parents so long ago squeezes my heart.

When Logan catches my expression—no doubt I look emotional—he stalks over to me. "You okay, Jojo?"

Nodding, I smile up at him, sighing contentedly when he takes me in his arms and presses a kiss to my forehead.

I freeze when I see Bev studying us closely, her lips curling up slowly.

A hot flush of embarrassment rises in my cheeks at the thought of the many naked things I did with her son this weekend, and I glance down, afraid she'll see it on my face.

I brace myself for her to say something, to call us out on the PDA or highlight the obvious change in our BFF status the way Ethan has, but she doesn't. Just gives me a wink before pointing a finger at her son and barking, "I need to talk to you later," before walking away.

Oh, God.

Leaning closer to Logan, I lower my voice. "Is Bev going to

give you a hard time about us being together?" It never crossed my mind that she might be against us having a relationship.

He shrugs. "I doubt it. You're like a daughter to her, so it's not like this is a stretch."

That warms me from head to toe for two reasons.

One. Logan expects me to stick around. He might have said this wasn't just a vacation fling, but it's taking time to let my guard down and trust him. Which makes me sound like a crappy friend, but it's been tough to reconcile the heartbreaker I grew up with and the man I've been bunking with for the last week.

And two. Bev's fondness for me isn't just my imagination. That she considers me a daughter is a compliment of the highest order.

Ethan and Tori hug the kids, who are jumping around and excited to see what Ethan brought back for them.

"Ma, did my heathens behave?" he asks Bev.

"Mostly. We only had to do one public flogging," she jokes, looking tired once again. I'm sure hanging out with the kids the entire weekend did her in. Even if she had Tori's cousins to help, Mila and Cody have a lot of energy to burn.

I help unload the caravan before I drag myself into the house. I'm relieved we have five days before the rehearsal dinner because I'm wiped out. All that sunshine and frolicking did me in. Well, and naked midnight activities.

Everyone has congregated in the living room except for Logan and Bev, who are arguing quietly in the kitchen. She waves her hands around, and Logan looks pissed. The vacation vibe he wore so well on the way home is gone. They immediately stop talking when they see me.

"Sorry to interrupt. Sorry. I'll just wait for you—" I point back toward the living room.

Weird. Those two never argue. Not really. She might want to

knock him over the head for being stubborn sometimes, but I've never known Bev to get really upset by much. Other than Ethan's ex, that is. Allison riled up Bev like nobody's business.

Logan's quiet on the way back to his house.

I wait for him to tell me what's going on, but he doesn't, so I finally break down and ask.

"Is everything okay with your mom?" *Please don't say she's mad about us.* I'll die a thousand deaths if Bev's against Logan and me having a relationship.

He sighs wearily. "Yeah. Just..." He pauses a long moment. "She forgot to refill a prescription, which I would've been happy to do before I left had I known." Another sigh.

Relief that she's not upset at me and worry about her health shoot through me so quickly, I can barely make sense of it.

"Is she sick?" I almost choke on the words. Watching my mother die of cancer was one of the worst things I've ever gone through, and the thought of losing Bev is crippling.

"Uh..." He shakes his head slowly. His eyes meet mine and soften when he sees my expression. He reaches for my hand as he drives. "There's nothing to worry about, babe."

I'm hoping he tells me more, but he doesn't. And I guess I understand. It's really none of my business, but I can't deny being disappointed that he doesn't confide in me.

His mood doesn't improve when we get back to his place. Rambo and I curl up on the couch to watch reruns of *Friends*, but Logan heads back to his bedroom to make a few phone calls. When he returns, he reaches for his keys.

"Gonna refill my mom's scripts. I need to drive to Austin since the pharmacy here is already closed, so I might be a while. Don't wait up."

It sucks to have to drive to the city on a Sunday night when he has to get up at the crack of dawn tomorrow.

"Do you want me to keep you company?"

"Nah. I got this." He kisses me on the forehead and is out the door before I can respond.

I can't shake the feeling that there's more to the story than what he's telling me, but it's not like I'm entitled to know Bev's private business.

Two hours later, after I get ready for bed, I stand in the hallway between our rooms and look back and forth at the doors, trying to decide what to do. I've only ever slept in Bev's bed while I've stayed with Logan. But me staying in his room while at the coast is different than me sleeping in his bed at his house for the duration of my stay. Would that be too much for him? Would it cramp his style? Am I even staying in town after the wedding?

Jesus, this relationship stuff is exhausting. I rub my face in Rambo's fur. "What should I do?" About all of it, but I'm too tired to articulate the finer points of this conundrum to my dog.

Bev's room is safe, I decide. Logan can come and get me if he wants me to sleep with him.

Except I fall asleep alone.

25

LOGAN

THE VERY LAST THING I WANT TO DO TONIGHT IS SPEND THE NEXT hour and a half in my truck after that five-hour drive this afternoon. What should've been a four-hour trip home turned into five and change when we stopped three times for gas and piss breaks.

I'm in a foul fucking mood as I haul ass to the one pharmacy on the other side of the city that will fill my mom's prescription.

I feel like shit for lying to Joey, but my mother's secrets aren't mine to tell.

Fine. I didn't overtly lie, but I didn't tell her the whole story, which feels like lying all the same.

My mother nearly went off the rails when she tried to refill her prescription this afternoon and found out how much those little pills cost. Usually I get her scripts, and I've let her think our insurance covers everything. She was royally pissed when she found out it doesn't. But like I'm gonna let my mother go without her medicine? Fuck that. I'd do anything for that woman, and if I have to work a second job to afford what she needs, so be it.

I'm pulling into the pharmacy when my phone lights up with a call.

I answer automatically, assuming it's Joey or my mom.

It's neither.

"It's about time you answer."

Goddamn it. I throw my truck in park and lean my head back to take a deep breath, annoyed with myself for not checking the caller ID first.

"What do you need, Samantha?" She acts like I ignore her. I've only answered a half dozen of her texts over the last three days.

"Zach's not feeling well."

"Still?"

"I'm worried, Logan. Can you please come and check on him? I'm not sure if I should take him to the ER. I don't have a grand to blow if they're just gonna turn us around and send us home. Unless you wanna foot the bill."

Fuck my life. Why does everything always fall on my shoulders?

"Does he have a fever?"

"I'm not sure."

Jesus Christ.

"Can you use a thermometer and check?" I ask as calmly as possible.

"I don't have one."

Of course not.

I pinch the bridge of my nose, hating what I'm about to do. Not because I don't care for Zach. I love that kid with every fiber of my being, but dealing with his mother overwhelms me to no end. A throb takes residence in my temple, and I add painkillers to my internal list of items to buy.

After another long-ass sigh, I nod. "I'm at the pharmacy. What do you need besides a thermometer?"

Zach went to a carnival with some friends yesterday and threw up last night, but I thought he was feeling better this morning. My brother and I puked our guts out when we were kids after we ate hotdogs and immediately hopped on a roller-coaster, so I didn't worry too much because Zach's a tough kid.

When I reach their apartment almost an hour later, Zach is resting peacefully on the couch. Sam's hands twist, and she gives me a pained smile. "Sorry if I overreacted. I was just worried," she whispers. "He finally kept down a Gatorade and passed out."

I feel his forehead. It's cool to the touch, and his breathing isn't labored. He appears to be resting comfortably.

After I unpack the groceries in their kitchen, I make a cup of instant coffee. It tastes like shit, but I'm so fucking tired, I'm not sure how I'll make it home.

I ignore the fact that Sam's barely dressed, only covered up in a tiny silk robe that barely reaches her thighs. Doesn't matter because I have no intention of seeing what's underneath that fabric.

"Make him some soup when he gets up." I motion to the mountain of juices and other get-well necessities.

She picks up one of the Gatorades I bought for him. "Orange is his favorite flavor."

"I know. That's why I bought him four." I might have felt a fat wave of guilt at the pharmacy so I overcompensated by purchasing enough supplies to last through the next ice age.

But the lead in my gut won't go away. Zach was sick, and I was on vacation. Nothing about this situation is his fault, yet he's the one who had to suffer. I should've brought him with me. He would've had a blast.

If you'd manned up and told Ethan the truth, you probably could have.

As I look at Zach sleeping in the other room, I vow that the next time I head off on a family vacation, the kid is coming with me. He's family after all. Even under these unusual circumstances.

After I chug the rest of the coffee, I rinse out my mug. "Call me tomorrow if you're still worried."

"You'll pick up?" she huffs.

This again.

"Sam," I say gently, "you know we've talked about having boundaries."

Her eyes well with tears, and it makes me feel like shit. I know this isn't entirely her fault, but this isn't an ideal situation for me either.

"I just..." She sobs quietly. "I'm lonely, Logan. Why can't we keep each other company? It's not like you're a saint. I thought you might want to..."

God, please don't finish that thought.

I'm gonna have to give her a hard pass. For so many reasons.

I start talking before she can say anything else. "I know moving here was tough and you miss your family. Did you enroll in classes like I suggested? You'll meet more people like that. Just send me the bill, and I can reimburse you for the credits."

"I don't care about the fucking money, okay?" She lowers her voice when she realizes she might wake up Zach. "I mean, yes, I need the cash, but why do you only care about Zach and the bills? Why don't you care about me?"

I'm not really sure how to answer that tactfully. I take a deep breath. "Sam, come on now. You know I care. I give you a huge check every month to make sure you can afford everything you need. I take Zach to lunch every week and fix the broken shit in your apartment. Don't say I don't care. I just can't be what you need in a man. That's not me. That will never be me, okay? But I will support you each and every step of the way until you get on your feet. I care. As a friend."

A wild look in her eyes flashes for a moment, but then it's gone. She nods slowly as she wipes away the tears, and I relax.

There are only so many ways I can emphasize that she and I will never get together. Not in this lifetime or the next.

Samantha is a beautiful woman with red hair, a curvy figure, and big green eyes. Which she bats at me every chance she gets.

Still, I'm not interested.

I hope Sam understands. That she really gets it this time.

More importantly, I hope Joey understands when I tell her about Samantha.

26

JOEY

A WARM, HARD BODY SLIDES BEHIND MINE UNDER THE COVERS, AND I smile sleepily into the pillow.

"What time is it?" I ask, my voice a rasp.

"It's late. Sorry I woke you, baby." Logan's cold nose presses to my neck, and I wiggle back to nestle against him in our cocoon of two.

"Missed you." A sad admission since we've been glued at the hip the whole weekend, but still true.

"So much that you're not in my bed?"

I chuckle and rub the gunk out of my eyes. "You should've heard the internal debate I had about that at bedtime."

"I bet." He kisses my shoulder, rests his giant palm on my breast, makes a manly sound of contentment, and passes out.

Poor baby. I want to ask him a million questions, like why it took him so long to get the meds and if Bev is really okay. I worried he had car trouble or couldn't get the prescription, but right now I'm just glad he's home and wrapped around me.

In the morning, there's a note on my pillow to call him when I'm up, and he'll try to join me for lunch. I forgot to tell him Tori was picking me up today so I can test out a hairstyle for the wedding, so I send him a text that I'm headed his way.

The house is filled with people when I get there—Tori's parents, her cousins, Bev, and the kids, who perch on their dad's lap in the kitchen. This might be Ethan's second marriage, but I never saw him this happy with Allison. His smile is wide and relaxed even though Mila and Cody hang off him like he's their personal jungle gym.

Although the wedding is a few days away, you'd think it was this afternoon from the smiles on everyone's faces.

When the kids spot me, they bound over and tackle me for a hug. "Hey, guys." I smooch their little heads. "I just saw you last night, you know."

Mila grabs my hand. "Yeah, but Uncle Logan says we hafta convince you to stay in Texas." She leans up to me like she wants to tell me a secret and whisper-yells, "He says he'll die if you leave. So don't leave, okay? Plus, Cody and I love you."

Oh, my heart. Dang. He's good.

I kneel in front of Mila and talk to her as honestly as possible. "I haven't figured out how to stay yet, but I'm working on it, okay?"

She nods solemnly, and I hug her tightly.

I've been putting off that conversation with my cousin. Dawn let me stay with her when I was flat broke and helped me get on my feet. Her family was there for me when Gran passed. It would be so crappy to bow out on her. I made a commitment. My dad and brother might bail at the drop of a hat, but I don't. Never mind that my money is wrapped up in her salon. Honestly, though, nothing pains me as much as the idea of letting down someone who's stood by my side.

The back door slams, and Logan strolls in, flushed from the heat and sweaty, and looking so edible, I want to gobble him up.

A thick knot rises in my throat at the thought of going back to Florida. How can I give up Logan? After being in love with him for so long and we finally get a chance...

Now that we're back from the coast and the reality of leaving after the wedding starts to sink in, my heart feels like it might disintegrate.

Two fingers lift my chin, and I look up until I'm staring into Logan's baby blues.

"Whatcha thinking so hard about, Bitsy?" He kisses my forehead, and tears well in my eyes.

"Just... How I'm supposed to leave next week."

His brows pull tight, and then he's tugging me against his chest. He smells like leather, clean sweat, and sweet hay. I don't even care that his skin's damp and now mine is too. I wrap my arms around him.

His voice rumbles in my ear. "Don't want you to go. There's still time to figure out something, Jojo."

I nod against him and blink back the heat in my eyes.

That's when I notice the kitchen has gotten quiet.

Turning slowly, I laugh nervously when I see everyone staring at us.

Tori's mom motions between me and Logan. "Are you two dating?" She glances at Tori. "I thought they were, what did you say, BFFs?"

Tori winks at me and whispers something to her mother, who nods and points at us again. "This is new, yes?"

I chuckle. "Yes, ma'am."

Logan tucks me under his arm. "Only 'cause I was too stupid to get a clue sooner."

Everyone laughs, and my heart swells ten times bigger. I'm so gone for this guy, it's ridiculous.

My eyes meet Bev's. She's grinning from ear to ear, and I blush. I've never told her how I feel about Logan, but she's a smart lady. I'm sure I must've looked like a sad puppy following her son all over town when we were young.

One of the kids burps, and suddenly everyone's attention is off of us, thank goodness.

Logan's fingers thread through mine. "When you're done doing wedding stuff with Tori, wanna go for a ride? I thought you might like to take Cinnamon Pie for a spin. Maybe this evening when it's not so hot. We could have a picnic down by the creek."

Emotion rises in my chest again, and I swallow. "I'd love that."

In this moment, it starts to sink in how differently he views me from the other women he's been with. A picnic down by the creek? Call me crazy, but that sounds like a date, which I've never known Logan to do.

My stomach flutters when I think about having a legit relationship with Logan and what that could mean. It's a familiar daydream. Him working on the ranch and me meeting him for lunch after I take a couple of clients. Long nights watching Netflix and making love and laughing. Hanging out at the Carter farm and taking turns with Tori to watch all of our kids.

Our kids.

They'd have Logan's eyes and his determined attitude. Maybe with light blond hair when they were little that would get darker as they got older. They'd love the farm and the horses and running wild in the fields.

I sigh deeply, wishing my emotions didn't always get the best of me. I'm pretty sure these aren't the things a girl's supposed to be dreaming about five seconds into a relationship.

Logan studies my face like he's trying to commit little details about me to memory. "We'll figure it out, Jo," he whispers, wrapping me in his strong arms again, "but let's have fun this week.

Let's make some new memories. We'll get back to real life after the wedding."

That's the best idea I've heard all day, and the smile that sweeps across my face is genuine. Nothing sounds better than making more memories with Logan.

I tilt my head up to look at him, and he grins down at me before he tucks his sweaty face into the crook of my neck and licks me. I squeal and push him away, but I don't get far before he starts to tickle me, not caring that his entire family is a few feet away.

I love playful Logan. The expression on his face reminds me so much of when we were kids, and he and my brother ran around like cyclones, always getting in trouble.

And if my emotions are any indication, I'm in so much trouble when it comes to Logan Carter, and I don't even care.

27

LOGAN

"HAVE FUN ON YOUR PICNIC!" TORI WAVES AT US AS ETHAN SMIRKS.

"Yeah. Have fun on your 'picnic.'" My brother uses air quotes, and I give him the finger behind Joey's back.

Jo and I ride our horses out of the barn and down a path that leads behind the property. The horses amble along side by side as dusk settles over the horizon. Butterflies meander lazily in the breeze that smells of cedar and earth, and I take a deep breath, maybe for the first time all day.

Joey does that for me. Settles me somehow.

My phone buzzes in my back pocket, and just like that, my calm disappears when I see Sam's name flash on my screen.

After I scan the message to make sure Zach's okay, I turn it off and tuck it away. I'm tired of Sam sucking up my time and mental energy, and I vow to myself to keep tonight fun for Joey. She deserves that much. Hell, I do too.

Thankfully, Jo doesn't sense my preoccupation. She sports a megawatt smile as though riding our old mare is the best thing to happen to her. It's so easy to please her. Ever since she was little, she's always been grateful for anything people do for her. Always appreciative and kind.

I don't remember the last time she rode Cinnamon Pie, though Joey always stopped by to give her treats and brush out her mane. It bothers me that I can't remember, that before now, I never made it a priority to do something for her I knew she loved.

"Bitsy, why didn't you ever ask me to take you riding? You know, before." I don't say the rest. *Before you left for Florida.* I don't want to remind her of the decision she has to make next week, but I'm sure as hell hoping it involves staying here.

She shrugs, but doesn't give me an answer.

"You love riding. I'm sorry I didn't offer to take you more often. I'm just curious why you never asked," I say gently.

Another shrug. "It seemed selfish to ask when you spent such long days with the horses." Her eyes meet mine, and the devotion there nearly knocks me off my saddle. "I know how hard you work. Guess I didn't want to add to that."

Fuck. This girl kills me in the best ways.

We ride silently the rest of the way. I'm lost in my thoughts, lost in her shy smiles and calm spirit. A part of me wishes we could run away and not ever have to deal with real life.

When we get to the creek, I secure the horses and toss a thick quilt under an old oak tree.

Her eyes widen when she sees the spread—dinner, dessert, and wine. "When did you have time to do this?"

"I have to confess that my mom and Tori helped." This morning I mentioned wanting to take Joey on a picnic, and Tori and my mother sprang into action.

Jo laughs, and that sound makes everything better. "This is amazing. Thank you." Going up on her toes, she kisses me, and I take a moment to breathe her in. She smells sweet and familiar. Like home. I close my eyes and rest my forehead on hers.

I don't know when this went from giving the relationship thing a shot to being all in, but I'm fully invested now. And it's scary as hell. Because if I don't work out my shit, I might lose the best thing that's ever happened to me.

"Are you okay?" she asks hesitantly.

"Yeah. Just a lot on my mind, but I'm glad we're getting a chance to go riding." I kiss her again and speak from the heart. "We'll do this more often, Jo. You're important to me, and I know I've taken you for granted for a long time now. I won't anymore. I want you to know you're my priority."

She tears up, and it guts me. I think back to that horrible argument with my father and wonder if things would be different today if he'd encouraged me to wait for Joey instead of telling me I was the last thing she needed.

Children aren't supposed to hate their parents, but I've always hated my father for the things he said to me that day. The fact that those were the last words he spoke to me before he died makes it worse. Then there's the guilt, the guilt that maybe I made him so upset when we argued he suffered a fatal heart attack.

The concern in Joey's beautiful gray eyes does me in, and I give in. "After the wedding, I have some things I need to share with you."

She stills and stares up at me. "What's wrong?"

"Nothing. I mean, it's not the end of the world. Just some things I need to share with you and the family. Some things I've been meaning to for a while, but with the wedding..." I shake my head, already having said too much.

Two small lines form between her eyebrows. "Why after the wedding? Why can't we discuss it now?"

I shift uncomfortably. "I, uh, I need to talk to Ethan and my mom about this, and... I don't want anything to fuck up my brother's big day." After marrying that shrew Allison and enduring a contentious divorce, Ethan deserves to be happy this week.

And my news will not achieve that goal.

Joey's eyes fill with concern. "Is it about the business? You and Ethan have been working your little hearts out these past few years, and I know you've been worried about it."

"It affects the business, yeah. But like I said, no one's dying or anything." Yet. Ethan might strangle me. And my mom? Fuck, I can't even think about how she'll react.

Joey gives me a reassuring smile. She strokes my jaw, and I lean into her palm. "I'm sure you'll figure it out. You always do. Who dug me out of that well when I was eight and all of your friends panicked?"

I shake my head. "Like I was gonna leave you down there?"

"Silas did. His buddies did. But you didn't. You came for me."

The memory is seared in my brain like a hot cattle prod. That was one of the most terrifying moments of my life.

We'd been playing cops and robbers near an abandoned property when Joey fell through the decaying boards that covered a well. I'll never forget Jo's scream or seeing her muddy and wet at the bottom of the dark well, crying and shivering in the waist-high water.

"We were too far from the farm to get your parents," Jo recalls, "so you cut the rope from the old tire swing by the pond and tied that to a tree trunk." She shakes her head. "But I wasn't strong enough to pull myself out, so you scaled down and got me."

"Damn right, I got you."

"And then you carried me home."

"Your ankle was swollen twice its size. There's no way you could walk."

I don't remind her of the rest. Of how she was afraid to tell her parents what happened because they'd be pissed at her. She told them she twisted her ankle when she tripped and fell into the pond. Because she knew, like we all did, that her father would find fault with her somehow. And since Silas was scared shitless Bill would beat the crap out of him if he figured out Silas was the one who suggested we play there, we somehow managed to keep Joey's accident a secret.

She stares up at me like I have all the answers. I don't, but I like that she sees me as more than I am. I want to become that man, the man she needs. I want to deserve her, and right now I don't. I'm a long way from the kid who crawled down into a well. Unfortunately, I'm probably closer to being the fuck-up my dad thought I was.

I swallow thickly. "Let's eat."

We settle on the blanket and unpack the roast beef. I open the chilled wine and fill our Dixie cups.

I'll admit I'm not getting any points for style. I should think through this better next time. At least I took a shower at Ethan's before we left.

Everything's delicious. I make a mental note to bring Tori and my mom some flowers.

I glance over at Joey, who's nibbling on a strawberry. Her hair blows in the gentle wind, and I'm overwhelmed by how good it feels to be by her side. The sun has almost set, and she's silhouetted against the darkness, but as my eyes adjust, I can see her smile.

Once we're done eating, I lie back on the blanket and draw her to my chest. She comes willingly, tucking herself against me. Around us, the trees rustle in the wind and crickets chirp.

Joey's wearing a babydoll top and jeans that accentuate her perfect curves. I stroke her back and draw her leg over my thigh.

I don't know who kisses who first, but it doesn't take me long to want more. Since no one comes back here, I'm not worried about anyone interrupting.

Knowing Jo had a bad first time, I've kept the physical stuff to third base. I'll wait as long as she needs to be comfortable. But I can't deny the dance we're doing around the main event is hot as hell.

Slowly, I unbutton her jeans and slide them down her toned legs. She helps me kick them off, and then I pull her over me so that she straddles my lap.

The moon is brighter in the sky now, so I can see her pouty lips and flushed cheeks. I drag a finger over her neck and catch the fabric of her top and tug it over her shoulder.

"Mm. Wanna bite you right here."

Her eyes heat, and she swipes her long hair over her shoulder and leans down, presenting her tilted jaw to me. "Maybe you should."

Fuck. I really like this side of Jo. I lick her bare shoulder slowly before I sink my teeth into her just a little. I've never bitten a woman before Joey, but for some reason, I really like biting her.

She moans and grinds down on me. My cock responds, angrily pushing against my zipper.

My hands slide to her ass, and I work her over me while we kiss. I can feel her heat through her thin panties, and it's driving me out of my mind. I want to tell her I'm dying to fuck her, dying to feel her tight pussy clench around me.

When I can't take it another second, I flip us around, making sure to cradle her head so I can lay her gently beneath me. I yank off my T-shirt and slide down her body. Her legs open for me, and I smile, loving how she's grown comfortable with me seeing her like this. I slip my fingers beneath the hem of her top that barely covers her mound.

Dragging my nose over her, I rub her through the fabric of her panties. Her hands yank at my hair while her hips wiggle beneath me.

"That's right, baby. Make yourself feel good." Her other hand reaches into her top, and I hate that I can't see what her fingers are doing. "Pull your top down so I can see your beautiful tits."

When they're bare before me, I reach up and gently push two fingers into her mouth. She sucks me, licks me, makes me so hard I wanna fuck her until she can't remember her name.

My cock kicks in my jeans, but I ignore it. When I'm good and wet, I drag those fingers over her pink tips and watch her nipples tighten. Perfection.

I lick her through her panties until she moans loudly.

"Logan, please," she gasps.

"Please what, baby?" I love teasing her. She pushes down her underwear, and I smirk up at her from between her legs. "Oh, you want me to lick your pretty pussy?"

"Yes. Lick it. And..." I wait for her to finish. I'm torturing both of us right now, but I don't care. The longer we hold off, the more amazing this will be when she comes. After a moment, she whispers, "And use your fingers."

"Want me to fuck you with my fingers?"

"Yes." She's panting, trying to catch her breath. "Hard. Do it hard."

Fuck, yes.

I slip two fingers into her tight channel while I take a long lick up one side of her and then the other. Mesmerized, I watch my fingers slide in and out of her. "You're so wet, baby." Her chest juts out as her knees pull up and lock around my shoulders. She's a vision under the moonlight. Beautiful full breasts and that tiny waist. Her gorgeous lean legs. Her thick blonde hair that cascades behind her. "Jojo, you're so fucking sexy."

I love that she's comfortable enough now to tell me what she wants. That she trusts me to do this.

I've never gotten this riled up by getting a girl off before, but seeing my sweet Jojo so uninhibited makes me hard as hell. I know she's close, and watching her writhe on my hand is such a goddamn turn-on, my dick throbs.

Taking care to avoid her tight nub, I lick around and around until she yanks my hair. When I finally give her a long lick up her center and settle in on that one spot, she comes with a scream and pulses on my fingers.

Once the final shudders work through her, I gently slide out of her. I wipe my face with my T-shirt, collapse next to her, and pull her to me.

Closing my eyes, I will my body to calm down. I'm not a quid pro quo kind of guy. Getting a woman off is its own special treat. I don't expect reciprocation, and if Jojo's too tired, I would understand.

"Did you enjoy that, baby?"

"Mm-hmm. So much."

I kiss her forehead and run my hand up and down her back. I'm starting to wonder how I'll ride home with this monster erection when she settles over my lap.

"Let's do that one thing we haven't yet." That gets my attention.

She unbuttons my jeans and reaches in to free me. I'm leaking on her hand, and she uses it to lube me up.

I hiss through my teeth when she strokes that one spot on my swollen head.

"Do... do you have a condom?" She bites her lip.

I jerk in her hand, unable to mask my body's enthusiasm. But I want to be sure this is the right thing for her.

"Babe, we don't have to do this if you're not ready. I don't wanna rush you." I brush my thumb over her lower lip to release it. "Only what you're comfortable doing."

She looks me in the eyes. "I want this with you. I want you."

"I want you too." So damn much.

28

JOEY

A COOL BREEZE BLOWS OVER MY HEATED SKIN AS LOGAN SHIFTS ME to the ground. When I see the look in his eyes, my heart goes crazy, skittering in my chest like a runaway colt. Because we're really doing this.

Wanting to commit every moment to memory, I rub the stubble on his handsome face. Thread my fingers through his thick hair. Stare at the man who has always owned my heart.

I almost say the words, almost tell him I love him, but I force myself to hold it in. Just because I'm head over heels about him doesn't mean he feels the same about me. Logan cares about me, that much I know. Loves me as a friend. Cares for me as a lover. But is he *in love* with me? I'm too scared to test those waters, so I kiss him before I say something I might regret, though it runs through my mind:

I've always loved you.

I can't remember a time when I didn't love you.

Do you think you could love me?

He leans over me, pulling back at the last moment to rub his nose against mine, a small moment of intimacy that has me sighing and wishing I was brave enough to say the words in my heart.

We kiss until I'm out of my mind, and then we push down his jeans and reach for each other, desperate and hungry to connect.

His hard body moves over mine, shooting tingles over my sensitive skin. Feeling the way he fits, rubbing his steely length between my thighs, brings me close to the edge again. It reminds me of our first night together at the coast when I sat on his lap and made him come.

"Logan, I need you," I gasp.

He sits up, kneeling between my legs to reach for his wallet. I take that moment to appreciate his body. All of that lean muscle. The poetic grace in his slender hips and chiseled thighs. He's the picture of virility with that proud erection jutting between us.

He rifles through his wallet and pauses, only to drop his head forward with a loud groan.

"What's wrong?"

"Fuck." He scrubs his hands over his eyes. "I'm sorry. I don't have a condom." After a moment, he flops down next to me and covers his face with his arm. His chest rises and falls like he's out of breath. "I hadn't planned to get naked out here."

A twisted side of me smiles that Logan's bent out of shape at the thought of being denied sex with me.

I run my hand over his chest, down over the trail of hair on his lower abdomen, and I whisper, "I'm on the pill." He didn't ask before.

He lowers his arm just enough to make eye contact. "I'm clean. I got tested in the spring."

My brows rise because it's July. I don't want to think about his revolving bedroom door, but I'm not going to make a dumb decision because I'm being naive.

His eyes soften. "Jo, I haven't been with anyone in months.

Certainly not since I was tested, but it's been much longer than that. Probably not since last fall."

Last fall?

For some reason, that makes me emotional. Heat stings my eyes, and I turn away.

"What's going on, baby? Tell me what's wrong. Is this about having sex? We don't have to do anything else tonight. I told you—"

"No, that's not it."

He must sense I need time to collect my thoughts because he rubs my back.

Finally, when I can talk, it comes out a rasp. "I left for Florida to get over you. Because I didn't think you'd ever see me as more than a friend. And... I basically slept with someone because I thought it would help me move on, but it didn't." I swallow. "The whole time I was there, I figured you were back home being your normal player self, but now that I know you weren't, I wish... I wish I hadn't been with anyone else. I wish you had been my first."

I can't help the tears that leak out of my eyes or that I spilled my guts on him.

He pulls me to his chest where I cry harder.

When I can speak, I mumble, "You probably hate the idea that someone you're with could catch feelings for you, so we don't have to talk about it, but if you're serious about me staying after the wedding, I want to be honest with you. And I have my own baggage, which apparently results in me bawling all over you when we're supposed to be having hot, sweaty sex."

Another dream of mine that I've probably just shot to hell, thanks to my verbal vomit.

"God, Jo," he says against the shell of my ear. "I wish I'd done so many things differently. I wish I'd been your first. I can't go back and undo my mistakes, but I can clear this one thing up right now. I'm a damn lucky man to have you in my life. And you're not alone in this relationship. I have feelings for you too."

We lean apart until a few inches separate us, and he cradles my face to wipe away the tears with his thumb.

"You mean so much to me, Joey." He repeats the words that have me melting. "Of course I have feelings for you."

When I see the earnestness in his expression, I smile, and he smiles back before kissing me softly. He kisses me until we're tangled around each other. Until that frantic need has built again.

Pausing, he tugs off my shirt, which has pooled around my waist, before we fit our bare bodies back together. I shudder at the intensity, at the intimacy of feeling every part of him against every part of me.

I feel him nudge my entrance.

"Yes." It's the answer to his unasked question.

He stares into my eyes. "Babe, tell me if something hurts or if you need me to slow down."

His hand snakes between us. My attention dips to where he grabs himself and runs his head through my folds, finally notching his head at my core.

Instinctively, I spread my legs farther as he pushes into me.

We both groan, and even though it's a snug fit, once he lets me adjust to his size, he feels so good, I have to squeeze my eyes shut.

"Tight," he grits out. "So wet. So tight. You feel amazing."

I'm shocked by how good this feels after my horrendous first time, but then this is Logan. Everything with him is always better.

Then he starts to move. Slowly at first, while he stares down at me with so much heat in his gaze, I might combust.

He increases the tempo, building us. Finally, he pumps and

thrusts until our bodies slap together. Until I'm gasping and panting and desperate.

"Oh, God. I'm gonna come." I reach between us and focus on getting to the goal, but a glance at what's happening down there, just barely visible in the moonlight, gives me inspiration. I lower my hand and spread my fingers on either side of him and squeeze just before he slides back into me.

"*Fuckkk*. Do that again."

Somehow, he's thicker inside of me, and I arch my back, overwhelmed by sensations and so close. Logan latches onto my nipple and sucks and bites, and that's all it takes for me to fly apart. Every part of me tenses. Every cell and nerve ending in my body catches fire and detonates. I'm still shaking with my release when I remember to do that finger move again for Logan, and then he pulses into me.

We're breathless and sweaty, and I'm so sated, it doesn't matter that we're only lying on a quilt because I might sleep into next week.

Logan presses a soft kiss to my forehead and rolls to the side, bringing me with him so that we stay entwined.

"You're amazing, Jo." His hand travels up and down my back in a sweet caress. "That was—Christ, I don't have words." He mumbles something to himself and then kisses me again. "I didn't even know you were the part of me that was missing."

I'm speechless, wondering if this is a dream.

A beautiful, perfect dream.

After a few moments, he gently separates us and gives me a playful smile. "I think I made a mess."

I'm not prepared for anything to gush out of me, but that's a dumb realization since he went in bare. But before I can consider how I'll be able to ride Cinnamon Pie back to the farm like this, Logan grabs a few napkins and quickly wipes me down. I want to be embarrassed because this has to be the most intimate thing I've ever done, but he's sporting a giant grin as he kneels between my thighs.

"You're getting a kick out of this?" I ask, laughing.

"Kinda. Yeah." He shrugs. "That's hot." He motions to my very exposed area, and I feel my whole body flush. My eyebrows lift, and his smile widens. "What can I say? I'm a perv." But then his smile disappears, and gone is the teasing tone from his voice. "I've never done it without a condom before. You're my first." We stare at each other. "I like that, Bitsy. I want more firsts with you."

"Yeah?" I hate how eager that comes out, but tonight feels too surreal.

He flops down next to me, naked and still hard, and wraps his arms around me. "In case I haven't told you lately, you rock my fucking world."

No, Logan. You rock mine.

29

JOEY

Sleeping in the nude is a new experience for me. One I'm thoroughly enjoying.

I wake in Logan's bed with his hand on my breast, his hard chest at my back, and his thick length against my rear.

"Morning." I reach behind me and thread my fingers through his hair to gently scratch his head, and he grunts in approval and kisses my neck. His whiskers scrape against my sensitive skin, and I shiver.

It's a small miracle we made it back home last night after our romp by the river. We collapsed into bed and woke once in the middle of the night to make love again. Fortunately, I didn't cry again. Couple goals!

"Are you sore?" His sexy voice, thick with sleep, sends another round of chills down my body.

"A little." I squeeze my thighs together and still. "Okay, yeah, I'm sore."

"Sorry, baby. We shouldn't have done it that second time."

I grind back against him because even though I'm achy, he feels too good to stop. "I'm not complaining."

"Mmm." He thrusts against me. "There's something to be said for waking up with a beautiful woman."

"You sweet talker. Bet you say that to all the girls."

I'm smiling and starting to wonder if I could test the waters today if we go slow when Logan rolls me onto my back.

His hair is going in every direction, and his jaw is covered in stubble. But it's those piercing blue eyes staring down at me that I want to get lost in.

"Jo, you're the only woman who's ever stayed the night in this bed."

Oh.

Remembering those sweet words he told me last night, I palm his chin, and he leans into me. "I like being the first."

What I mean to say is I like being the only one, but I can't take back this Freudian slip, and the idea that someone likely will come after me smacks me like a Mack truck.

Fortunately, he's kissing me and not parsing my words. I remind myself to take what I can get. To enjoy being together for however long we have. After all, we might end because *I* have to leave, a thought that could make me cry again if I let myself think about it too long. But if I get emotional again while we're in bed, I might give both of us a complex, so I try to focus on the positive.

I'm grateful for the distraction of Logan's dirty words in my ear and the sharp bites he gives my shoulder and breasts.

After a mutually gratifying shower where I come so hard against his mouth, I'm pretty sure the next town over hears my screams, we get dressed for the day and head to his brother's.

"You're awfully sweet to help out at the ranch." Logan gives me a lopsided smile as he drives one-handed, his other hand on my thigh.

There's nothing special about how he's dressed—just faded jeans, a fitted T-shirt, boots, and a baseball cap with a rounded bill—but it's quintessential Logan. Playful and sweet and so handsome, it hurts to look at him.

We turn the corner and the sun streams through the window and down on my face. I close my eyes to soak in the heat and bask in this quiet moment of happiness. "I love hanging out at the ranch. Nothing I've ever done there has felt like work to me. Tending to the horses, hanging out with the kids, watering the garden—it's a pleasure."

He makes a sound like he doesn't believe me.

"What?" I open my eyes and turn toward him.

"What about that time I somehow talked you into cleaning out the stalls? I think you were in middle school. That couldn't have been fun. Hell, the pitchfork was bigger than you."

He chuckles, and I shake my head with a laugh.

"I got to hang out with you the whole afternoon, and your mom gave us ice cream when we were done. We never had ice cream at home. Besides, I've always adored the horses." *And you too, dummy.*

He'd gotten in trouble—what else is new?—and had to clean and polish the tack and shovel out the stalls. So I did the stalls and he did the rest, since the saddles were too heavy for me and I had a hard time reaching the upper pegs in the equipment room. We kept each other company, joking all afternoon.

I shrug. "The hard stuff isn't so difficult when you love the rest." This is something Tori and I talk about often, how unexpected blessings blunt the sharp edges of life.

Logan doesn't say anything for a moment, but then he reaches for me and kisses the back of my hand. "You're a pretty kickass girl."

My heart skips a couple of beats. I smile back. "Because I helped you with your chores?"

"Because you've always got my back. Every fucking time. And you have the best attitude of anyone I know."

I'm not sure anything can wipe the smile off my face for the rest of the drive.

As we stroll up the front walkway of Ethan's house, Logan tosses his arm over my shoulders and says, "Been meaning to ask... Where'd you learn that finger move you used on me last night? It was hot as fuck."

He pauses to pull me in front of him so he can rock his erection against me.

I blush furiously and giggle. "Where else? Porn. And seriously, how can you be hard again?"

"Because I've gotten off with you three times in the last twelve hours?" He presses a wet kiss to my neck, and I reach back to grip his hair, the laughter dying on my tongue because, yeah, I'm ready to go too. His mouth is on mine a hot second later.

We're in our own little world of two when Mila opens the front door, turns around, and hollers, "Logan and Joey are making out on the front porch, y'all. Kissy, kissy, kissy!" She makes smacking sounds, and I cover my face with a laugh.

Logan drags me into the house by the hand. "That wasn't making out," he grumbles. "I was merely appreciating my girlfriend."

"Ohhhh." Mila bats her eyelashes as she hops around and sing-songs, "Logan has a girlfriend! Logan has a girlfriend!"

I'm Logan's girlfriend. Officially. I smile like I just won a million bucks.

Mila stops suddenly, and her eyes widen. "If y'all get married, does that mean you'll be my aunt, Joey?"

Logan and I both freeze. I cringe, hating that I might need to strangle this child whom I love so dearly.

Because I might be new to relationships, but I know better than to talk weddings this early. Especially with a guy like

Logan. A woman starts talking marriage, and he probably wants to bolt for the fences like an escaped convict.

I look up and see Logan's entire family and Tori's hovering in the kitchen, watching us, waiting for us to say something.

Ethan chides his daughter. "Mila. Honey, stop teasing your uncle."

Tori mouths, "Sorry."

Ignoring my mortification, I put on the fakest smile of my life and joke, "Marry Logan? It's *way* too early too know if he's the right guy for me." I saunter with a forced bravado toward the counter to grab an apple. "What if he picks his nose or leaves wet towels on the floor in the bathroom? A girl has to know these things before making that kind of decision."

Mila considers this and turns to Logan. "Do you pick your nose?"

"I pick my nose *and* my butt. Every day." He reaches for her face and pretends to pick hers while she squeals and laughs.

When she darts under the table, he reaches for me and sticks his finger in my nostril.

"Oh, my God, you're gross." I laugh and slap him away while he bites my neck affectionately.

When we stop, the room is still staring at us.

Ethan clears his throat and smirks. "How did the horseback ride go last night? Did ya get a lot of *riding* done?" Tori smacks his arm with a snort.

Bev looks positively delighted.

Oh, sweet Jesus. She totally knows I've slept with Logan.

I feel like I'm a teenager who just got busted for having a guy in my bedroom.

Flushing redder than the cherry tomatoes in Bev's garden, I smile weakly, but I don't have time to figure out what to say because Logan grabs Ethan in a headlock, and next thing I know, they're wrestling on the ground like idiots, laughing and razzing each other. Everyone clears back.

"Boys!" Tori claps. "I swear, if either of you ends up concussed for my wedding and sports black eyes, I'm gonna pour laxative in your coffee when you least expect it."

That does the trick. The brothers break apart, although they're still trash-talking. It's mostly G-rated, of course, since there are little ears.

I'm still chuckling about the guys' antics twenty minutes later when the women settle in the living room to help Tori assemble the party favors her sister made for the wedding.

"This smells incredible." I take another big whiff of the lavender sugar scrub before I replace the lid.

"I brought extras if anyone wants to try this out before the wedding," Kat says from behind a giant pile of tulle.

Always the hostess, Tori hands out drinks to everyone and then reaches for a glass.

With a sigh, Bev sits next to me and starts tying ribbon. "All I wanna know is when I'm gonna get some more grandbabies."

Tori chokes on her water, and Kat pats her on the back.

I nudge Bev. "Dontcha think you should take it easy on the bride-to-be?" I tease.

Her right eyebrow spikes up. "Who says I wasn't talking about you?"

That shuts me up, and everyone snickers. At least the guys are out in the barn and not here to witness this conversation. Bev winks at me, and I shake my head at her antics, a smile on my lips.

She leans close. "You know you're like a daughter to me, right?"

The smile stretches across my face. "Thanks, Bev. That's a lovely thing to say."

"I mean it. And because of that, I get to tease you from time to time. It's part of parental privilege."

My parents never teased me affectionately. To them, I was too shy, too awkward, too annoying, and it got me in trouble. It taught me to mind my own business and keep to myself. To keep my mouth shut. If ever the real me came out, it was with the Carters and their wild child Logan. Who's not so wild these days, I'm realizing.

"Well, I'm honored."

"It's really good to have you home, kid. I was wondering if you might want to help me with the garden this week."

"I love your garden. Of course I can help."

She takes a sip of her sweet tea. "I have photos of you where you were this tall"—she motions with her hand—"tilling that soil for me. You planted the first tomatoes, carrots, peppers, and potatoes."

"Your garden is my happy place."

"I've never seen anyone with a greener thumb than this girl," Bev tells the room.

I might never win an award for anything, but this right here, praise from a woman I admire, means so much to me.

Kat perks up from across the room. "Are we talking gardening? Honestly, there's nothing more satisfying."

I nod. Granted, I've never grown fields of lavender like she has, but the modest garden I helped Bev maintain over the years inspired me. "I always wanted to have my own garden and grow everything I put on the dinner table. I binge-watch this guy on YouTube who grows most of what his family eats, and his four adorable sons pitch in."

And if I imagine it's Logan and our kids from time to time, well, no one has to know that.

Kat pulls out her phone. "Bev, you have to see that show. I watch it too. I'll email you the link."

Bev turns back to me. "I'm thinking of expanding the garden. I can't run around the way I used to, but maybe you'd like to help me? I'd pay you, of course—"

"No, I can't take your money. You know that. I can help because I love you and your garden." *And your son. So much.*

She pats my hand. "Well, we'll see about that. Anyway, Kat has me composting, but I'm not sure where to go from there."

We talk about her plans for the next half hour, and I'm so happy to be included. I hadn't realized how much I missed these moments. My extended family in Florida is wonderful, but I didn't grow up with them, so it's not the same. But I've always felt invested in the Carter ranch and in their family, ever since I was little. This feels like home. Like where I belong. And if Logan and I work out...

I stop myself from the fantasy because, *hello*, this is not my ranch or house or garden. But it gives me a vision for my life that I never truly thought was possible. Could Logan and I do something similar? Plant a garden in his backyard? Harvest everything for our family? Enjoy having our kids tumbling around in the fields, helping us?

It seems almost too good to be true.

30

LOGAN

THE NAME ON MY CALLER ID MAKES ME DO A DOUBLE-TAKE.

"Holy shit, dude. Where the hell are you?" I drop down on the steps of Ethan's porch and strain to hear the voice on the other end.

"A Bolivian cantina." Isaiah Walker's deep laughter sounds in my ear. As does loud music and female banter. No surprise there. That guy has always been the life of the party.

I shake my head. "After that email you sent me, I was shitting my pants about your next gig."

This asshole forwarded me a copy of his last will and testament "just in case."

"The Death Road is no joke. Didn't think I should take any chances."

And people said I had a death wish growing up. It's nothing like Zey's.

"Please tell me you're done and headed home."

"And give up this glamorous life?"

I roll my eyes. According to his emails, he's living in a damn hut, eating nuts and berries, and shitting in holes he has to dig on the side of the road.

I love this guy like my brother, but I get why Liberty broke up with him. Speaking of...

"Dude, did you talk to Liberty about that will?" God forbid something happens to Isaiah, she's supposed to get everything. He's amassed a small fortune in the last couple of years, but you'd never know it based on how he lives.

"No. It's a worst-case scenario type of thing anyway. She's busy living her life. I don't want to intrude."

That's the dumbest fucking thing I've ever heard, but I don't want to argue with him while he's on the other side of the planet. Still, I can't help but nudge him.

"I'm sure she still cares about you. That was the whole point of why you guys broke up, right?"

"There's a saying here. *Me has llegado hasta la copete.* It basically means 'you've worn me out' or 'I'm tired of your crap.' And yeah, Liberty might care about me, but she's over my shit and has moved on. *That's* why we broke up." He sighs. "Anyway, I just wanted to make sure you got that document. I need to focus on those trails, and I can't if I'm worried about something that big."

"Then I'm glad you called. I got your dumb will, and if you die, I will be one pissed-off motherfucker, asshole."

We both chuckle. "So how you been? Still dealing with Samantha?"

I groan and look around to make sure I'm alone on the porch before I respond. "It's worse than ever. I swear the more I do for her, the more she wants."

Zey is the only person who knows about this situation. I tried to bury my sorrows in a bottle of Jack a while back when he came over and found me three sheets to the wind. And since he couldn't remember the last time I'd been that drunk, he knew something was up and chatted my drunk ass up until I confessed everything.

I fill him in on the last few months of drama. Until I get to the most pressing issue in my life.

"Joey's back."

"No shit."

Not sure why, but my palms are sweaty. I wipe them on my jeans. "We're, uh, we're together now." Silence. "Dating." Still nothing. "You know, each other." The silence drags on. "Zey?"

"Yeah. I heard you. I had to look out the window to see if pigs were flying."

I shake my head with a chuckle. "Is it weird we're dating?"

"Not as weird as it is to hear you admit you have a girlfriend. Never thought I'd see the day when our little Logan would grow up."

"Shut up, dick."

He laughs. "I'm happy for you, man. Joey's a great girl, and she's always had a thing for you."

"I don't know about that. I'm just glad we're working out now." My lungs fill with a deep breath. "I really like her."

Jesus. I sound like I'm in middle school. But then I'm flooded with images from last night and have to bite back a groan. There's something about Bitsy's vulnerability and her girl-next-door vibe that's such a turn-on. Hopefully our first time together meant as much to her as it did to me. I can't lie—thoughts of last night bring out the caveman in me. There's nothing more I want to do than drag her back to my house and strip off every stitch of her clothing.

He chuckles. "I figured as much." People yell in the background, and it sounds like he moves to somewhere quieter. "I almost hate to ask this question, but does she know about Sam and Zach yet?"

There goes my boner.

"No. I'm planning to talk to everyone after the wedding." Isaiah makes a sound of disbelief. "What?"

"Not sure you should wait to tell her with the rest of the family. I understand why you want to wait, but she might not take it well."

A knot forms in my gut. "But Jo always gets me. If it weren't for Silas always being up in her grill, I would've told her sooner. You know the rumors he spread about my family. Joey's the only reason I didn't beat his ass for being such a cocksucker."

"I hear you about Silas. He can be vengeful, but you need to trust Joey to have your back. She's not a kid anymore. You gotta trust her to handle Silas." He laughs humorously. "Take it from the guy whose last relationship imploded, don't put off an important conversation too long. I'd hate to see you screw up a good thing."

I swallow, wishing I hadn't dug this hole for myself. "I do excel at screwing up, so..."

"Dude, it takes a screwup to know one."

We laugh, and although I might not be a particularly religious man, I send up a prayer that my buddy makes it home safely.

When we get off the phone, I stare out at the fields and wonder how I begin to untangle this mess.

I guess it starts with the truth.

And Joey needs to hear it.

31

LOGAN

When I come around the corner, I spot Joey taking a selfie with Cinnamon Pie, who's leaning out of the stall. I've missed seeing Jo in the barn. She looks at home here.

I try to shake off the somberness lingering since Isaiah's phone call. As much as I want to take his advice, this isn't the kind of convo I can handle if my brother interrupts. It'll have to wait until Jo and I are back at my place.

Besides, the barn has too many bad memories. If I wanna jinx myself and fuck up my life permanently, this would be the perfect place to do it.

"My feelings are hurt, Bitsy," I tease, knowing she'll be able to get me out of this funk. "You've been home over a week, and you've taken a selfie with a horse but not with me."

She rolls her eyes but reaches for me. I swing her into my arms, relishing the giggle she lets out.

She wraps those gorgeous legs around my waist, and I hold her up by her ass while she takes pics of us.

"Gonna post those on your Instagram?"

"Do you mind?" She pins me with those big gray eyes. "I just realized I didn't take any photos when we were at the coast."

"Tori can share hers with you. She took a bunch." I nibble her neck, feeling better already. "I thought you hated Instagram."

She shrugs. "I never had anything that exciting or interesting to post."

Leaning back so I can see her face, I wag my eyebrows. "Am I exciting enough to post?"

Her soft palm lands on my face. "You're probably more excitement than I can handle."

"Oh, I think you handle me just fine." I press her into the stall behind us and kiss her until we're both out of breath. "Fuck, you make me so hard."

I've been a walking, talking erection all day, thanks to memories of last night, but nothing compares to having her in my arms.

And even though I'd like nothing more than to relive every naked moment in real-time, one of my nosy family members could walk in here at any moment. The barn isn't isolated like the creek.

Reluctantly, I set her down on her feet and rearrange my junk, which she palms.

"I'll take care of that when we get home." She winks at me and struts out of the barn.

I laugh and shake my head. I don't know when she became so carefree and flirty, but I'm really digging this side of her. A side only I see.

I'm not sure how to explain the emotion careening through my chest. How to explain the way it's easier to breathe when she's with me. How fucking elated I am when she sends a smile my way or touches me.

Damn. I love this woman.

I stare at Cinnamon Pie, dumbfounded by the revelation.

I consider those words and frown.

Never did I think I was the kind of guy to lose it over a girl, but based on how it's physically painful to be separated from her, Joey Grayson owns my dumb ass.

"Holy hell, I do love her," I declare to my horse.

That's when the memory of my father standing just a few feet away hits me so hard, it sucks the air out of my lungs.

"She's not the girl for you, Logan. You'll never make someone like Josephine happy. She'll want to settle down, and son, that'll grow old, and you'll move on to the next pretty thing who glances your way and break her heart. Trust me. I know a thing or two about this sorta thing."

When the man you've looked up to your entire life says you're basically not good enough for your lifelong best friend, it makes you question everything.

At least it did at the time.

Shaking my head, I stalk out of the barn, determined to prove him wrong.

Joey's thumb rubs across my wrist as we turn off the main drag. The sun sets as my truck slows in the drive-thru of the burger joint. We're both wiped out. While I'm enjoying these family festivities stretching on until the wedding on Saturday, it doubles my responsibilities since Ethan has been hanging out so much with everyone. Not that I mind. I'm just tired as hell.

At least Sam has chilled out. She texted me yesterday to let me know Zach is feeling better. That's a load off my mind. I'm tempted to text back to see how he's doing today, but I don't want to invite more conversation with her than necessary.

After Joey and I scarf down our meal in my truck and start back home to my place, I see the turnoff for her grandma's house, and it gives me an idea. Even though there's nothing more I want than to crash in front of the TV with Jojo wrapped in my arms while we relax, she needs to be my priority.

"What are you doing?" she asks hesitantly as we bounce along the torn-up road to her grandma's property.

"You haven't stopped by here since you've been home, and I figured they might have some of your stuff in boxes or something."

She leans forward in her seat, her expression melancholy. "I've wanted to come by, but we've been so busy."

"I figured." That's just like Jo. Always putting others first. Never asking for herself. That shit stops right now. I love that she's so nurturing, but it can't be to her own detriment. "Babe, if you need something, *anything*, you just need to let me know. I'm not always that intuitive."

She smirks at me. "You have no idea." With a chuckle, she presses a sweet kiss on my lips and then hops out of the truck when we park in front of the modest home.

I link our hands together and then knock on the door. A young couple answers, and I explain that Joey used to live here and her brother sold the property. I leave out the drama because there's a lot of it. "We were wondering if he left any of her belongings behind."

"Oh! Yes, we were just about to toss everything out. I'm glad you stopped by!" The woman, Melanie, ushers us in past her husband, who gives us a friendly wave. "I would've felt terrible if you'd been too late."

As she leads us to the back bedroom, I note the house has been painted and the floors shine like new. It's obvious this couple is taking good care of it, and a part of me is pained I couldn't buy this property for Jo and renovate it for her the way this family did.

"Take your time, and let us know if you need help carrying

anything." Melanie shuts the door behind us, leaving us in what used to be Joey's old room.

"That asshole left my things here!" Jojo takes in the piles of clothes and memorabilia. It's been shoved into the corner to make room for a crib and a rocker. It's a strange sight since half of the room looks like a scene from that TV show *Hoarders*. It's not just Joey's stuff. It's a mixture of household items and random things piled high on what I'm assuming are her belongings. At least, I hope they are.

I rub her shoulders. She has to be pissed because she rarely curses. I don't blame her for being upset, but I hate to see her on the verge of tears.

"Look on the bright side, Bitsy. At least you're getting your things back. Silas could've just tossed them into the garbage."

That asshole is always hurting his sister. The next time I see Silas, I might have to break his goddamn face.

Forcing myself to calm down, I take a deep breath.

She starts to sniffle, and I wrap my arms around her. "It's okay, baby. We'll get your things organized again."

I don't mention the other questions I have, like what happened to her grandmother's or mother's belongings. Maybe some of them are in the pile, but it's hard to tell.

Silas wasn't always a dick. When we were kids, he was rough around the edges, but given who his father was, I figured he was doing better than his old man. Turns out, he's just like that asshole—an abusive addict who only cares about himself. And I'll be damned if he hurts Joey again.

By the time we're done loading the truck, it's late. Although most of what we boxed up were Joey's clothes and random kitchen stuff we'll probably toss, she found an old box of photos. Thank God she was able to rescue something of sentimental value. At the end of the day, while I know she's grateful to get some belongings back, those photos are worth more to her than anything else she owns. Those might be the only pics she has of her mom.

Joey's quiet the rest of the night. I undress her and tuck her in my bed before I spoon her from behind. We don't talk. We don't have to. I guess that's what being in love with my best friend is like.

The thought doesn't scare the hell out of me like I figured it would.

"I love you, Jo," I whisper against her neck, the need to say it overwhelming any of my reservations. After talking to Isaiah this afternoon about his damn will, I don't wanna hold back with Joey.

She stills. After a moment, she turns to face me. Her eyes are glassy with unshed tears.

"Don't cry, baby. I'm sorry about your grandma's house. I feel like an asshole for not taking you there sooner. I'm sorry for so many things. For not knowing what your brother was up to and trying to stop him from selling the house. For not helping you more with your grandma. For not stepping up to the plate and trying to build something real with you sooner."

It kills me to know she's hurting. I start to apologize again, but she places a finger over my lips.

We stare at each other, and even though she's been crying and her eyes are puffy, she's still the most beautiful woman I know. She's pure of heart and loving and means the world to me.

She takes a shuddering breath. "I love you too, Logan."

We grin at each other. I lean down to kiss her, never wanting this moment to end. It feels too good to have her in my arms. To know I mean so much to her.

As we move together, it strikes me that we haven't been having sex. This isn't fucking. As cheesy as it might sound, we're making love. There's no other way to describe it. I've been a damn fool to not see it sooner. The thought that I could've lost this, lost her, because I was too busy screwing around or being preoccupied is overwhelming.

She needs to know about Samantha.

My conversation with Isaiah rings in my ears. He's right—I can't wait until Ethan gets married. I have to tell Jo now. I don't want to keep anything from her anymore.

My eyes travel over her. The girl's been through the wringer tonight, so maybe right this moment isn't the best time. But tomorrow. As soon as I get home from work, I'll sit her down and tell her everything. Joey is the most supportive person I know, she'll understand. As long as I can explain how it happened, it'll be okay. It has to be. Because I can't lose this girl.

32

JOEY

Laughter bubbles out of me as I scramble across the bed. I'm buck naked, the sun is out, and I can't seem to give a flying flip that Logan is getting an unobstructed view of my backside.

"I'm not done with you," Logan growls. "Get over here."

His hand wraps around my ankle, and I squeal as he drags me across the mattress. He pins me down, and I giggle into the pillow when his fingers slide across my ribs.

"Not fair!" I gasp.

"This is totally fair, baby." His hot mouth latches to my shoulder, and he knocks my legs apart to make room for his big body. "This is what we call tickle torture. And this is what bad girls get as punishment."

I yell and kick and laugh so hard, I can barely breathe, but oh, my stars and stripes, am I turned on.

Did I mention he's not wearing a stitch of clothing either? And his hard muscles are pressed against me, from chest to thigh.

I'm so grateful Ethan told us to sleep in today. He texted late last night that he'd pick up Logan so I could keep the truck and run a few errands for Tori. But even with the extra rest and a more relaxed plan for the day, I couldn't figure out why Logan looked so pensive this morning.

I was afraid he wanted to talk about last night, and I'm so over my family's drama. I just wanted to lighten the mood. So I rubbed the sleep out of my eyes and told a joke.

"What do you call a herd of cattle masturbating?"

A laugh erupted from him.

"That's not the funny part."

"You trying to tell a dirty joke is funny."

"I can work with this. Okay, so what do you call a herd of cattle masturbating?"

"No idea." He looked amused.

"Beef stroking off."

He chuckled. "Speaking of, I got something you can stroke off." He kicked off the blankets, and his giant member saluted me.

I gave him the hairy eyeball. "You can't just whip it out like that."

"I can't?"

"No. I need a prelude."

He lifted an eyebrow. "You need a prelude for my morning wood? That sounds awfully formal considering you've ridden my face."

"Don't be vulgar. I gently perched on your face." I poked his penis and watched it wave like a pendulum. And then giggled.

You'd think I'd committed a crime.

"Did you just laugh at my cock, woman?" He looked so darn serious.

Squinting at his flagpole, I turned my head sideways and decided to razz him a little more. "It's cute. I kinda want to draw a smiley face on the end of it."

He gasped in horror, and I grinned.

Except then he got a mischievous look in his eyes that made

me scramble away seconds before he pounced on me like a jungle cat.

Which is why he's tickling me so hard, I might pee my nonexistent pants. He has no idea how lucky he is I already ran to the bathroom this morning.

I howl as his fingers wiggle against my stomach. "You weigh a ton more than I do, you big lug! This isn't fair!"

"Baby, you called my cock 'cute.'" Said member slides between my thighs and through my wetness. "I'll show you how cute he is when I fuck you through the mattress."

My laughter turns into a moan because it's difficult to keep that quiet when he's squeezing my breast and rubbing my mound.

Needing more, I lift my hips and he notches himself into me from behind. His large hands grip my waist and with a quick tug, he yanks us together.

We both groan.

"Fuck," he pants in my ear. "Sorry, baby. Shoulda warmed you up more. You okay?"

"Yeah." My eyes are crossing from the invasion, but I love it. "Don't stop." After a moment, he starts to move until we're two bodies slapping together. I'm not trying to go X-rated porn star, but suddenly dirty words start tumbling out. "Oh, my God. Your cock feels amazing."

I swear it swells inside me.

"Aww, hell, baby." Grunt. Slap. Grunt. Slap.

Everything in me tightens.

"Don't stop." I gasp for breath. "I'm gonna come."

Stretched out beneath him, I fist the sheets as his finger swirls tight circles on my clit. My back arches, and he somehow slides in deeper, and I scream my release into a pillow. He pumps twice more before he follows me over the edge, and we collapse on to the bed.

Somehow, I find myself being spooned, and I close my eyes with a smile and relish the sated, warm feeling of being in his arms. Nothing has ever felt better.

You're my density.

He squeezes me tighter like he heard me quote that line from *Back to the Future*. He would know what I really mean by that. *You're my destiny.*

I'm not sure how much time goes by, but we must snooze for a while. Only when I hear a horn out front do we budge.

"Damn, time flies when you're having fun." Logan kisses my shoulder and drags himself to the bathroom. "Can you text Ethan and tell him I'll be out in a few?"

"Sure." Yawning, I grab his phone by the bedside.

When Logan runs out of the bathroom, he's dressed in jeans and a T-shirt. He grabs his phone and presses a kiss to my forehead. He's halfway out the door when I yell out. "Check your messages! You had some texts from a guy named Sam."

He freezes for a second and then turns back to me, all traces of his good mood erased. At first I think something's wrong, but then he clears his throat. "Let's have dinner here tonight. Just the two of us. There are some things... some things I need your help with."

I smile, loving that I'm his person. "Sounds great. I'll make us something yummy. Just give me a heads up when you think you'll be home."

The fantasy of living here for real, of loving Logan and building a life together, flashes in my mind. And I start to feel like everything I want is finally within my grasp.

33

JOEY

With a flick of a finger, I post the pics I took of me and Logan yesterday on my Instagram. My silly heart soars when I study them closer. We look like a couple. I'm in his arms, and he's kissing my temple while I smile at the camera. In another shot, we're cheek to cheek, mugging it up. My cousin will probably give me some hard eye rolls when she sees this. I shoot Dawn a quick text, asking if we can catch up later today.

Once I feed Rambo, I hop in Logan's truck to run a few errands for Tori. I've barely pulled out of the driveway when my phone vibrates with a text.

Silas: You around still?

And just like that, my brother lands in my life like he hasn't been MIA for months.

Relief and anger vie for the most prominent emotion in my chest, but after reminding myself that he sold our house without telling me, anger wins out.

After I take a few calming breaths, I compose several texts, but end up deleting everything. I can't tell him off via text or he'll ghost me again with nary a look in his rear view mirror. Finally, I settle on something unemotional and hope we can sit down to talk.

Me: Yeah. You in town?
Silas: Maybe for the weekend. Not sure.

God forbid he commit to anything.

Me: Want to grab coffee?

He must want to talk since he texted in the first place, but I'm still surprised he agrees to meet me at the Lone Star diner.

When I pull open the door to the restaurant twenty minutes later, I immediately spot Silas sitting in the back corner.

Grungy. That's the only way to describe him. A dirty T-shirt. Ripped Jeans. Greasy hair. Silas used to be a handsome guy. Now he looks homeless. My big, tough brother doesn't look so tough all of a sudden.

"What happened to you?" I slide into the booth.

"Nice to see you too, Josephine."

"Cut the crap. You sold Gran's house, fell off the face of the planet for months, and show up suddenly like it's no big deal, looking like something the cat dragged in."

His eyebrows lift. "Aren't you a ray of fucking sunshine?"

Silas is not the only one who's surprised. I never talk to him this way, but I'm done tiptoeing around him.

Carol pulls up to take our order. "Hey, darling. Nice to have you home! What can I getcha?"

I ignore my sorry excuse for family and smile at Carol, who's always been the biggest sweetheart. "Hey, Carol. Nice to see you too! I'll have a sweet tea and a slice of your amazing pecan pie, please." I don't think I can stomach much food and talk to Silas at the same time.

"No problem. And for you?" Her smile disappears when she turns to my brother.

"Coffee. Black. That's it." He rubs his hands together, and I take in his scrawny appearance and the dark circles under his eyes.

I roll my eyes at myself. I shouldn't care. Silas doesn't give two flips about me. And yet I know myself. The guilt will eat me alive if I don't get him a meal. "Carol, can you please bring him something to eat? Maybe the pot roast and mashed potatoes with extra gravy. Oh, and some biscuits." That used to be his favorite. I turn to him. "You still eat meat, right?"

"Yeah. I like that stuff. It's just..." He rubs his hands again and looks away.

I sigh. Leave it to my brother to blow through thousands of dollars in the blink of an eye. Because he's undoubtedly broke. Again. "It's on me. Don't worry about it."

Carol gives me one of her parental smiles like she thinks I'm doing the right thing even though she doesn't like Silas.

When she's out of earshot, I drop the niceties. "What's going on with you? And why don't you have any money when you just sold Gran's house?"

After a long, dragged-out sigh like I'm the biggest pain in his ass, he tosses an arm over the back of the booth. "I've been in rehab." He waves the other hand over himself. "Obviously, it's doing wonders."

"That's why you sold the house? You wanted to go to rehab?" I feel like I'm speaking a foreign language with how unexpectedly this conversation is going.

"I wouldn't say I *wanted* to go to rehab."

It takes me a minute to process what he's saying. "So you got in trouble, and what, had to go to rehab instead of jail?"

"Ninety days of court-mandated rehab, to be precise."

"And you didn't think to mention this to me?" Tears sting my eyes. I hate myself for showing any emotion right now.

"Don't start blubbering over that old pile of bricks. The house was barely worth anything anyway."

Furiously, I wipe my eyes with the back of my hand. "I'm upset about you, you pompous jerk. Why didn't you tell me you were in trouble?" I lower my voice. "And did you seriously forge Gran's signature on the deed or something? That's how you afforded rehab, right? The house?"

He shrugs, and it takes everything in me not to reach across the table and strangle him because I know that's as much of an answer as I'm gonna get.

The food comes, and I sit there shell-shocked and watch Silas shovel down mashed potatoes. I have eighty-five dollars to my name, and as much as my brother hurts me down to my soul sometimes with his selfishness, I have to ask if he needs anything.

"Do you have money for food and rent? Where are you staying right now?"

"Got a girl. She'll feed me."

Good Lord.

"And you're done with rehab? You... you're feeling better?"

"Yeah. I'm off the hard stuff."

My eyes drift to his arms where the track marks have faded. "Silas, please take care of yourself."

He pauses with a fork of food halfway to his mouth. "Really. I'm cool." He studies my appearance. "What about you? Where you staying?"

"Logan's." I answer without thinking.

His whole body tenses. "What the fuck, Josephine? Don't you have other friends you could stay with?"

I clench my hands so I don't reach for a blunt object. "Where was I supposed to stay? You sold our house. Without bothering to mention it to me."

I'm annoyed with myself for bringing up Logan when I know the topic triggers Silas, but why should I have to hide things about myself? All I ever did was hide who I was growing up to make my parents happy. I was too awkward? I shut the hell up. I giggled too much? I stopped laughing. They didn't want me to show too much skin? I wore freaking overalls. Well, they're not here to tell me what to do.

Before he can respond, I shake my head. "Why do you care if I'm with him?"

"What do you mean you're 'with him'?" His eyes narrow into tiny slits. "You're *dating* him?"

Here we go.

"You could give a shit what happens to me as long as it does not involve the Carters. Why is that?"

With a clang, he drops his fork on his plate and jabs a finger at me. "You know why. You know their fucking father cheated with Mama. Hell, if you hadn't been born before we met those people, I'd wonder if that man was your sperm donor too."

I'm so disgusted I can barely talk. "Not this again." I shake my head. "Daniel Carter would never cheat on Beverly. Besides, the man has passed, rest his soul. And it's in poor taste to talk ill of the dead, Silas. I know you harbor this misplaced resentment, but those rumors aren't true. Mama might have cheated, but I seriously doubt it happened with Mr. Carter. I always thought Daddy was delusional, all hopped up on drugs, and imagined the whole thing."

"You're a fucking fool. It happened right under your nose, and you refuse to see it."

"See what? Tell me what I'm missing. Are you mad because Mr. Carter laid off Daddy because he was coming to work drunk or high? I can't say I blame him for that."

He pushes his plate away. "Daniel Carter slept with Mama and laid off Daddy while he had the whole town thinking he was a saint. That's why I hate that fucking family. Logan's just a carbon copy of his old man, and you're a dumbass to think he won't do the same thing to you. With the way you've chased after him your whole life, he probably decided to go for the easy lay. So don't go thinking you're special. He'll be on to the next pretty thing who spreads her legs in a few weeks."

I suck in a breath at his hateful words.

Heat stings my eyes, but I refuse to let the tears overflow. "If anyone is like their daddy, it's you, Silas. Maybe you should look in the mirror before you go casting stones." I toss down some money to cover lunch. "Funny, but I used to look up to you when we were younger. I honestly don't know what I ever did to make you treat me this way, to act like you hate me." With a swipe of my elbow, I wipe my eyes. "You always said you wished you didn't have a sister. Congratulations. You're getting your wish. I hope you have a nice life."

I'm surprised to hear him call my name as I race out of the restaurant, but there's no way I'm going to sit there and let him talk to me that way.

My days of being a doormat are over. Even if it breaks my heart to lose my brother.

34

LOGAN

TODAY IS NOT GOING THE WAY I IMAGINED.

Last night, when Ethan texted to say he'd pick me up late, I decided to sit Jojo down for breakfast while I explained why I'm at this other chick's beck and call. The more I thought about what Isaiah said, the more I realized he was right. Jo deserves for me to talk to her, one on one, and explain how I got myself into this situation.

Instead, I fucked her like an animal and overslept in a post-sex haze.

Real mature, asshole.

Worry gnaws at the back of my mind. I didn't mean to be so savage with her this morning. We fucked like the world was ending, and it was hot as hell.

I'll be honest, though. I'm having a hard time melding Joey, my childhood best friend, with Joey, my girlfriend, the woman I want to fuck until I can't move.

It takes me a second to realize I'm feeling shame. Shame that I took her that hard. She was practically a virgin ten minutes ago, and I mounted her like a damn animal. I lost all restraint.

Like when I came on her tits at the coast. Not my proudest moment.

Well, that's a lie. I liked marking her and seeing the evidence. Liked it quite a bit. But it feels wrong to do this to my sweet Jojo. Even if she tells me it's okay and she likes it.

Scrubbing my face, I let out a curse. Truthfully, I could really use a brother-to-brother chat with Ethan. Though I'm not sure how to bring this up. Just add that to the whole host of things I need to talk to him about.

The worst part is he would know exactly who I'm talking about, and I'd rather have my nails pulled out with a rusty plier than share details about what Jo and I do in bed.

I'm filling the tank at the gas station when a familiar car pulls in.

"Hey, man." I lift my chin to Patrick, who gives me a weird look.

He comes over and shakes his head, but doesn't say anything.

"What's your deal? You pissed about something?" I haven't seen him since we got back from the coast Sunday night.

"Why're you messing with Joey when you got some chick on the side?"

I frown. "What are you talking about? I don't have anybody on the side."

He rolls his eyes at me. "Samantha? Ring a damn bell?"

I still, my heart thudding in my chest. "How do you know Samantha?"

"So you *do* know her? Red head. Legs for days. Tits like melons."

Christ. This guy. "What about her? We're friends." Sorta. "And what does this have to do with Joey?"

"Just had a really interesting conversation with Samantha on

Monday, and she was surprised to hear you've been boning Joey when you're supposed to be with her."

What the hell? I grab him by his T-shirt. "You have no clue what's going on here, and before you go spreading some nasty rumor about the people involved here, I need you to think long and hard first. Because if you tangle up Joey in some bullshit that hurts her, I swear to God, I will kick your ass until there's nothing left. You hear me?"

I push him off, and he stumbles away and mumbles, "I hear you, but I'm not sure I believe you."

"I'm not fucking Samantha."

Still shooting daggers my way, he sniffs. "I'd just hate to see Joey get her heart broken because you can't keep your dick in your pants."

"And I'd hate to see your mouth get broken because you can't keep it closed. This is the last time I'm gonna say it, I'm not stepping out on Jo. I made you a promise I wasn't gonna hurt her, and I meant it. That girl is my entire world."

Sliding in the truck, I slam the door shut while talking myself out of running over Patrick. I get that he has feelings for Joey and has a wild hair up his butt as a result, but there's no excuse for the shit he's saying.

My fingers fly over my phone as I send a text to Samantha. I can't figure out if she's really telling people we're together, or if Patrick was talking out his ass.

With one more errand to run for the day, I try to focus on my job and head for the lumber yard to pick up a delivery for my brother. As soon as I'm done with this, I can finally get back to Jo so we can talk.

All of a sudden, my phone starts blowing up. I don't recognize the number, but the person calls back three times in a row.

When I answer, I listen to the frantic voice on the other end for only seconds before my blood runs cold.

35

JOEY

Despite how angry and hurt I am with my brother, I manage to get my act together enough to pick up the wedding supplies for Tori. With a truck full of votive candles and hair accessories for the wedding, I head back to Logan's house and crawl into bed. Rambo must sense how upset I am because he curls up on my neck and whimpers.

Silent tears fall when I think of my messed-up family. In some ways, I know Silas never stood a chance. Our father was a grade-A asshole who roughed us up, cited scripture when he was good and high, and only thought of himself. My mother was a saint for putting up with his bull. Or a fool.

In some ways, I understand why Silas hates the Carters. They were everything our family wasn't. Loving. Financially stable. Respected. And they always loved up on us like we were theirs. But Silas doesn't know how to accept love.

Too tired to keep my eyes open, I pull the blankets over me and Rambo, ready to block out the world.

I'm not sure how long I sleep, but it's getting dark out when I crack open my eyes at the sound of the front door closing.

That's when I remember I was going to make us dinner so

Logan and I could hang out. Dang it. I didn't mean to sleep so long.

A notification on my phone catches my attention. It's a lame-ass apology from my brother. *Didnt mean for things to get out of control today.*

Annoyed, I text back. *I'm with Logan. Deal with it. Get over yourself and your petty issues and support me for once in your life. I've always had your back. Why don't you have mine?*

In the last few months, I've learned a few things about myself. I hate gray areas. My brother can either put up or shut up.

I decide to put things in his court. *You can make it up to me. Come to dinner tonight at Logan's.*

I probably won't hear from him for another three months.

Wishing I could erase what happened with Silas today, I stumble into the hallway ready to launch myself into Logan's arms for a much-needed hug when I freeze.

A strange woman with long, auburn hair is standing in the kitchen.

Logan never locks the door if someone's home. It's one of the things I've always loved about country living. How everyone knows everyone out here, reducing the need to lock up.

Obviously, that's a mistake.

She's wearing a tight tank top, a tight pair of jeans, and red heels, and she's putting away groceries like she owns the place.

Before I can ask her what she's doing in someone else's house, she starts to speak.

"Logan, baby, I know you said you were busy this evening, but I couldn't go one more day without seeing you. I haven't seen you since Sunday night." She makes a pouting sound.

Logan's not home yet, but she obviously doesn't know this.

But the familiar way she talks to my boyfriend makes the hair on the back of my neck stand up.

I clear my throat. "Who are you and what are you doing in Logan's house?"

Her breath catches, and she spins around with wide eyes. Rambo finally decides to bark.

"Oh, hey, Rambo," she coos. "How's my puppy?"

Who the hell is this woman? I pick up my dog before the psycho does.

Her eyes narrow as they travel over me. I'm just wearing one of Logan's T-shirts and underwear.

I lift my brows. "Again, who are you?"

She looks so familiar, it's eerie. Where have I seen her before?

Her red lips tilt up. "I'm Logan's girlfriend, Samantha. And you would be?" She says it with such authority, I take a step back.

I open my mouth and close it again. At this point, it feels weird to argue that *I'm* Logan's girlfriend.

"Oh!" She laughs, and the sound sends chills down my arms. "You're his little friend. The one who's always tagging along everywhere. Back from Florida for the wedding?"

How does this woman know so much about me?

I nod hesitantly, my head spinning in a million different directions. "You look really familiar. Do I know you from somewhere?" She shrugs and flicks her hair over her shoulders, a mannerism I remember. "Wait. I cut your hair once, right?"

Nothing about her expression changes. She completely ignores my question, but I know who she is. At least I think I do. She's the woman who pitched a fit at the salon last winter and got me fired. I didn't think her name was Samantha, but maybe I'm misremembering.

Jesus, what is going on?

A bad feeling settles over me, and all at once, it dawns on

me. Those texts Logan's been getting for the past several days. The ones he got this morning from *Sam*.

No, not Sam. *Samantha*.

I never bothered to read those messages. Didn't think I needed to. Even if I was concerned, snooping isn't my style.

But now *Sam* has definitely piqued my interest.

"Did you say you saw Logan on Sunday?" I hear myself ask as I lean against the wall. Bracing myself for her response, I cringe when she smiles again.

"Sunday night." A giggle shakes her ample chest. "I can't turn him away when he wants to get some, you know? He's insatiable. He sure does like his booty calls."

My stomach lurches because she's talking so confidently, with so much assurance, it rattles me.

"I... Can you tell me what time he... visited on Sunday?" I feel like I'm clinging to a life raft in the middle of a storm. Maybe this woman is a nut job. Maybe she'll tell me the wrong time, but all the hope I have burns to ash when she responds.

"It was after he stopped at the pharmacy for Zach, so it was late. Like almost midnight. Poor Zachy got sick and needed some soup, and Logan drove to my apartment in the middle of the night, bless his heart. And then he tucked me in, if you know what I mean."

Bile crawls up the back of my throat.

Sunday night. When Logan left for several hours to allegedly refill his mother's prescription and came back well after midnight exhausted.

My brother's warning rings loud and clear in my mind. That Logan's a cheater. That he'll toss me away once he gets what he's looking for. That I'll never keep his interest.

I shake my head. I've known Logan my whole life, and he might be irresponsible from time to time, but I can't see him sleeping with another woman right in my face.

"Is he gonna be home soon?" Samantha curls a shiny lock of hair around her finger. "I figured he'd be here since his truck is parked outside."

"I borrowed his truck. He took his brother's. He was supposed to be home for dinner, but I guess he's running late..." I trail off. I'm not sure why I'm telling her this.

She takes a step closer. Samantha is really beautiful, I admit ruefully. Tall and buxom with gorgeous long hair.

"Logan's so proud of Zach. Want to see some photos?"

I have no clue who Zach is, but this doesn't seem to deter her.

Without invitation, she sidles up next to me and pulls out her phone. She's so much taller than me, her being this close is freaking me out. When she taps on the screen, several texts from Logan pop up. She swipes it, but not before I see him asking where she is. That he's been trying to reach her. That he really needs to talk to her.

My unease deepens. God, am I being a complete idiot? Is she telling the truth about dating him or hooking up or whatever they're doing? I cover my mouth with my hand, afraid I'm going to be sick.

She smiles at me like my world isn't on the cusp of destruction. "Here we have a photo from last summer at the lake."

"La-last summer?"

"I have some from the year before, but last summer's shots are adorable."

"So you guys go back years?" I ask weakly.

Nodding, she looks at me like I'm a moron. "Well, Zachary is seven, so you do the math."

My heart thuds painfully in my chest, and I swallow back the acid in the back of my throat, my eyes finally focusing on the image in front of me.

It's a pic of Samantha and Logan. He has his arm around her shoulders, and they're both smiling.

And they're standing behind a little blond boy.

One who's the spitting image of Logan.

I stare at it long and hard.

She runs her finger over the boy. "You can tell what side of the family he takes after."

The answer is like a knife to my shredded heart. *His father's.*

36

LOGAN

Rage is an interesting thing.

The emotion can spin you out of control or make you so deathly focused, you swear you could fight like Neo in *The Matrix*.

Right now, I'm so pissed, I might spit fire.

My legs can't carry me fast enough up the stairs of Samantha's building. When I get to the top of the stairwell, I go to the apartment across the hall from her place and pound on the door.

A petite older woman opens it. "I'm so sorry. I didn't know who else to call. I have to go to work tonight, and—"

"It's okay, Carmen. This isn't your fault. I'm glad you called me." I'm kicking myself for not having her number in my phone to begin with. If I had known she babysat for Zach, I hope I would've thought to get it.

Zach hops off the couch and comes racing into my arms.

"Hey, buddy. You doing okay?" It takes everything in me to calm the hell down. Seeing that he's safe helps. I give him a big hug and let out a sigh of relief.

Zach nods, but it's obvious he's been crying. "Hey, Logan."

Carmen motions for us to sit, and I take Zach over to her kitchen table and sit next to him before I turn to her.

"Tell me what happened again."

Her hands twist together. "Mr. Logan, Samantha asked me to watch Zach on Monday morning for a few hours, and by late afternoon, I started to get worried, wondering where she was. By night time, I had Zach sleep on the couch and hoped she would come home after her job. It was strange because she wasn't returning my messages. And then yesterday morning, when I took out the trash, I saw her run to her car. I was shocked to see her. She acted like nothing was wrong, even though she had left her son with me and hadn't stopped by to check on him or anything."

What the fuck? I'm about to blow a gasket, but I take a deep breath.

"And you're sure you didn't maybe misunderstand? Is it possible she wanted him to stay with you for a couple of nights?" Although the fact that Samantha dumped him here and hasn't checked in with Carmen this whole time has me seeing a haze of red.

"Zach has never stayed overnight with me before." She turns to the kid. With a sad smile, she pats his hand. "But *mijo*, you know you're always welcome here, right? I was just worried about your mama, and I was afraid I'd miss work tonight."

He nods, big tears welling in his eyes.

I tug him into my arms and give him another hug. "Hey, bud, everything's okay. We'll get this sorted out. How about you go and play for a few minutes while Carmen and I finish chatting? You hungry? Maybe we can grab some burgers after this."

That makes him smile. Once he's settled in front of the television, I turn back to Carmen and lower my voice. "How much does Samantha pay you for childcare? I want to be sure to settle her bill." I didn't miss the tremble in Carmen's voice when she talked about missing work.

But she shakes her head, pink rising in her cheeks. "I've never asked for money. She's a single mom."

There's a question in her eyes. "Yeah, she's a single mother. But I give her more than enough to pay for childcare if she needs it."

In fact, I've offered to take Zach for a few days to give her a break, and she's never taken me up on it. Samantha, though emotional at times, seemed like a good mom. She was flexible with me at the beginning, and I was afraid to rock the boat and talk about getting more time to see the kid. Sure, that might've pushed me to finally tell everyone in my family what's going on, but I didn't want her thinking she had to raise a child by herself.

Maybe that's what I've fucking needed—to face the reality of the situation.

I scrub my face, so tired of dealing with this by myself. Who am I kidding? I need people in my life to know what's going on even if it hurts them. More than anyone, I'm desperate to tell Joey, desperate to finally have this out in the open.

Grabbing my phone, I try calling Samantha again, irritated as fuck when I get voicemail. So I rifle off several more messages, wishing I had my brother by my side and sorry as hell I'm gonna have to burst his bubble before the wedding.

And then I call our lawyer.

By the time I'm done, the sun is starting to set. Zach and I drop off Carmen at work, before we grab some drive-thru and head to the ranch. It's time to talk to Joey.

37

JOEY

For one long, agonizing minute, I stand there and do the math.

Seven years.

Samantha's child is *seven* years old.

That means Logan got this woman pregnant *in high school.* His senior year. Back when I was busy writing his name in my binder like a lovesick fool, he got this girl knocked up.

"Oh, honey. I know this must come as a shock to you." Samantha pats me on the shoulder.

It's only then that I realize I'm crying. I'm not sure why. Logan and I weren't together until I came back from Florida. We certainly weren't dating in high school, though I had hoped we could.

Deep down, I'm mostly crushed he never told me. That he had a child with another woman and never mentioned it to me, his alleged best friend. And here I've been daydreaming about the life Logan and I could have together when he's been lying to me about something so huge. For *years.*

Is Samantha being honest about being with him now? I'm not totally sure. This is the same woman who got me fired after all. I mean, I think it is. Ugh. I feel like I'm losing my mind, like I don't know anything anymore. Who is Logan? Is he my best friend? Or is he the guy who's kept this enormous secret from me and his whole family? Because I can guarantee Beverly doesn't know about Zach. She's nothing if not a proud grand-mother, and she'd raise hell if Logan didn't bring his baby around.

"Do you want to see more pictures? I really should post a few of these to my Instagram." Before I can tell her no, she's scrolling, pointing out the places she and Logan went with their freaking kid.

What is it they say? A picture speaks a thousand words? Zach is obviously Logan's clone. Same blue eyes. Same light blond hair Logan had when he was younger. Same nose and playful smirk.

Photo after photo. From last winter, last Halloween, last summer, the previous Christmas, at various dinners. Finally, I cover my eyes. The pain of seeing him with this woman and their kid in a parallel life cuts me to the quick.

I want to rage and scream at Samantha, but it's not her fault Logan lied to me.

All signs point to him being this child's father. Because what else could be going on here?

As I wipe my face, I remember telling Logan that a *guy* named Sam had texted him this morning. He could have corrected me, but he didn't.

No, he was walking out the door, and he paused.

And then deliberately omitted that Sam is a *woman*.

More tears fall.

Why is Logan such a liar?

I can barely breathe. Has our whole relationship been a lie? Is he really dating this woman, and I'm just a convenient fuck? Is he expecting me to go back to Florida and thought he could get laid while I was in town and then go back to his real girlfriend?

Rambo squirms in my arms, and I put him on the ground as I attempt to hold in a sob. Tugging my shirt down, I try to cover my bare legs.

"I-I'm gonna go put some clothes on." My words are barely above a whisper. "Make yourself at home, I guess."

"Honey, I'm sorry to say this." She looks me over, and a little piece of me dies from embarrassment to be scrutinized by Logan's beautiful baby mama. "But do you really think you should be staying here? It's kinda inappropriate. Don't you think?"

I nod, feeling like I just got sucker-punched by life. Though I'm not sure where I can go. I need to talk to Logan. At the very least, I plan to give him a piece of my mind and maybe my foot up his ass. But I'm not sure I can carry on that conversation right now. What I need is a night to pull myself together.

"Let me get my things."

She nods. "I can give you a ride wherever. And you're probably headed back to Florida soon, right?"

"Yeah." It's impossible to see through the tears. "I'll be going back to Florida."

As soon as possible.

38

LOGAN

ZACH AND I ARE HALFWAY BETWEEN AUSTIN AND MY PLACE WHEN I get Joey's text. *I'm leaving. I'll talk to you tomorrow.*

I'm not sure what that means. Why would she be leaving? Unless maybe she's staying with Tori tonight. But she told me she was making us dinner, and she knew I needed to talk to her about something.

Am I so late that she's pissed?

A glance at the clock on the dash tells me it's possible. I cringe. Yeah, I'm an asshole. I should've called her earlier to let her know I was running behind schedule.

I'll have to make it up to her. I want to send her a text, but I'm driving. At this point, it would be faster for me to just head home and try to catch her than to pull to the side of the road to send a message. And I don't really know how to explain the child in the passenger seat over text.

Zach smiles at me while he stuffs his face with a burger, and I smile back, relieved to have him with me. When I got Carmen's call earlier today and heard he'd basically been abandoned, I freaked out. It's taking me a minute to calm down. I try to find something mellow to talk about.

"I'm glad to see your appetite is back. Did your mama tell you I stopped by on Sunday night? Gotta be careful with those carnival rides."

His eyebrows knit together. "What carnival rides?"

"Didn't you get sick this weekend after you went to the carnival?"

He shakes his head, looking at me like I'm a little touched. "I was home this weekend by myself. Mama had to work."

I let that settle in, and when it does, my hands tighten on the steering wheel. "She left you at the apartment by yourself?"

What the fuck is going on? My brother would have my ass if I left his kids at home by themselves.

If I'm calculating this right, Samantha left this kid alone all weekend except Sunday night when I stopped by, only to drop him off at a neighbor's on Monday, never to return. Here we are on Wednesday. And I know she's been around because my messages are showing up as read. Plus, Patrick saw her on Monday, and Carmen spotted her yesterday. I'm ready to punch my dash, I'm so frustrated.

I'm hoping this whole thing is some major misunderstanding, but if it's not and she's leaving this boy wherever for days at a time, my lawyer is gonna chew her up and spit her out.

Doing my best to stay calm, I motion to Zach, who polishes off his burger. "Your mom said you were sick to your stomach Saturday night and puked, so I brought over some Gatorade on Sunday because you still weren't feeling well."

That gets me another head shake. "I didn't get sick this weekend."

Jesus. Is Samantha a diabolical liar?

The bad feeling in my gut grows. As soon as I reach a light, I call Joey, but it goes straight to voicemail.

But it's the incoming text from Samantha that fills me with dread.

I'm at your place cooking dinner. See you soon!
And now I get why Joey is leaving.
Fuck!

39

JOEY

Ten minutes later, I've thrown on some jeans and tossed what I could into my rolling suitcase. There's no way I can carry all the stuff we got from Gran's, but that's a problem for another day. I'm too upset to deal with that given the bombshell Samantha just dropped on me.

My hands are shaking when I text Logan to say I'm leaving. I consider telling him his baby mama is standing in the damn kitchen eyeballing me like I'm a homewrecker, but I don't want to give him time to get his story straight. If he's been lying to me, I want him to look me straight in the eye when he admits the truth.

I don't wait for a response before I shove the phone in my purse.

Samantha is curled up on the couch with Rambo when I roll my suitcase out of Bev's room. When Sam sees me, she grabs her purse. "Where can I drop you off?"

"It's okay. I don't need a ride."

She frowns and stands up. "It's no trouble at all."

"I'm not going very far." Tori and Ethan's house is a twenty-minute walk that will probably take ten minutes longer because

I'm dragging my luggage behind me, but it's still a trip I can make on foot. Even though Logan's truck is outside, I'm not about to drive it again.

"Did you let your friends know you'd be coming?" she asks as she takes a step closer.

What an odd question. I shake my head. "I'll text them on the way."

I head toward the door. It feels really freaking weird to leave this stranger alone in Logan's house. I might be mad as hell at Logan, but I can't deny the strange vibe I'm getting from Samantha.

Maybe she's giving you the stink-eye for boning her boyfriend. What do you expect, Josephine?

I'm so confused right now, I want to crawl back into bed and never come out from under those covers.

Seriously, how did I end up being the other woman?

Samantha gives me an impatient look, and I debate whether I should ask her to leave.

Clearing my throat, I motion to her. "Can I ask how you got in the house?" I don't mention it was probably unlocked, but I'm not sure how to broach the subject otherwise.

She blinks slowly. "Logan gave me a key." Reaching into her bag, she pulls out a keyring and rattles it in my face. "See?"

A deep sigh wells up from my chest. I really want to leave this woman here so Logan can deal with her, but she is a stranger, to me at least. And I'm not about to test out each and every one of her dozen keys to check whether one works on the door.

"Um. Would you mind waiting for him in your car? I'm the guest here, and it would be rude of me to leave someone in Logan's house without him."

Of course, it's rude of him to have a child with someone else and never bother to mention it to me, but who's keeping the dang score?

What is it with the men in my life? Do they all have to be such assholes?

Sam's nostrils flare, and she lets out a huff of annoyance. "Sure. I get it." She points behind me toward the kitchen. "Actually, I think I'll wait for him at my place. Do you think you could help me carry some groceries back to my car?"

Lord, grant me patience.

"Sure." I leave my luggage at the front door and head to the kitchen, but I don't see the groceries. She must have put them away.

When I turn back to ask Samantha what she needs me to carry, she's right behind me.

"Sorry." She shrugs. "I was hoping it wouldn't come to this."

Unease crawls up my spine. "Come to what?"

Suddenly, everything goes dark.

40

LOGAN

ZACH AND I STAND ON THE PORCH AWKWARDLY. ETHAN LOOKS AT the little boy next to me for several heartbeats before turning to me.

"You gonna explain?"

Lowering my voice, I whisper, "Look, I just need you to watch him for an hour. Maybe two. I'll tell you everything when I get back. I swear. It's just... I have a situation."

Thank God our mother is hanging with Tori at Kat's place tonight. I couldn't handle it if she was here right now.

Ethan laughs, but it lacks amusement. "You don't say."

Ignoring him, I kneel in front of Zach. "Okay, bud, I know you've had a rough day, but I'll be back in a bit, and then we'll stay at my place tonight. Ethan has my number, so he can reach me if you need anything." After what he's been through with Samantha, I feel like Zach needs reassurances.

His eyes light up. "Can we ride the horses tomorrow? Mama is always telling me you have horses."

Damn. I'm so gutted that Zach doesn't have the first clue about our family business. I put my hand on his shoulder. "Absolutely. I'm gonna give you the grand tour tomorrow." I turn to my brother. "Is Mila up?" When he nods, I motion to Zach. "They're the same age. Let them play together."

I give the kid a quick hug and race down the steps to hop into the truck.

Now that I'm by myself, I lose my shit. Because not only is Joey not answering my calls, she wasn't at my brother's house. So that means she's still at my house. Possibly with Samantha.

I'm praying she left before Sam thought to randomly drop by my house, which she's only done once.

Pebbles fly out from under my wheels as I tear down my brother's driveway. I didn't bother to ask if I could borrow his Ford again. I'm guessing he gets this is an emergency. Time drags like thick molasses despite the fact I gun it home. I swear my heart is in my throat when I reach the turnoff.

The first thing I notice is my truck is parked next to my house. Its windows appear intact, so at least Joey hasn't gone Carrie Underwood on my ride. Not that I don't deserve it. In some ways, I know I do.

But that brings a different kind of worry. If Jo didn't take my truck, did she go somewhere on foot? Did someone pick her up? Or is she still here?

I get out of Ethan's truck and slam the door. As I'm trekking around my house, I notice Samantha's car is parked out front. Anxiety races through my veins. Because who knows what she told Joey. This has clusterfuck written all over it. I debate what to do. My lawyer specifically instructed me not to confront Samantha face to face, but that was before I knew she was at my house. And what is she doing here when she hasn't checked on Zach in days?

When I get to my front porch, I pause to listen. It's quiet. Strangely quiet. I pull out my phone. Joey hasn't read my texts, but Samantha has read the ones I sent her. I don't know what that means.

The door is unlocked. I poke my head in, surprised as hell to see Samantha sprawled out on my couch, petting Rambo. But she's breathing hard like she was running around seconds before I walked in.

My eyes dart around. Everything seems normal. Except my rug. Which, for some reason, looks like it's been tugged out from under my Barcalounger.

Impatiently, I turn to Samantha. "Where's Joey?"

"Who?"

I swivel to her. "Don't fucking play games with me. Where's Joey?" I call out her name, hoping she'll come bounding out from the bedroom, but she doesn't. "Where's my girlfriend?"

The shrillest laugh I've ever heard bubbles out of Samantha. "Oh, come on now. She couldn't have been that good a girlfriend. She just left." She motions toward the driveway with her thumb. "Got a ride."

My eyes narrow. "Oh, yeah? With who?"

"How should I know? She said she was headed back to Florida."

"She's in a wedding in three days. I'm pretty sure she didn't go to Florida."

Sam shrugs. "Well, she was pretty upset."

"And why would that be?" I swear to God, if she lied to Joey to hurt her...

"How was I supposed to know you hadn't told her about Zach?" I grind my teeth, but she goes on. "Look, she took her suitcase. I'm telling you the truth. She left for Florida."

Before she can say anything else, I head down the hall. I flip on the lights in my room. The bed is messy, but I can't tell if anything is amiss. It's not as though Jo had a lot of stuff in this part of the house, but when I enter my mom's room where Joey keeps her suitcase, it looks likes looks a tornado tore through here. Except for the boxes we brought from her grandmother's last night, most of her things are gone.

I'm trembling when I return to the kitchen. I look for a note, something to tell me that Joey is on her way to see Ethan and Tori right now. Because I don't know where else she'd go. She hasn't talked to Silas since she got back from Florida, and she doesn't have any other family nearby. Our ranch is walking distance from here. Kat's farm is farther, but maybe someone gave her a ride?

I text Ethan, Tori, and Kat in a group message just in case anyone has heard from Joey since I left my brother's.

About to blow a gasket, I stalk to the living room and get in Samantha's face. "I'm not sure what you're doing right now, but in case you're not aware, I picked up Zach this afternoon from Carmen's. Care to tell me why you ditched him there three days ago and never bothered to pick him up? Only to show up here like nothing's going on?"

Her lower lip immediately quivers, and tears fill her eyes. "I needed a break, okay? Carmen doesn't mind watching Zach. She does it all the time." She picks up Rambo, who struggles to get out of her arms.

I don't mention that we'll be discussing this in court because I'm two seconds from losing my shit.

Her tears dry up enough for her toss her hair over her shoulder and push out her tits. "I was thinking we could go to the coast this week. Just you and me. I know you went with your friends last weekend, and that's fine, but maybe you and I could hang out. I'm starving, though. Why don't you run out and grab us something to eat first. And I can... clean up around here."

I feel like I'm in the fucking *Twilight Zone*.

When Rambo jerks in her arms, she sets down the dog, and he runs to the hallway and starts barking. With a groan, I press my palm into my pounding temple.

"Samantha, I'm giving you one more chance to tell me what's really going on. Zach already told me he didn't get sick last weekend. I don't know why you're lying or what you think you're doing here, but if I don't hear something that sounds like the truth in the next sixty seconds, I'm calling the cops, and you can explain to them why you abandoned your kid and broke into my house. So one more time, where the fuck is Joey?"

Rambo starts scratching at the hallway closet and whimpering and barking, drawing my attention.

There's water on the hardwood floor that wasn't there a minute ago.

I look to Sam, and her eyes widen as she pleads, "I-I wa-was just trying to get clo-closer to you."

My heart thunders in my chest as I turn back to the closet where that water is spreading.

But it's not water.

It's blood.

41

LOGAN

Bolting to the hall, I fling open the door, and my whole world collapses in on itself when Joey's limp body tumbles out.

"What did you do?" I yell at Samantha.

Why is there so much blood everywhere?

"WHAT DID YOU DO?"

For some reason, all I can think of is that time when Joey was little, and my mother got her a dress, and she was obsessed with twirling. When she spun, all of her blonde hair would get caught in the sunlight and look like spun silk. Even when we were kids, even before there was any hint of something more between us, she's always been my sunlight. Everything that's good and sweet and genuine in my life is wrapped up in this girl. And I can't fucking lose her now.

Leaning down, I gently wipe her hair out of her face. It leaves streaks of blood. "Joey. Baby. Talk to me."

I don't notice the gun until it's right in my face.

Samantha is crying, her hands shaking as she waves it at me. "It doesn't have to be this way. We can get away! Just the two of us!"

"The two of us?" What the fuck is she talking about?

"Zach's like a son to Carmen, and I bet she wouldn't mind keeping him."

She says this so matter-of-factly, it's like we're talking about what kind of toppings she wants on her pizza.

I stare down the barrel. "Samantha, the only way I'm going anywhere with you is if you shoot me and drag my dead body along. Do you hear me?" My voice is a low growl, but this is what happens when you eviscerate me. The thought of losing Jo now, after everything we've been through, sends me right to the fucking edge.

I scramble closer to Joey and feel for a pulse. From this angle, I can't tell if she's breathing. "Come on, baby. Come on."

There. It's faint, but her heart is beating. I place my hand over her chest and nearly collapse in relief when it rises. *Thank God.*

As carefully as I can, I try to pull the rest of her out of the closet so I can see where the blood is coming from and try to stop it.

Samantha releases the safety and wails, "Don't be like this, Logan. Let's go somewhere and talk. You don't need this bitch. She only brings you down. I tried to get rid of her for you last year. I tried so hard, and it worked and she went to Florida, but then she had to come back for this stupid wedding. But I have a place we can put her, and no one will ever know."

I'm about to punch this psycho in the fucking face when someone comes flying in from the living room and tackles her down to the ground.

Silas.

I have no idea what he's doing here, and I don't have time to ask.

Because the gun goes off.

42

JOEY

It flickers, in and out, like a clip at the end of a movie reel.

The lights.

Red and blue.

Colors flashing.

So much flashing.

I'm not sure if it's from actual lights or the nuclear explosion happening in my brain.

I groan and crack open my eyes only to slam them shut again when the brightness of the room stabs me in the cranium.

"She's awake. Thank God. Logan, honey…" I recognize the voice. Bev. It's such a comfort to me, I let go and fade back into the darkness. I'm so tired.

At some point, Logan's whisper in my ear drags me back. He sounds so sad. So desperate. I want to tell him I'm fine and not to worry, but I can't move my lips.

I'm supposed to be mad at him. Vaguely, I remember he broke my heart.

I've always loved Logan. Does he know this? I get the distinct feeling I shouldn't. Like he's done something so terrible, I'm supposed to hold it against him. But I don't want to be upset with him. I love him too much. It'll shatter me if what he did was really bad.

Did he cheat on me? Like Daddy thought Mama cheated on him? That would be devastating.

Logan's apologizing. Telling me not to cry. Wiping gently under my eyes.

But I must be dreaming because I hear Silas too, and I know Silas would never be anywhere near Logan. I let that thought take over and allow myself to fade. I could sleep forever and never wake up, and that would be fine with me.

"Baby, I love you so fucking much." Logan's voice is rough, raw. He sounds gutted.

When my lashes flutter open, I see him hunched over me, holding my hand, looking like someone killed his best friend.

"Am I dying?" I croak, my throat so dry. Because why am I in the hospital?

His head jerks, and he laughs when he sees me awake. He wipes his eyes. "Holy shit, Bitsy. You scared me. I was so afraid I was gonna lose you."

He's kissing me, and nurses rush in who poke and prod me. A doctor ushers everyone out so he can examine me more carefully. He says something about a lot of blood loss and a concussion and low blood pressure. How I'm lucky to be alive. About how they'll have to wake me every so often so I don't die in my sleep. That sounds ominous, but I'm too tired to care about the details. Everything feels fuzzy, like there's a layer of gauze over my thoughts. It's hard to speak, hard to think, exhausting to move.

I sleep until dawn becomes day. At least I think it's day. Nurses nudge me every so often, and I grunt at them until they leave me be.

It's not until I'm alone, when the room is still and so quiet I can hear the drip of the faucet in the bathroom, that I remember what happened.

My eyes fly open on a gasp.

An alarm sounds by my head. Wincing, I reach up to rub my temple, but there's gauze, and the pressure is intense from the light touch of my palm.

"Sweetie, calm down." A nurse jogs in and pushes some buttons that shut off that ungodly sound. She listens to my heart and lungs. Takes my blood pressure and temperature.

Logan runs in with Bev on his heels.

It's the expression on Logan's face that does me in.

His bloodshot eyes sport dark circles. He looks devastated. Like he cares about me. Like I mean something to him, and he's worried I got hurt.

But I can't trust anything because he's a liar.

Seeing him here, knowing how wrong I've been about him, hurts worse than whatever injury landed me in this room.

When I try to talk, I can only cough.

The machines start beeping again.

Finally, I can say the words. "Why did you lie?" I swallow past the sandpaper in my throat. "How could you not tell me?" For the first time in my life, I'm too angry, too hurt, to cry. He had a kid with another woman, *seven years ago*, and never bothered to tell me. "I can't stand the sight of you."

I can't even roll away because there are cords and IVs hanging off my arm.

"Joey, I swear I—"

"Leave me alone!"

"Sir, I need you to leave." The nurse tries to usher him out, bless her. "We don't want to upset her right now..."

Their voices fade, and I cocoon myself under blankets.

That nice nurse returns, and I make sure she understands I don't want any visitors. No one. Not a single soul. I'm not sure I've ever felt this alone before, but I have a feeling I need to get used to it.

When I wake again, it's dark outside.

I want to check the bus schedule and find out how much it'll cost to go back to Florida, but in the back of my mind, I know there's a reason why I can't go yet.

There's something I'm supposed to do or somewhere I'm supposed to be...

Holy shit, the wedding.

With trembling hands, I punch the nurse's button. A different nurse pokes her head in.

"What day is it?" I ask.

"I'm sorry. What do you need, hun?"

"What. Day. Is. It?"

She smiles. "Sunday. Are you hungry? I'm supposed to get you to eat more during my shift. We can get that catheter out tonight, and..."

I don't hear anything else she says.

I missed the wedding.

There really isn't anything to keep me here.

Finally, those tears fall. I couldn't stop them if I tried.

Logan is with another woman. Silas doesn't give a shit about me. Tori and Ethan got married. I mean, I wouldn't expect them to put their lives on hold for me, but I'm so upset I missed their wedding, the blow is crushing when added to everything else.

After a minute, the nurse pats my hand. "Concussions have a tendency to make you emotional. I've seen grown men bawl like babies when they've gotten a good goose egg, so I just want to let you know this is okay. Let it out, hun."

Oh, I will.

Before the nurse walks out, she adds, "By the way, the police are going to need to question you about what happened. You weren't in any condition to talk before, but they'll be stopping by tomorrow to get your statement."

She walks out before I can process what that means.

Because honestly, I'm not sure what happened.

43

JOEY

I'M LOOKING FOR MY CLOTHES WHEN THE YELLING STARTS.

Gingerly, I walk toward the door and listen. The nurse got me out of bed to get me mobile last night, but I was too exhausted to do more than go to the bathroom and crawl back into bed. Since I'm being released soon, though, I'm trying to do more for myself.

"This is bullshit!" Logan's voice booms from the hallway. "Joey's my fucking girlfriend."

I push open the door, shocked to find two security guards looking like they're about to toss Logan out of the hospital. "It's okay. Let him in."

Now that I'm feeling better, I need answers.

He rushes into my room so quickly, I have to take a step back. Then his hands are cradling my face, and I wince.

"Shit. Did I hurt you?" He studies the stitches that run along my hairline where the psycho apparently laid me out with a baseball bat. At least, that's what one of the nurses told me.

I shrug out of his hold and sit on the edge of the bed, aware that I probably look like crap since I'm sporting neon-blue hospital socks, a gown with questionable stains, and greasy hair, but I can't conjure the effort it takes to care. The only thing I need right now is the truth.

Absentmindedly, I pick at the Band-Aid on the back of my hand where I had an IV.

"So tell me. Get everything off your chest." My voice sounds hollow.

Logan collapses in the chair next to my bed and drops his head into his hands. "You have no idea how long I've wanted to talk to you about this."

"Well, since everyone already knows your dirty secret, I'm not about to give you points for doing it now."

He shakes his head, his eyes squeezed shut. "Please don't call Zach that. This isn't his fault."

My heart pangs in my chest. Even now, even after everything, it still hurts to see Logan in pain. "I wasn't talking about the boy, though, yes, he is shocking. I meant Samantha. I meant you living this whole other life and lying about it."

"There's really no excuse," he admits before turning to look me in the eye. "I thought I was protecting my mom. She's been through so much, and—"

I cut him off because I'm confused, and he's starting to piss me off more. "What does Beverly have to do with *anything*? Please tell me you're not blaming the way you hid your child on your mother." I'm about to go on a rant about having character —maybe after I knee him in the balls—but the expression on his face stops me.

"My *what*?"

That gets him a hard eye roll. "*Your. Child.* The one you had with Samantha. *Zachary*. The kid you've been hiding for *seven fucking years*." In the span of a heartbeat, my temper is volcanic. Gone is the canyon of loneliness and despair. Now I want to scorch the earth.

Logan has the audacity to gape at me like this is shocking

news, and then he's out of his seat and trying to grab my hand. "Fuck, baby. No—"

"Don't call me baby. And don't touch me."

I go to move off the bed, but my legs are weak, and I start to stumble. Logan's arms come around me, and I try to push him off, but he's too strong, and my limbs feel like saplings.

His voice is low in my ear. "Calm down. Don't hurt yourself over this. Zach's not my son."

He kisses my temple, the one that didn't get bashed in, and I close my eyes before I cry. I'm so frustrated and upset, and I hate myself for being in love with Logan when he's been this deceitful. I wish it didn't feel so good to be in his arms. I want to scream and break shit and demand that life stop trying to screw me.

"Stop lying!" I choke out. "Tell me the truth for once!"

He doesn't let me go. "Listen to me." He shifts me in his arms until we're practically nose to nose. "Zach is not my child." I'm about to scream in his face that he's a filthy fucking liar, when he shocks the hell out of me. "Zach is my *brother*."

"He's your... Wait. What?"

"My brother." A long sigh leaves his lips. "Well, my half-brother." He gently kisses my forehead, and I'm too shocked to protest. "Maybe we should sit down for this."

44

LOGAN

SEEING JOEY WITH STITCHES ON HER FOREHEAD, BRUISES ALONG her eyes, and as thin as can be, shakes me to the core.

This is the worst time to unload the whole story on her, but she's right. I can't stuff this down anymore. Deep down, I realize she's stronger than I'm giving her credit for. I'm sick to my stomach thinking she believed Zach was mine and I kept this from her.

We sit on two hard chairs next to the bed, and I shift in my seat to get the pressure off my left thigh, which is throbbing. "The short version of this is my father had an affair with Samantha about eight years ago. She got pregnant just before he died."

Her mouth drops open, but she doesn't say anything, so I continue. "I didn't find out about Zach until the summer before last. Samantha came by, wanting child support, talking about suing my father's estate. We were already dealing with Ethan and Allison's divorce. Shit was ugly between them, and I was scared as hell we were gonna have to sell the farm to pay out Allison. I figured Samantha entering the picture at that point would make it a foregone conclusion, and we'd lose the ranch.

So I talked her into letting me pay the child support myself without going to court."

Joey makes a face. "How old is Samantha? She must've been young when she hooked up with your father. And what the hell? He really cheated on Bev?"

"Samantha is three years older than me, so yeah, she was young at the time."

A nurse pops her head in, checks something on a chart, and tells Joey not to overdo it out of bed. We wait until she leaves to continue.

I clear my throat. "I was pissed at my father for so many fucking things, but that wasn't Zach's fault. The kid should get a stake in the farm at some point, but he was five at the time, and I figured that could wait. And until Samantha showed up on our doorstep with a little clone of me, I'd never given credence to those rumors that my father had cheated on my mom before."

Her eyes widen. "You heard those?"

"I did."

After a long moment, she sighs. "Silas always thought he cheated with our mother, that their relationship was the reason our dad took off."

I wince, hating the toll my father and his selfishness took on Joey's family. "I'm so sorry, Bitsy, but that's probably true."

"I just went off on Silas about this the other day. I saw him the afternoon Samantha came over." Her eyes meet mine briefly, and I nod, encouraging her to continue. "I thought he was crazy for thinking your dad had bedded our mama. I mean, she used to quote scripture to me. How does someone like that have an affair with a married man?"

Bowing my head, I run my hands over my jeans and try to think back to that time. "Maybe your mom needed some help or attention. Your father wasn't around, and my dad, the charmer himself, took it upon himself to comfort her?"

"Ugh. That does sound plausible. What dicks. All of them."

I hate that this whole situation disparages her mother. "Did your mama know she was sick by then?"

"I'm not sure. Maybe." She nibbles her bottom lip. "But if she did, that would explain why she wanted someone in her life other than Bill Grayson, the town drunk."

"I know it doesn't make it any easier to accept, and we'll probably never understand, but don't let any of this tarnish the good memories you had of her."

She sniffles, and I look away, knowing this is rough on her. I want to grab her hand, I want to hold her tight, but I'm not sure we're there yet.

After a minute, she coughs. "How's Beverly doing? Is she heartbroken?"

"She's hanging in there. She didn't outright say she knew my dad had stepped out on her, but I'm guessing a part of her sensed it."

My mother didn't tell me she's heartbroken, but I'm pretty sure she is.

A long silence stretches out between me and Joey, and I shift uncomfortably.

Finally, she groans. "I'm still having a hard time understanding why you didn't say something about this. Why keep it to yourself for so long? For two years? Why did you hide this from everyone?"

I rub the scruff on my chin. "When Tori came to live with us to nanny for my brother, my mother left for Chicago to visit family for a few weeks. Remember?"

"Yeah," she says slowly.

"She didn't go to Chicago. She went to San Antonio to have a procedure. My mom had dangerously high blood pressure and an arterial blockage, and she needed a stent. Bottom line is she didn't want anyone to know. She thought Ethan was stressed out with the divorce and had enough on his plate." My mom and I have had some long talks this week, and she knows I need to tell Joey the whole story. I have her full permission to give Jo the details of my mother's condition.

"So... you didn't tell anyone about Zach because of Bev's health."

Nodding, I sigh. "The doctors told me they didn't want her in any stressful situations. That she needed to rest. And maybe I overreacted, but finding my father face down in his own vomit after he had a massive heart attack shook me up pretty fucking bad. So there was no way I was gonna let a shitty situation that wasn't even my mother's fault affect her health. But yeah. That's why I didn't tell anyone."

When she doesn't say anything, frustration gets the best of me. "Put yourself in my shoes, Jo. Would you have wanted to deliver the bad news to my mom? So yes, I procrastinated. I'm not proud of that, but I couldn't bring myself to tell her that her husband of almost thirty years couldn't keep it in his goddamn pants." I scrub my face with my palm. "Anyway, I felt like I owed it to my mother to tell her first before I talked to Ethan or anyone else about it."

"I know that was a rough time for you," she whispers. For a moment, it looks like she wants to say more, but doesn't.

We're quiet for a long stretch as I mull over the events of the last few days. "I had no idea Samantha was so unhinged. I feel responsible. Like I triggered her or something."

Joey fiddles with a tie on her hospital gown. "Samantha told me she was your girlfriend. That y'all have been together for years, and Zach was your son."

Pure hot rage boils up in me at the thought of Samantha trying to manipulate Joey. That she went to such lengths to hurt my girl. No wonder Joey didn't want to see me while she's been in the hospital. "Samantha and I have *never* been like that.

Honestly, the idea grossed me out. She slept with my dad and then wanted to get with me?" I shudder. "No, thanks."

"What... what happened to her? After she knocked me out, I mean." Joey glances at the door. "Is she here? Do I need to be worried she's going to come after me again?"

"No. She's not here. She was arrested the night she attacked you, but I've been camped outside your door since you were admitted, so even if she was on the loose, she'd never get to you." I sigh, relief rushing through me to finally see Bitsy. "I swear to God, Jo. I've never been more scared than coming home to find you like that."

Needing a moment, I lean forward and close my eyes. "After she took a goddamn bat to your head, she stuffed you in the closet." The cops found the bloody bat under my couch.

I share the details of how I came home and the strange conversation I had with Samantha before Rambo started barking.

"Rambo found me?"

For the first time in days, I smile. "He did. Our little guy wouldn't stop barking at the hallway closet. He knew you were in there." But the smile drops off my face when I remember how close I was to losing her. "Jo, there was so much blood. I was terrified, baby." I reach for her hand, and she lets me take it. "The doctor told me that if Samantha had shifted a hair to the right, she could've crushed your eye socket. If I'd come home any later, you could've died."

I clear my throat. "I'm so fucking sorry for everything, Jo. For putting you in this position. If I had just told you what was going on, you could've protected yourself." As gently as possible, I hug her. She's stiff in my arms, and I get it. I fucked up. Badly. Even if Jo forgives me for what happened, I'm not sure I can forgive myself. I let her go, hoping like hell she'll give me another chance.

The door opens behind us, and I turn to wipe my eyes.

"What's up, assholes?" Silas smirks from his wheelchair. He's being pushed by a petite blonde.

Joey sniffles and tries to stand. I hold her elbow so she doesn't wobble. I don't think she realizes the toll her body's been through.

"What happened to you, Silas?" she asks quietly.

I smile at my former best friend, not caring one bit about the dumb shit he's said about me and my family over the years. In the moment of our greatest need, he was there. But more than anything, he came through for his sister. "Silas is the one who saved your life. Mine too, probably."

Silas chuckles and points to me with the hand that's not in a sling. "That bitch was waving a gun in Logan's face, and your crazy-ass boyfriend is hovering over your body and trying to help you. He's freaking the fuck out. There's blood everywhere. And Logan sounds just like Clint Eastwood in *Dirty Harry* when he tells that psycho, 'The only way I'm going anywhere with you is if you shoot me and drag my dead body along.'"

He's talking like he's recapping some *Red Dead Redemption*, all laid back and shit, but I know better. Silas was just as upset as I was that his sister was hurt.

"Your brother came over that day to apologize for that argument you guys had." I give him a pointed look before I continue. The sheepish expression on his face tells me he hasn't made it yet to Joey. "He overheard the yelling from the front porch and saw you were hurt. He flew through the air like a damn ninja and took down Samantha. He ended up with a bullet to his shoulder, but still managed to restrain her so I could try to stop your bleeding until the paramedics arrived."

Joey gasps. "Oh, my God. Are you serious?" She reaches over to hug him and almost lands on her ass. I grab her just in time to keep her from toppling over.

"Whoa, there. Not sure you're ready for that maneuver yet." As I stabilize Joey, I grin at Silas, whose face is turning red. He's not used to being the center of attention.

"No big deal, really," he says gruffly.

"It was a big deal," I note. "Since Silas had just gone through rehab, he refused the good painkillers after the doctor dug that slug out of his shoulder."

I'm glad to see he's straightening out his life. It's been a long time coming. But I shouldn't talk. I've had my own shit to work out too, I suppose.

Even though he's been banged up, Silas looks pretty good. But that's what Beverly Carter's home-cooked meals will do for a man. When my mother heard he came to our rescue and basically saved our lives, she parked him in the guest bedroom to recover and made him three squares a day.

"But why are you in a wheelchair? Did you get hurt anywhere else?" Joey looks him up and down, fear etched on her pretty face.

"Nah. Darlene here just offered me a ride. I'm gonna offer her another kind of ride later." He winks at his nurse friend over his shoulder, and I snicker while Joey rolls her eyes.

It's surreal to be having a normal conversation with Silas again after all these years.

He points at me and cocks an eyebrow. "Did lover boy here tell you he got shot too?"

"What?" Joey's eyes widen.

"It's nothing. Just grazed my thigh." Mostly.

"Jesus. She shot both of you?" Joey asks, her expression stricken.

"I got nicked when Silas tackled her, and he got a slug when they went scrambling for the gun, but he got the worst of it."

A smile pulls at my lips when she wobbles toward her

brother and leans down to hug him again. I reach behind her and close her hospital gown before she flashes everyone.

"Knock, knock." One of the nurses comes in with the cops on her heels. "Josephine, the police need to take your statement, and I'm thinking you've been out of bed long enough this afternoon."

"Jo, I'll be out here if you need anything," I say as the nurse ushers us out. I'm not sure what I'm looking for. Just something to know Joey understands, that she gets why I did what I did. But she doesn't make eye contact. She doesn't say anything. Just gets back into bed slowly.

My heart sinks as I wonder if I've fucked up too bad this time. Because I'm not sure she's gonna forgive me.

45

JOEY

SQUINTING INTO THE BRIGHT SUN, I TAKE A DEEP BREATH. CEDAR and a hint of barbecue scent the air. My stomach grumbles. At least I'm starting to get my appetite back, but I still feel pretty crappy.

Yes, I have stitches on my head and a gnarly concussion and bruises everywhere, but that's not what hurts the most.

Even though I got the full story from Logan yesterday, or what I'm hoping is the full story, I'm still wrecked.

Because deep down, I don't know if I can trust him.

Granted, two years of keeping this enormous secret is exponentially better than seven or eight, and knowing Zach is his brother and not his son is huge, but my heart is still battered and my faith in Logan is shot. I guess a baseball bat to the brain will do that to a girl.

The nurse wheels me to the curb where three trucks are lined up: Ethan's, Logan's, and Brady's.

Guilt tightens my chest for not wanting to see my friends when they stopped by the hospital. Even after I spoke with Logan and somewhat cleared the air, I wasn't ready to see anyone. I don't know if I am now, but everyone's here, and the hospital is releasing me, so it's not like I can hide out anywhere. I'm a little ashamed I want to. I'm embarrassed for so many things, but I can't begin to decipher why I feel this way.

My doctor said "emotional lability" is one of the side effects of this kind of head injury, and I can expect mood swings and extreme highs and lows as a result.

I'm definitely in touch with the lows.

Ethan and Tori hop out and the next thing I know, I have a bouquet of flowers in my arms and Tori hugs me.

I pat her awkwardly. "What are you doing here? Aren't you supposed to be on your honeymoon?"

She pulls back like I slapped her. "Didn't Logan tell you? We postponed everything for two weeks."

"Oh, my God, why?"

"Because of you, knucklehead. Look at you. You can barely stand, and you have two black eyes. I can't believe that wench did this to you." Now she's crying.

"Ugh. Please don't tell me I ruined your wedding." I'd cry too if I had to postpone my wedding.

"No! What? Of course not! We just want to make sure you're better so you can be a part of it."

Ethan squats down next to me. "I'm so fucking glad you're okay, squirt. I'm sorry you got the brunt of this." He gives my hand a squeeze, and emotion brims in his eyes.

"It's okay. It wasn't your fault."

Everyone gets quiet, and someone coughs. Logan. He's got his hands in his pockets.

"Now, y'all," Beverly interjects, bumping Ethan out of the way. "Don't you blame Logan. This started because he was covering for me. And... and he couldn't bear to tell me what Daniel had done." She sniffs, and Ethan wraps his arms around her shoulders. I can't imagine what she must be going through after finding out that her husband had a child with another woman. I'd be devastated.

She pokes Ethan. "Did y'all know Logan's been working nights? All those times we teased him about carousing, he was putting in hours at the Stock Yard so he could pay for child support when it wasn't even his kid? So he could pay for my medications and procedures. Don't you give him grief on top of everything else."

Bev kneels down next to me. "Honey, I wanted to let you know that I'm good with Silas. He's apologized for being a jackass, and I've accepted, especially after he jumped in to help y'all the way he did, but the truth is he's one of the reasons Logan didn't tell you what was going on. He was afraid your brother would read your texts like he did a few years ago. That he'd learn something he shouldn't and blab it around town to hurt us like he did in the past. You know what a hothead Silas was when he got messed up."

Huh. That does make sense.

I nod slowly, embarrassment over my messed-up family creeping up on me. Of course Logan was afraid to tell me anything with my doped-up brother always in my business. "I hear what you're saying."

Ethan pulls his mother up off the sidewalk. "Cool down there, Ma. I get all that, but no one told Logan he had to go it alone."

Bev smacks his chest. "Did you hear what I said? I made him swear he wouldn't tell you about my medical situation. And then, well, everything avalanched after that."

Logan makes his way closer, and he squeezes his mom's shoulder. "It's okay. I understand what Ethan's saying. I should've been honest." He turns to Ethan. "Bro, I swear I was gonna come clean after your wedding. It took you so fucking long to get to a place where you were happy, where you weren't stressed out over the ranch and Allison's demands, and I didn't want to bring you down again. But you're right—this is a big deal. I screwed up and nearly got Joey killed." His voice gets rough, and he clears his throat.

"I'm okay, everyone. Seriously." I try to ease myself out of the wheelchair. Four hands land on my arms to steady me. "No one needs to be blaming anyone on my account, except maybe the lady who picked up the bat."

Samantha was arrested, and at least I don't have to worry about her stalking me anymore.

According to the police, who searched her apartment over the weekend, they found a notebook full of details about me— places I worked, where I hung out, names of my friends, and photos from my Instagram. I told them how I thought she was the woman who got me fired, and we discussed the likelihood that she's also the person who vandalized my grandmother's car last winter.

I rub my temple, wishing I was in a bed so I could curl up. "Really. I'm fine."

The words surprise me. I don't know I feel that way until the words are out of my mouth.

I mean, I am fine. I'm bruised, and I'm at the center of too much drama, but I'm alive. That has to count for something.

Looking back and forth between the brothers, I sigh. "Don't y'all have better things to do than be upset with each other? Hug it out or something."

Tori gives me a grateful smile, wiping her eyes. Strangely, I'm not crying at the Hallmark commercial in front of me when Logan and Ethan do that bro hug thing.

Mostly, I feel numb and disconnected and want to go home.

I don't even know where that's supposed to be. Where is home for me now?

The one thing I do know is I don't want to go home with Logan.

46

LOGAN

Low voices in the kitchen come to an abrupt halt when Zach and I enter. Ethan gives me a nod. Tori gives me a half-hearted smile and pours me coffee. Yeah, we've been a hot mess since shit went down with Samantha.

I knew my brother would be upset that I'd kept so much from him, but it's a painful realization to think I might have damaged something permanently in our relationship. He worshipped our father, so I'm sure the news that Daniel Carter was a womanizing playboy behind the backs of his devoted wife and family has hit Ethan hard.

I motion to Zach. "Hey, buddy, why don't you go wash your hands so you can eat breakfast."

The kid has been staying with me, but I bring him to Ethan's every day to play with Mila and Cody. The police let me keep him after I showed them the DNA tests I had done when Samantha initially brought him around. I'm supposed to check in with Children's Protective Services, but since Samantha is probably going to prison for the foreseeable future, my lawyer says they won't care who gets the kid as long as he's with family.

It's a depressing thought, the idea that we could shuffle him around like a chess piece and no one would give a shit. I told Ethan I want to petition for custody, so Zach knows I want him. Ethan is supportive and says he plans to be in Zach's life every step of the way and help pay for whatever he needs.

And Joey? She's staying at Kat and Brady's. She says she needs time to think, so aside from talking to her at the hospital, I haven't seen her since. Not for almost a week. It's fucking killing me.

She'll return my texts, but she doesn't carry on conversation. Just answers my questions. I stop by there every day and drop off flowers. Sometimes a stuffed animal or some pie from the diner. Things I hope she likes. Mostly I want her to know I'm thinking about her and sorry as hell I hurt her.

Kat and Tori are worried about her. They tell me she doesn't say much. That she was pretty shaken by the attack and doesn't seem like herself even though the bruises are fading.

A knock at the front door makes me turn. "You expecting anyone?" I call out. Not sure why I ask because I'm opening the door before I hear the response.

Solemn gray eyes stare back at me.

"Jojo. Hey." I'm so damn excited to see her, she's in my arms before I realize she might not want me hugging her. And ain't that a kick to the nuts. I let her go and step back. "Sorry. Don't know if you're still sore or anything."

She shakes her head. "I'm better. Thanks."

"How'd you get here?"

"Kat dropped me off."

When we get to the kitchen, Ethan and Tori bound over to give her gentle hugs. Zach tugs on my shirt, and I clear my throat. I don't know why, but I'm nervous as hell at the thought of introducing the kid. It's not fair that he gets any residual shade because his mother went off the deep end, though, and I'm really hoping Joey feels the same way.

"This is our brother Zach. Zach, this is my... my best friend Joey." I almost call her my girlfriend, but right now, I'm not sure she is. It's gut-wrenching to think we might not work out, but I don't want to pressure her.

I hold my breath as he grins up at her.

Her eyes soften. "It's nice to finally meet you. Your brothers have said such wonderful things about you. I know they're really happy to have you here on the ranch."

The kid looks like he falls in love with her a little. *I know how that feels, buddy.* Of course she put him at ease. I don't know why I doubted her.

After a few minutes of conversation, Joey leans over to me. "Can we talk?"

"Of course." My heart beats erratically, and I wipe my palms on my jeans.

When we reach the living room, she settles on the couch. I join her, anxious as hell to hear what she wants to say.

"I'm sorry I haven't been ready to talk. Mostly, I haven't felt like myself. But thank you for the gifts. They've been thoughtful."

"I'm so relieved you're feeling better."

"Logan, I want you to know I'm not trying to punish you. I understand why you did what you did." She sounds so resigned, the tone of her voice morose, and the hope in my chest deflates.

"But?"

"But I'm not going to lie. It really hurt my feelings that you didn't tell me about Zach. That you had a second job. That you were helping this... this woman. You have so many secrets, Logan." Her eyes shift to the ground. "How can I trust you now?"

Fuck.

God, she's right. Why would she trust me?

Her hands twist in her lap. "Samantha told me you went to

her place on Sunday night after the pharmacy. She was telling the truth, wasn't she?"

One look at my face, and hers falls. But she has to know that Samantha made it sound salacious. "I went for Zach. She told me he was sick. I never touched her, Jo."

"I figured. Eventually, I mean. I just... How could you do that, be there for her, and then not tell me? Spend time with her and then crawl into bed with me and not mention it. That's what I can't resolve."

Isaiah was right. Joey needed to hear this from me.

"Baby, I almost did so many times. Remember when I said there was some stuff I wanted to talk to you about? That day even. The morning we fucked like animals."

She blushes. "I remember. Yes, you mentioned that right after you got texts from her and allowed me to think *Sam* was a guy."

Fuck me. This is not going how I intended. "Babe, come on. I was going to tell you. I swear to God. Ask Isaiah. We—"

Her brows furrow. "You told Isaiah about Samantha? You wouldn't tell me, but you told Isaiah?"

Shit.

I close my eyes, hating that I didn't have the good sense to confide in her. I could have warned her not to text me about it. Told her I was worried about someone finding out and concerned that Silas might hack her phone again. Why didn't I trust her?

"It's not like that. I got really drunk one night. I was so fucked up about my dad and about Zach, and worrying over how I'd tell my mom. And he happened to swing by. He found me completely shit-faced and prodded it out of me." I sigh and rub the back of my neck. "That's who I was talking to last winter. That conversation you overheard at the River Walk, the one that made you think I was calling you a burden. I was complaining to Isaiah about Samantha."

She huffs out a breath. "Jesus, Logan. Don't you think you could've told me that at the coast? Why wouldn't you just tell me then?"

"You're right. You're totally right."

An uncomfortable silence draws out between us until she finally says, "This isn't why I came here." She rubs her stitches along her hairline. "I didn't intend to get into all of this again. I know, at least in my head, that you did all of this for Bev. That you were protecting her confidence, which I respect. I'm just... I understand it in my mind, but my heart doesn't want to catch up. Does that make sense? And on top of everything else, the only emotion I'm feeling these days is anger or this weird detachment. I can't explain it."

"You don't have to." I take her hand, relieved as hell that she lets me. "You've been through a lot."

"Kat suggested I see a therapist." She hesitates. "Kat and my cousin have been talking and trying to find me someone. In Florida."

My heart sinks like a stone. "You're going back to Florida?"

"Don't you think that's for the best? After the wedding, I'll go back, and you can figure out what you want now that you're not dealing with so much."

A fierce wall of frustration and love wells up in me. "I know what I want, Josephine. I don't need time to figure it out." The conviction in my voice must catch her off guard because her eyes widen. I don't tone down my intensity because I don't want her to think I'm confused. "I love you. You're fucking wrecking me right now. I know I've been an ass, and I would like the opportunity to make it up to you, to prove that you can trust me, before you decide to run away again."

Her nostrils flare, and she yanks her hand out of mine. "I'm not running away. I'm sitting here discussing it with you."

"But the end result is the same." I know I'm being a dick, but if I lose her because of this, I'll regret it forever. And for some reason, I feel the need to challenge her, even if it pisses her off.

She's not the fragile, delicate Joey I've always made her out to be. She took a damn beating last week, came back like a champ, and now there's steel behind her gray eyes. "Fucking fight for this, Jo. Don't give up on me. On us. I know I screwed up badly, but I swear I'll do right by you. Stay here, and challenge me like you always do. Let's make a life together."

She stills. "Don't say things you don't mean."

"Why do you think I don't mean them?"

"You feel guilty because I got injured. Don't confuse that for something deeper."

"You want deeper? I would've taken that bullet right fucking here for you." I pound my chest. "When I thought you were dying, Jo, when I found you pale and covered in blood and not moving? I was so fucking scared. I knew right then and there I'd do anything to have you back, no matter the cost. So you need more time? Fine. You want me to prove myself to you? No problem. But don't think for a minute I'm letting you go." A frustrated breath leaves me. "Do what you got to do. If that means returning to Florida, fine, but know I'm gonna be right behind you."

Her eyes soften. "You're nuts."

"Damn straight. I'm fucking crazy about you, Josephine Marie Grayson."

Her lips pull up slightly in the faintest of smiles, but then that somberness returns to her expression. "And Zach? Are you dragging him to Florida too?"

I shove my hand into my hair. "You never told me what you thought about him moving in with me." I called and left a message after I'd discussed it with Ethan. I didn't want Joey thinking I left her out of the loop again. "I haven't talked to the kid yet, 'cause if you're really opposed to him living with me permanently, well..." Anxiety riddles up my spine at the thought she'll hate this idea.

"Of course he should stay with you. He knows you better than anyone else, right?"

I nod, the relief swift. And just that little bit of under-standing from her fills me with hope, hope that we can connect again. Hope that I can get her to trust me once more. Leaning closer, I cup her face and draw her to me so I can kiss her forehead.

"Give me a chance. Just one."

That's all I'll need.

47

LOGAN

ETHAN'S QUIET AS WE FINISH UP IN THE BARN FOR THE DAY. FOR once in our lives, he hasn't been giving me shit this week.

It's unsettling.

I wouldn't say he's giving me the silent treatment. He seems preoccupied. Given that his wedding, the one day he'd been looking forward to for months, got postponed, I'm not surprised his easy smiles have disappeared.

"Bro. Wanna get out of here and maybe grab a beer?" I wipe my hands on an old towel. "My treat."

"Not really in the mood, but thanks." He cleans the tack methodically, the way our father taught us.

A horse snorts in his stall, and I debate how to bring this up, but Ethan beats me to the punch.

"What's on your mind? You're obviously thinking big thoughts over there. Problems with Joey? Is she still considering going back to Florida?"

I nod and tell him about the conversation I had with her this morning.

"So what are you gonna do?" he asks when I'm done.

"Not really sure. I was planning to write her notes."

His eyebrow lifts. "Notes?"

"Yeah." I shrug, uncomfortable, but I'd like to get his thoughts. He and Tori went through a rough time after they first got together but managed to work things out. And Ethan's always been a serial monogamist with serious girlfriends. If anyone can help me maneuver these relationship waters, it's him. "I wanted to remind her of the good times we've had growing up. Things I remember about her that maybe she doesn't realize. Let her know I'm in this for the long haul."

My brother smiles. "Gotta say that's pretty sweet. Bet she'll love it."

"Can I ask you something?" This question has been on my mind since last week when I pounced on Jo like an animal. My brother is really the only person I can ask. And if it gets him talking to me again, even better. "Hell, this is awkward." I wipe my palms on my jeans. "You know I've never been in a long-term relationship, and I have questions. Is it... wrong to be... *adventurous* in bed with someone you're serious about?"

"Adventurous?"

"Yeah. You know. Rough." Images of the bite marks I'd left on Joey's body flash before my eyes. Bite marks she didn't seem to mind, but still. "Maybe a little debauched. I just—" Rubbing the back of my neck, I clear my throat. "I sometimes feel bad if I do things with Jo. Since...." Add this to the kind of conversation I never wanna have again. Fortunately, my brother finishes my sentence.

"Since she doesn't have a lot of experience."

Nodding, I lean against the stall. "Not that we're doing anything right now. I'm lucky if she lets me hug her, but I need to figure this out in my head."

Ethan looks down at the ground a moment before he turns his eyes toward me. "I can see why you'd be concerned. But as long as y'all are communicating, and she enjoys what you're doing, then you should be good to go. What you do and how you do it is one hundred percent up to the two of you. No one gets to judge that."

I let out a sigh of relief and wipe my palms again. "FYI, it feels super weird to be asking you for sex advice at my age."

He laughs, and it lights up his whole face. "Happy to be of assistance to you, little brother." He smacks me on the back. "Joey's a great girl, and I know I might've given you shit at the coast, but I can see you're serious about her. Just wanted you to know I'm pulling for you."

That chokes me up just a bit. I cough. "It means a lot to me that you'd think that." I take a big breath, needing to get this off my chest. Been doing a lot of that lately. Figure it's better than keeping this bad stuff inside. "I never told anyone this, but Dad and I argued that day. About Jo."

Ethan stares at me. "The day he died?"

"Yeah. I was running late because Jo and I were hanging out, and he busted my balls."

My brother gives me a small smile. "Sounds about right."

"Except he wasn't just pissed I was late. He didn't want me hanging out with Joey so much."

"'Cause he was pissed at Bill?"

I shake my head. "No, because he thought Joey was too young for me to get any ideas, and I had 'too many oats to sow.'"

"She was, what, a freshman when you were a senior?" When I don't say anything, he motions to me. "Was he right? Could you have been serious about her then?"

"I knew she was young and we probably needed to wait a year or two before we dated, but I thought maybe I could. Wait for her, that is."

"No shit."

"He told me I'd just break her heart. That I was a fool to think like that. He said I'd only be young once, and not only was

I not the kind of guy for one girl, he said I'd probably regret it if I tried."

My brother grits his teeth. "Well, damn. That's a fucked-up thing to say. Especially in light of the fact that he was a cheating bastard himself."

I kick at a twig on the ground. "After that, I couldn't bring myself to pursue her. Kept hearing that conversation. Kept thinking I wasn't any good for her."

"That's some straight-up bullshit. I know you've got a lot going on in your head right now, and I may have questioned you before when I didn't have the whole story, but if this has proven anything, it's that you're as loyal as they come. Hell, loyalty is what got you into this mess with Samantha in the first place, 'cause you were protecting the family. Who knows how the news might've affected Mom that summer?"

We stand there, mulling over everything, when he sighs again. "I haven't meant to be surly toward you this week. I realize you've been doing your best. I plan to repay you for my half of the child support you gave Samantha. Tori and I talked about it and agreed it's the right thing to do."

I wave him off, not wanting to talk about money right now. I have every confidence we'll work out those details later. "I'm real sorry you and Tori had to postpone the wedding. Been meaning to ask how much extra that's gonna cost. I can help with that."

"My girl isn't going anywhere. And you know how persuasive she can be. We might've lost the hotel, but everyone else accommodated the date change. It'll work out. Besides, we can't get married without Joey. Waiting was the right thing to do."

We're quiet for a long time before I nudge him with my elbow. "Sorry I never told you about that conversation with Dad. Felt weird telling everyone I'd argued with him before he died. Had a lot of fucking guilt over it. Like maybe I pissed him off so bad, it pushed him over the edge."

"You didn't push him or punch him, right?"

"Fuck, no. Just yelled a bit before I stomped off."

"That's what I thought." He grabs my shoulder and turns me so that we're eye to eye. "You got to stop blaming yourself for everything. Maybe Dad's heart condition was worse because he was busy lying to everyone. That's on him. Not you. And you've been looking after his kid for the last two years."

I didn't know how badly I needed to hear that until now. But I'm not the one who was close to our father. "How are you doing with that? With Dad having another son?"

Ethan sighs and runs his hands through his hair. "Still pretty pissed off, to be honest. It helps that Zach's a great kid, though. Looks like ranching is in his blood. Did you see the way he ran around here today?"

I smile, loving that Zach is getting comfortable around the horses. "He's an easygoing kid at home too. Didn't realize Samantha was leaving him by himself so much, though. Wish I'd known."

"You did your best. We'll make it up to him."

"I was thinking about finding him a counselor. Someone to talk to." Since Joey mentioned she wanted to talk to a therapist, it's been on my mind to find someone for Zach too.

"Sounds like a good idea." He frowns. "You sure Mom's doing better? You said she has a procedure scheduled while Tori and I are gone, right?"

"I got it covered. It's minor, I promise. And when she's done, she's kicking back with her friends in San Antonio for a few days of R and R. She'll be good and refreshed when you get back from your honeymoon."

"I appreciate you keeping an eye on her the last two years. I hate that you had to fly solo, but you were right—I was stressed as fuck when Allison and I were getting divorced. I'm relieved that whole phase is over."

"When we hired Tori to nanny for you, I wasn't lying. I was worried about your health too." I shove my hands in my pockets. "You know, in case I haven't told you, you're a great brother. When I was staring down the barrel of Samantha's gun, I was worried I'd never told you that before."

"That's fucked up, bro." He smacks me on the back. "But I *am* a good brother, aren't I?"

I chuckle. "Damn straight. The best."

48

JOEY

Standing on Kat's front porch, Beverly gives me a careful smile, the one everyone has been sending my way since I got released from the hospital.

"I know I'll see you tonight, but I wanted to make sure you had your notes first." She places the small bundle in my hands.

It's kinda crazy she's worried about me. She's the one whose husband of nearly three decades cheated, and she's concerned about my well-being.

Now that my brain doesn't hurt constantly, I'm starting to get some perspective. Like the fact that Samantha waved a freaking gun in Logan's face.

What if he'd died? If something had happened to Logan, I'd be devastated, plain and simple.

Or what if Silas had died before we'd had a chance to make amends?

What if Logan had been too late, and I'd croaked in that closet?

The words from that sweet lady I took the bus with from Florida come back to me. *Life is too short not to say what you mean and live the life you want.*

She's not kidding.

With the notes in one hand, I give Bev a hug with the other. "You're the best. In case I haven't told you, I really appreciate you coming over every day to drop off these messages."

"Logan wants to give you the space you need, but I know how much he cares about you." When I let her go, she shakes her head. "I feel terrible that I asked my son to keep my health situation a secret. I'm sure that's what led him to think he couldn't talk about this to anyone. I hope everything will be okay tonight?"

Tonight meaning the wedding. "I've needed time. I... I guess my feelings were really hurt, but—"

"You don't need to explain anything to me." She pats my hand. "Just don't give up on my son. He's a knucklehead, but that boy loves with a big heart and is loyal as the day is long. Look at the hullabaloo he went through for me. Now that's the kind of man you want by your side." With a wink, she trots off down the front steps before I can respond.

Back in my room, I line up Logan's cards on the dresser.

Even though I don't feel quite like myself yet, even though some part of me is still upended by what happened with Samantha, I can't deny a glimmer of hope flickers in me when I read Logan's slanted handwriting scrawled across the pages.

Sometimes, you're the only person who can make me smile.

When you were in high school you were quiet around so many people, but you always talked to me. I loved that. You've always been special to me, Jojo.

Do you remember when you were seven and found that bird with the injured wing? Everyone told you it was going to die, but you refused to listen. You nursed it and cared for it until it could fly again. That's what you do for your friends and family. You love us until we can fly again.

A lump in my throat forms every time I read those words.

A lump that forms into a boulder when I unfold the letter Logan sent me yesterday.

The one that describes how his father warned him away from me in high school because he thought we weren't a good match. Because Mr. Carter thought I was too young and Logan too much of a player to ever settle down.

But the more I think about it, the more I wonder if that warning had more to do with Mr. Carter's inability to curtail his wandering eye than Logan.

And to learn that conversation happened on the day Mr. Carter died? It explains so many things. Like why Logan stopped hanging out with me and started partying again. I mull over those words, and oddly, it helps me make sense of our past. Of the way Logan distanced himself from me after his father passed.

That's one of my greatest regrets. I should've waited for you.

I'd always thought I'd imagined him liking me. That, like a lovesick teenager, I had deluded myself into seeing something that wasn't there.

Knowing he had feelings for me back then stitches back something I didn't know was broken.

My lips tug up when I open the notes Bev dropped off this morning.

I almost asked you to my senior prom. I'm still sorry I didn't.

The first time I kissed you, I finally understood why people write love songs.

Excitement bolts through me when I think about seeing Logan today. I missed last night's rehearsal dinner because I'd had a headache that concerned everyone. Even though it subsided by the time Kat and Brady left, we decided not to take any chances. That it was better if I was rested today.

Honestly, I'm prepared to drag myself down the aisle this evening if it's the last thing I do.

Leaning closer to the mirror, I finger the angry scar across my hairline. The stitches just came out. I figure it doesn't look that bad considering it's been just a little over two weeks since that wackadoodle took a bat to my noggin.

Kat knocks on the door and pokes her head in. "Do you need any help loading up the truck?"

"No. I packed what I needed last night except the dress so I wouldn't forget anything." Because I'm not exactly a hundred percent. Sometimes my mind feels fuzzy, but I've sworn to Kat and Tori I'm well enough to do their hair for the ceremony. I'm sure as heck not going to let Samantha take this away from me.

When I'm alone again, I open the last new envelope.

I hope you'll marry me someday and that our kids look like you.

They'll be hellraisers like me, no doubt. Sorry in advance if they are, but just think how much fun we'll have wrangling our brood. I love you, Jo. I think I have for a while. I'm sorry I didn't get my shit together sooner and figure it out. But I know what I want now. It's you. It'll always be you.

I wipe away the surprising tears that spring from my eyes. For the first time since I came face to face with Samantha at Logan's, the words I haven't been able to say to Logan rise in my heart.

49

JOEY

Tori grins up at me. "My hair looks amazing. Thank you so much!" She leaps out of the chair and squishes me in a hug.

"Thank you for waiting for me," I whisper in her ear, and she squeezes me tighter. "I'm sorry you had to go through so much trouble to reschedule everything. I hate that you lost the hotel—"

"Hush now. Of course we were gonna wait for you! You're *familia*, girl." She frantically waves her hand across her face. "Don't make me cry!"

I grab a tissue to dot at the corners of her eyes and then mine. We agree not to chat about any more mushy stuff for the sake of our makeup.

In the next hour, I do Kat's hair and one of the other girls'. There's something so special about styling a bridal party. Being part of someone's big day they'll remember forever and having a small role in creating that magic is why I wanted to get into this business in the first place.

But doing their hair only distracts me from my thoughts of Logan for so long.

By the time I slip on my dress, I'm ramped up with anticipation. His notes have helped me see him in a new light and understand what he was going through.

And never, not once, did he mention the fact that I was gone for six months out of those two years he dealt with Samantha. Now that I've had time to reflect on what happened, I don't blame him for not leveling me with this as soon as we started dating.

Ultimately, the letters were the perfect way to show he cared. That he missed me. That I'm someone he wants in his life.

That he won't hold back from me anymore.

Those notes, those words, they've helped me find my footing again.

I touch my lips to tone down the smile that wants to break out.

Heather, the wedding coordinator, ushers us into the hallway, and butterflies take flight in my stomach.

Tori sniffs the air. "Someone is eating a hotdog. Dear God, hotdogs sound so good right now."

I chuckle. "I swear you're part bloodhound. I don't smell hot dogs."

"That hot dog is nearby, and when this shindig is over, I'm totally gonna hunt one down."

"When this shindig is over, your husband is gonna toss you over his shoulder and run off with you to his lair," I joke.

"Yeah. He is." A dreamy look comes over her. "Fine. After the hot marital boning, Ethan and I are totally finding us some hot dogs."

All of the girls laugh.

Mr. Duran joins us and wraps his daughter in a hug. "*Mija*, you're stunning." Tori's hair is swept into an updo with a few soft tendrils framing her lovely face. She's glowing in a strapless princess ball gown.

He lets her go, and Tori hooks an arm through his. "Thanks, old man. You don't look too shabby either."

Her dad quirks an eyebrow. "You know, Ethan can't give you back after this. There are no returns."

"Dad!" She playfully punches his shoulder, and he laughs.

The giant doors swing open, and my gaze darts around.

"This is way cooler than that dumb hotel," Tori notes, taking in the beautiful reception hall.

When our friend Liberty heard that Ethan needed a wedding venue, she offered her grandparents' bed-and-breakfast, which has an enormous barn that just got renovated to host events.

White billowing fabric and twinkle lights crisscross the vaulted ceiling and meet at the front, where a huge chandelier hangs over the dance floor area. Along the tables that circle the perimeter, candles shimmer in open mason jars next to giant arrangements of pale pink roses, freesia, and peonies, casting a warm backdrop for the magical evening.

The coordinator leads us across the shiny hardwood floors to the other end while we ooh and ahhh at the decorations, like the photos of Ethan and Tori set up on a short wooden ladder by the bridal table. At the top is a pic of him down on his knee last Christmas. The look on Tori's face is priceless.

In the low light, I feel like I'm standing in someone's fairytale.

Heather lines us up out of sight of the guests as the back doors creak open, slowly brightening the barn.

Beverly and Tori's mom join us, and outside the music starts.

My heart kicks in excitement.

Bev is escorted down the aisle by one of her nephews, and I peek outside to see them make their way down a pebbled walkway, through the rows of guests, to a trellised archway where Ethan and the groomsmen wait.

"Holy shit," whispers Shelby, one of the bridesmaids who flew in from out of town late last night. "This is so stinking pretty."

Behind me, Tori pouts. "I wanna see."

One of the girls tuts and makes Tori wait behind the partition.

Then Shelby bumps me with her elbow and lowers her voice. "Who are the sexy beasts standing next to the groom?"

Without looking, I know she must be talking about Logan and Brady.

Across the aisles, my eyes connect with Logan's, and my heart beats triple time. He smiles, and it zaps me right in the chest. Suddenly, everything I've been wrestling with for the past two weeks, every moment of doubt and fear, every hesitation, dissolves. I smile. "That's the groom's brother Logan. He's mine. The other one is Kat's husband."

When it's my turn, I barely notice anything but Logan as I walk down the path. Sexy beast is right. Dang, he fills out that tux nicely.

When I reach the archway, Ethan gives me a big grin, and I whisper, "Good luck."

Then my eyes go back to Logan, who puts his hand over his heart and mouths, "You are so beautiful."

There are a million things I want to say, but the kids are about to walk down the aisle, so we turn to watch Cody and Zach, the ring bearers, make their way to the front.

Seeing how the Carters have welcomed Zach warms me in a way I wasn't expecting. But of course they'd welcome him with open arms. That's just the kind of people they are.

Ethan leans down to give both of the boys hugs and motions for them to stand in front of Logan.

Mila and Kat's daughter Izzy toss flower petals, pausing to twirl their poofy dresses when they get to the front. Everyone laughs. Ethan hugs the girls before they come to stand with us.

And then it's time.

A hush falls as Christina Perri's *A Thousand Years* begins to play, and the guests stand.

Mr. Duran and Tori pause at the top of the path, and her full skirt billows in the gentle breeze as the sunset backlights them.

"Damn, I'm a lucky man." Ethan looks like he's been struck by lightning. Or a powerful case of love.

Logan pats him on the back as everyone marvels at the beautiful bride.

By the time her father hands her off to Ethan, everyone's choked up.

After Tori gives Kat her bouquet to hold, she holds out her hand, and I place a few tissues in it so she can dab her eyes. We knew she'd never make it through the ceremony without crying.

Ethan has to clear his throat a few times during his vows. "Tori, you came to me at one of the darkest times in my life. You showed me what it means to really and truly love. You're my best friend, my favorite person, my lover, my everything. I promise to always cherish you, to always put you first and love you with my whole heart. And it would make me the luckiest man and father to have you as my wife. The three of us"—he pauses and Cody and Mila move closer to stand with him—"would be so honored if you'd join our little family. We promise to lift your spirits when you're sad. Cheer you on when you're happy. Support your dreams. To always love you, and to always stand by your side."

Tori wipes her eyes, and I sniffle. Some of the bridesmaids are full-out crying. Pretty sure half of the audience is too.

As I look at the emotion on Logan's face, I wonder if this will be us in a few years. And when he looks at me and mouths that he loves me, the anticipation that's been brimming in my chest overflows.

After taking a deep breath, Tori leans up to kiss Ethan. "I know we haven't gotten to the kissing part, but as my parents will tell you, I've never been that good about following rules." She pauses while everyone chuckles. "But every day that we've been together, I've counted my blessings. You and Cody and Mila have become such a big part of me, I can't tell where you guys end and I begin. And something about that tells me we've always meant to be. Ethan, you're the crunch to my peanut butter and the peas to my carrots. I consider myself the luckiest girl alive to have you as my husband. I promise to always be there for you in good times and in bad, no matter what challenges we face. To be your person. To love you and our children wholeheartedly. To encourage you every step of the way."

She smiles and wipes her eyes, adding, "Except I hope it's okay to let you know we won't be a family of four for long."

Taking his hand in hers, she places it on her belly.

We're quiet for a long breath until Ethan lets out a loud whoop, scooping her up to spin her around a kiss. "We're having a baby, y'all!"

Everyone stands to clap and cheer. The moms are crying, and the kids are jumping up and down. It's barely contained wedding anarchy.

The minister somehow gets in his final blessing, and I swoon when Ethan takes Tori in his arms and dips her for their kiss.

When he lifts her up, one of the groomsmen shouts, "It's official! Let's party!"

We pair off for the trek back down the aisle, and when Logan gives me his arm, he leans down to whisper, "This is gonna be us some day."

I give him a little side eye. "You want the babies too?"

"Hell yes, woman. I wanna have babies with you."

My smile grows.

Maybe my someday might come true after all.

50

LOGAN

WATCHING MY WOMAN WALK DOWN THE AISLE IS GIVING ME IDEAS.

And based on the shy smiles Joey gives me throughout the ceremony and the baby comment a minute ago, we're getting back on solid ground.

After ten million photos of the wedding party, everyone heads back to the reception hall, but I grab Joey's hand and motion to the photographer. "She needs to take some of us."

Bitsy's nose wrinkles in confusion. "But she didn't take any of the other couples."

"I asked her to take a few special ones for us." Because, some day, when we tie the knot, I want special pics like my brother has of his time dating Tori.

When the photographer asks us to smile, I turn Jojo's face toward me and cradle it in my palm while the flash goes off.

"Joey, I love you, baby."

I gently swipe my lips against hers. It's the first time she's let me touch her since her injury. And it lights me up like the fucking Fourth of July.

Especially when I see that smile again.

I keep going. "Never wanna be away from you." I steal

another kiss. This time, she kisses me back. Fuck yes. "If that means I have to follow you to Florida, then that's what I'll do."

The realization that we're okay makes me wanna bang on my chest like a damn gorilla and drag her away to my lair.

Her eyes get glassy. "You'd really do that for me?"

"Jo, I'd do anything for you. You're it for me." I keep telling her this, but I know it's taking time for everything to sink in. If the situation with Samantha has taught me anything, it's that I never want something to come between me and Joey again— time, space, other people, business, bills. This woman is my number one priority.

"Doesn't Ethan need you? What about your other job?"

"E and I have had a few talks this week. We're working it out."

Jojo smooths the lapel of my jacket. "My cousin said she's found other investors for the salon." I can see the hesitancy in her eyes, but I nod to encourage her, and she says, "She'd need me to help out for a month or two and it might take up to a year to repay me, but she says she understands and wants me to be happy."

I press my lips to her forehead. "I've always liked Florida. If you can wait until my brother gets back from his honeymoon, I can go with you."

Her voice wobbles. "But what about Zach? You probably can't leave when you're working out his custody."

Damn it. She's right.

But then she pushes up on her tiptoes to kiss me. "But what's a month or two? Nothing in the big scheme of things."

I hate the idea of being apart, but I'll be damned if I let a snag in the road deter us. "Can I write you more letters?"

Her eyes shine. "You'd better."

Heather calls out to us. "Come on, guys. The wedding party is about to be introduced."

I thread my fingers through Joey's. "We'll figure out the specifics. I promise."

She smiles, and it nearly knocks me on my ass. After feeling like I've been stumbling in the dark for so long, loving Joey is like living in the sunlight. I know where I'm headed. I know what I want. And I know who I want it with.

After Ethan and Tori dance, each couple joins them, and I pull Joey into my arms as Ed Sheeran's *Perfect* plays from the speakers.

We stare into each other's eyes, and I commit the vision of this beautiful woman to memory. "This is so much fucking better than prom." Though I'm still kicking myself for that.

A tender smile tilts her lips as she runs her hands up my lapels to the back of my neck. "I love you, Logan. I've loved you as long as I can remember, and that's probably why this scared me so badly. Thank you for your notes, for sharing your heart with me."

I pull her against me, forgetting to dance or sway or that we're in the middle of the dance floor. "You mean the whole fucking world to me, Jo. I'm never gonna give you another reason to doubt me again."

After several slow dances where I push the boundaries of decency with my gorgeous girlfriend in her sexy dress, I throw up a prayer of thanks for the dim lights, dark shadows, and packed dance floor.

A few hours later, as the festivities are wrapping up, Ethan smacks me on the back. "Thanks for watching my kids, brother."

"Starting tomorrow, right?"

He smirks, knowing full well what I have planned tonight. "They'll be home at six tomorrow. That enough time for... things?"

Mentally, I tally how much sex Joey and I can squeeze in

before I get bombarded with children. Thank God the grandparents are pitching in to watch the kids until then.

"Things. Yes. Lots and lots of *things*." A guy can hope, right? I give him a bro hug. "Have fun on your honeymoon. I'd say don't get into trouble, but ya already got a bun in the oven, slugger, so..."

We both laugh.

My smile grows as I watch Ethan swagger toward his wife and scoop her in his arms. He's got the right idea.

It's time to get my girl.

51

LOGAN

I'VE GOT MY ARM WRAPPED AROUND JOEY'S SHOULDERS AS WE climb the stairs of the B&B, and I'm envisioning all of the dirty things I plan to do to her when it hits me.

My girlfriend just suffered a concussion. We can't fuck like animals all night long.

With a regretful sigh, I let go of her to unlock the door. Jo and I might not be able to screw like bunnies, but at least she can get some rest.

"What's wrong?" Joey asks as we slip into our suite.

I flip on the light next to the bed. "Nothing."

She lifts an eyebrow, and I laugh.

Pulling her close, I place a chaste kiss on her lips and shrug off my tux. "Just thought you might be exhausted after the long day we had. You should probably get some rest." I run my hands through my hair. "It was probably presumptuous of me to book us a room. I can get another one if you want some privacy."

No, I'm not making this awkward or anything.

A frown tugs her eyebrows close. "So you don't want to get naked and have make-up sex?"

A wall of relief washes over me that she wants to be with me tonight. Even if we only cuddle or do some near-naked spooning, I'm just happy as hell to have her back.

I drag my thumb across her plump bottom lip. "Do we need to have make-up sex?"

"Yes." She smiles shyly and bites my thumb. "It's an age-old custom that goes back to the cavemen."

"What about your concussion? I don't want you having any kind of relapse."

A smile lights her face. "I just got the go-ahead from the doctor to do mild exercise because I'm recovering so well. He said some aerobic activity could help repair additional tissue."

"Babe, how can you categorize make-up sex as *mild* exercise?" I'm not sure banging her like a screen door in a hurricane constitutes mild exercise. "Maybe we should hold off."

"You want to hold off? After not being together for weeks?" She reaches behind her, the sound of a zipper filling the room before her dress drops to the floor. "Really?" Brain function deserts me at the sight of Jojo in a strapless, sheer lace bra, garters, and matching panties. Her nipples are hard little points on her perky-as-fuck breasts. "Cat got your tongue?"

"No, but I have an idea of where I'd like to put my tongue." I undo my bowtie, my attention riveted on her mouthwatering cleavage. "How about I do all the work?"

"Now you're thinking."

The way she watches me as I strip out of my clothes sends my blood marching south. By the time I'm in my boxer briefs, my cock wants to punch a hole out of the material.

"Baby," she gasps and reaches down to my thigh where that bullet took a chunk of me with it. The stitches are out, and it doesn't hurt much anymore. She runs her finger along the gouge.

"Gonna kiss it and make it feel better?" I smirk, wanting to forget that bullshit. Tonight is about me and my woman.

When her lips graze my thigh, my cock jerks.

But I don't want her on her knees. Tonight I wanna worship her.

I tug her gently to her feet. "You're wearing too many clothes."

With her eyes locked on mine, she steps back. One by one, she pulls a few clips out of her hair, and long wavy tresses tumble down her bare shoulders.

Damn.

The girl next door has got it going on.

My little minx kicks off her heels and crawls onto the bed, her ass swaying back and forth.

I might need to bite that ass.

"Get back here." I grab her ankle and drag her across the bed. She's all giggles and playful smirks.

This moment is so similar to our last morning together, the day everything went to hell, except now there's nothing between us. No secrets or half-truths. Nothing I'm holding back. I've never felt this good or certain about where Jo and I are headed.

The second she's in my arms, I let out a sigh. Fuck, it feels amazing to be with her again like this.

With my back to the headboard and Joey in my lap, I take my time to enjoy this moment. My lips drag against hers as I breathe her in, and I let my fingers leisurely slide up and down her thighs to play with her garters. "When did you get these? They're hot as sin."

Those lashes turn down, pink rising in her cheeks. "They were a gift."

I still. "Who the hell is buying you lingerie?" If Patrick bought her underwear, he's a dead man. Why didn't I think to do this? If anyone should be buying my woman lacy, sheer panties, it's me.

A smirk pulls up her lips. "Tori got it for me. She said if she was getting laid tonight, I should too."

Laughter breaks out of me. "Holy shit. That girl is too much." My new sister-in-law is definitely getting a good Christmas gift this year. I pull Joey's legs tighter to my thighs, so she can feel how she affects me. "Good thing I didn't know what you were wearing during the ceremony. It's probably rude to have a boner during someone's wedding."

She giggles, but the sound turns into a moan when I rock her against me.

"Relax, baby. Let me do the work." Through the lace, I take a taut nipple in my mouth and clutch her ass in my hands, grateful for the fabric between us slowing us down so I can savor tonight.

For the last two years, I've been running in circles and trying to put out fires. While I'll never regret taking care of my family, I'm ready to reclaim my life. And it starts and ends with this woman in my arms.

With a lust-drunk look in her eyes that likely reflects my own expression, Jo pushes up just enough to slide down my boxer briefs. I lift my hips to help her. Then it's just that tiny scrap of lace between us when she settles down on my hard cock.

"I can feel how wet you are." My hands tighten on her hips. "This meant for me?"

She nods, not taking her eyes off mine. I love that she can look me in the eye now when we're together like this.

Slowly I lower the lace on her bra so her beautiful breasts jut out. I lick one nipple, nibble it, before I bite, enjoying how she presses down in my lap. My baby likes the biting.

"Wanna make you come so hard. Been dying to get inside you all night."

A sexy smile teases her lips as she threads her fingers through my hair, and she whispers, "You looked hot as fuck tonight in your tux."

A groan busts out of me. Jesus Christ. I'm not sure I can handle her cursing when we have sex. I might go off like a fire-hose if she's not careful.

I slip a hand between us, eager to make her come, and move that scrap of lace out of the way. With slow strokes, I circle her tight little nub while she keeps my cock trapped between us.

"Lean back. Brace yourself on my legs."

Her head tilts back, her long hair dragging on my thighs, and she's such a vision, all delicate lace and flushed skin and warm woman. Mine. All fucking mine.

She's coating my cock with her arousal, and I'm hanging by a thread as I watch her unravel, her body going tight when she convulses in my lap.

When I've wrung the last shudder from her body, I scoop her in my arms and settle her next to me.

Her eyes are closed, but she leans up to kiss me. Her tongue, warm and slick, glides lazily against mine.

"Love you, Logan."

"Love you, baby. You fucking rock my world," I mumble against her mouth. When she reaches between my legs, I grab her wrist. "You sure you're feeling okay? No headaches?"

She makes a contented sound in the back of her throat. "I just came so hard, I nearly levitated. I feel phenomenal."

I smile and release her hand. She tugs off her underwear, and then she's back in my arms.

When her thigh hooks over my hip and my cock nestles against her pretty wet pussy, I groan. "Think you can come again?"

She shakes her head. "No, but it's your turn."

Screw that. I like a good challenge, though.

Grabbing her ass, I rock my hips, slicking myself against her, knocking against her clit every time I move forward. When I can't take it any longer, I lean back just enough to reposition myself at her entrance.

My thick head pushes into her slowly, but it's really fucking tight. "Jesus, baby, you feel so good." I shut my eyes, pausing to get control of myself.

It takes a few torturous moments to work myself in, and the needy sounds she makes drive me wild. By the time I'm fully seated, she's panting.

"Logan, fuck me before I die."

My balls pull up, and I moan into her neck. "You're so goddamn hot, Jo. I don't know how I ever resisted you." I bite her neck, relishing the gasp that comes out of her mouth. "I'm never letting you go. I hope you know this."

She spasms around my cock, and I thrust into her, unable to contain myself any longer.

We kiss and bite and suck on each other, while my swollen cock tunnels in and out of her.

"Need you to come," I grit out.

"Al-almost there."

I suck my finger and reach behind her, sliding between the globes of her perfect ass where I rub her tight rosebud. She stiffens, but I coo in her ear. "Just relax. I'll make this feel good." When my finger breaches her, she gasps, but her pussy tightens around me. "That's it. Take it, baby. Take my cock in that fine pussy and my finger in your ass. You feel fucking amazing."

She goes off so hard, she screams while she claws at my back, sending me spiraling toward the finish. Pleasure radiates through me on the last thrust, and I unload inside her.

We lie there, a tangle of sweaty limbs, sated and boneless.

Sleepily, I lean up and watch my gorgeous girlfriend stretch across the sheets. I drag my nose against hers. "Gonna make you so happy. In this life and the next."

Her eyes open with a radiant smile on her lips. She tangles her fingers through my hair, and whispers, "You already do."

EPILOGUE

Joey
Ten Months Later

TORI WIPES BABY NOAH'S MOUTH WITH A CLOTH. "SORRY, NOPE."

"Why can't I hold him?" I blow kisses at her precious son.

"Because you're dressed up, goober. My child will no doubt aim his puke in your direction."

"*You're* all dressed up."

She rolls her eyes. "No one cares if I get puked on, silly. Now quit your bellyaching and finish my hair before the boys pick us up."

I don't understand her logic, but she's right to rush me because the guys will be here any minute.

We're dolled up in high heels, fitted dresses, and updos for a night on the town.

"This was fun." I wave at the mess we've made in her bathroom. "I always wanted to get ready for a dance with my girlfriends in high school, but something always came up and I couldn't go." I clip the last chunk of her hair up with a bobby pin and then take a step back to admire how beautiful she looks.

Tori gives me a sympathetic smile, but does me a favor and doesn't bring up my grandmother. "In that dress, you'll upstage everyone tonight."

"I don't know about that, but I sure do feel pretty in this outfit. What's the charity again?" We're supposed to attend some gala, which is the only reason I'm wearing this much eyeshadow. For the record, we're not really gala-attending people, though I am looking forward to seeing Logan in a tux again.

"It's for abandoned horses."

I wrinkle my nose. "I thought it was for orphans."

"Yeah. Orphaned horses."

"What?"

"I hear the boys. Hurry and zip me up."

I pause to listen, but don't hear anything except Noah's little gurgles. Before I can respond, Tori waves a card at me.

"Forgot to tell you. Gina Hartley wants you to do her hair for her wedding next month."

I hiss through my teeth. "Next month is pretty booked." Since I came back from Florida last fall, I've done more weddings than I can count. Tori showed her friends photos of her hair and booked me several gigs, and since then, word of mouth has spread.

"Don't forget to take a pic of my hair for your Instagram."

"Yes, slave driver." I smile as she chuckles. Tori and Kat have been instrumental in retooling my social media so I can use it to attract new clients.

"Ladies," a male voice booms from the other room. "Your chariot awaits."

I pause to listen. "That sounds like Brady. I thought Logan and Ethan were picking us up."

She shrugs, not looking worried.

Before I follow her, I give myself a quick once-over and smile at the hot pink streaks that run along the back of my hair.

When we get outside, a stretch limo is waiting for us. "Holy crap. I've never been in a limo." The back door opens, and Logan hops out, looking mouthwatering in a tux. "Dang, honey. You look handsome."

I squeeze my thighs together, remembering what we did the last time we wore formal outfits.

He pulls me to him and growls in my ear. "You look so sexy, I'm rock hard."

"Logan," I chide with a laugh as tingles shimmy between my legs. Fortunately, no one pays attention to us. Ethan is busy smooching his baby before he hands the little guy off to the babysitter so he can kiss his wife.

I'm suddenly so glad Bev is watching Zach tonight. As much as I adore that boy, it'll be nice to have the house to ourselves so we don't have to keep our nighttime activities quiet.

Initially, I was worried about how Zach would take to me, given how his mother felt, but he's been the biggest sweetheart from day one. Logan and Ethan got in touch with Samantha's parents, and everyone agreed it was in Zach's best interest if he lived with Logan, but he and Ethan decided to share custody. Because Ethan wants Zach to understand how much they both want him in their lives. Zach has gotten really close to Mila and Cody, so he goes back and forth between our houses. He now has two big families here who love him to pieces.

We've been in counseling to deal with what happened last summer. Logan also realized he needed to work through some things that happened with his father, and I have a truckload of my own family issues to unload, so it's been an important time of healing for everyone.

Samantha faces a slew of charges and will likely get some hefty jail time. In many ways, I've made my peace with it. She has some serious mental health issues, and given what I've experienced with my own family, I only hope she gets the help she needs. Her parents expressed regret they didn't heed the signs she was having trouble more seriously and offered to pay my enormous hospital bill, which went a long way to assuaging some of Logan's fury over the situation.

I've decided I'm not going to let any of that bring me down. Life is too short to hold on to anger. So even though I was nervous the first few times I stayed with Logan because his house had some bad memories, I try to focus on the positive. With our full home—including Zach, Rambo, and sometimes Bev—I don't have much time to get scared about the past. I'm too busy enjoying the present.

Plus, Logan signed me up for Krav Maga classes, so I'm pretty sure I can kick anyone's ass if needed.

Once Kat, Tori, Ethan, Logan and I are comfy in the limo, Brady hands us each a glass of champagne. He holds it up for a toast. "Here's to living our best lives with our best girls."

We cling glasses. I'm all smiles, enjoying being pampered and hanging out with my best friends when the limo stops and the door opens.

"We're here already?" I swear, we only drove five minutes. When I get out, I pause, not sure why we're at our high school gym. The lot is so full, cars have parked along the sidewalk. "The gala is here?"

"Yup." Logan winks and tugs me behind him as we make our way up the front steps.

When we enter, there's a huge sign that says, *Welcome to the Enchantment Under the Sea Prom.*

I pull Logan to a stop. "Babe, we can't go in here. We're crashing someone's prom." He kisses me on the forehead and drags me in. I look to our friends, and they're from grinning ear to ear. Huey Lewis and the News blasts through the speakers. "Aww. Remember this song? *The Power of Love* from *Back to the Future*?" It's a movie we've seen a million times together.

We stop in the middle of the dance floor, and Logan pulls me into his arms. I swear the whole town is here, everyone from Bart the butcher to Carol from the diner. Wait. Is that Silas and his girlfriend standing by the DJ? But then the lights dim, and *Earth Angel* starts to play.

"Baby," Logan says against my ear as we sway to the music. "I have a surprise for you."

"They're playing the soundtrack to that movie."

He chuckles. "Yeah, maybe they are. It's the first movie you and I ever saw together. It was raining that day, and you and Silas came over, and we watched it."

I lean back to look him in the eye. "You remember that?"

"I remember everything about you."

Hopping up on my tiptoes, I press my lips to his. I'm two seconds from going full make-out session with my boyfriend when the MC cuts into the moment.

"Can I get our prom king Logan Carter and his queen Joey Grayson up here for a second? They have an announcement to make."

Everyone starts cheering, and I freeze.

"Come on, Bitsy. They're calling our names." Logan gives me the biggest smile, and my heart beats triple time.

Laughter spills out of me. "What did you do, Logan?"

We run up to the stage like two fools because this whole thing is crazy. When we get to the mic, I realize the MC is my old principal, Mr. McClusky, who pats us on the back before he steps away.

Logan takes the mic like he owns the place. "Hey, guys. Thanks for coming tonight." He reaches back for me and drags me next to him where I blush furiously. He clears his throat. "Back in high school, I wanted to ask Joey to prom, but, long story short, I didn't. And I want to rectify that tonight." Turning to me, he laces his hand through mine and smiles. "Jo, I'd like to ask if you'd be my prom date."

I laugh. He's ridiculous. And all mine.

I lean into the mic. "Hmm. I don't know, y'all. I had the hugest crush on this boy, and as I recall, he took Maggie Lynn Meyerson to prom." Everyone "awws" at my declaration, and I turn to the audience and squint into the darkness. "Oh. Hey there, Maggie Lynn."

"Hey, Joey! Sorry 'bout that. He and I never kissed or nothing."

"Damn straight they didn't kiss!" her husband yells, making everyone laugh.

I remember thinking it was strange Logan took one of the few girls he was friends with instead of a hookup.

"Ahhh, c'mon, Jojo." Logan places his hand over his heart. "I really think you should forgive me for being a bonehead. Everyone here knows I should've recognized what a fantastic, beautiful woman you've always been and fallen at your feet the first chance I had."

My lips tug up despite my best attempts to keep a straight face. I'm about to give in when he drops to one knee.

For one long moment, we stare at each other. Is this really happening? I'm trembling with excitement and love for this man.

"Actually"—he clears his throat again and reaches into his back pocket—"I have a more important question I need to ask." My breath catches when he opens a tiny black box and blinds me with a diamond ring. "Josephine, you're the best part of my day and the favorite part of my night. I wanna live with you by my side now and always. I love you, baby. Let's build our lives together, make our dreams come true, have babies, and ride off into the sunset. What do you say? Will you make me the happiest man alive and marry me?"

Tears spring from my eyes, and I bring a shaky hand to my mouth before I cup his face. "You're my density, Logan Carter. My axis and center of gravity." His smile widens. "And there's nothing more I want in this world than to be yours. Yes." I laugh. "Yes! I'll marry you!"

He sweeps me into his arms before planting a kiss on my lips.

In the background, the crowd is cheering. When we finally come up for air, our friends have gathered at the front of the stage with Bev, Zach, and Silas, where my brother is holding a big bouquet of roses for me. Patrick is here with his new girlfriend. I smile at our friends, overwhelmed in the best way. I may not have a conventional family, but mine is the best kind. The kind that chooses me.

With a happy sigh, I turn to my fiancé and kiss him one more time in front of everyone I know. Because he's mine, and he always will be.

A long time ago, a boy named Logan pulled a bedraggled girl out of a well, and her heart belonged to him ever since.

Now he's promising himself to her forever.

And she's never going to let him go.

TO MY READERS

Thanks for picking up *Breathless*! If you enjoyed Logan and Joey's story, I hope you'll leave a review on Goodreads and the vendor where you purchased it. I try to read them all!

If Kat and Brady's story piqued your interest, be sure to check out *Shameless*!

Want to stay connected? Head over to my website, www.lexmartinwrites.com, and subscribe to my newsletter. You'll get new release alerts and access to exclusive giveaways, like signed paperbacks.

Would you like a book for Isaiah, the extreme sport junkie, and Liberty? Let me know!

ACKNOWLEDGMENTS

I hope you enjoyed Logan and Joey's book as much as I loved writing it! One of the best parts of my job is getting to reminisce about some of the places I've lived. My favorite vacations as a kid were spent at Port Aransas, and I went into this story knowing Logan and Joy needed a good romp at the coast.

On another personal note, Baby Noah is named for my best friend's son. I met Angela in middle school when I blocked her view in class with my big hair. (And probably kept her from paying attention with my big mouth.) Our special brand of crazy reminds me of that line from *Stand By Me*, "I never had any friends later on like the ones I had when I was 12." Love ya, girl!

I have several people to thank for helping me finish *Breathless,* a story that's been on my mind since Logan first strolled onto the pages of *Reckless*.

My husband is the reason I remember to shower when I'm writing. He knows that if I start to cry, I've either been a hermit for too long, or I'm writing the epilogue. (I always cry when I write the end!) If you're ever charmed by my male characters, I'm proud to say the hubs provides endless inspiration. He's an amazing parent to our twin daughters and the best friend and spouse a girl could have.

Last year was tough for logistical reasons as we prepared to move across the country, but my family totally came to the rescue. They're the reason I didn't lose my mind! (Not to mention, my mom is the reason I was able to finish editing *Breathless*!) I may write about vile parents from time to time, but mine kick ass.

When life gets extra crazy, I'm reminded how lucky I am to have an amazing agent. Kimberly Brower is the best person to have in your corner!

Once again, Lauren Perry took some beautiful photos, and Najla Qamber worked her magic in designing my gorgeous cover. RJ Locksley, thanks for your edits and eagle eye!

Candi Kane PR, Kylie and Jo at Give Me Books, The Dirty Laundry Review, and Jenn and Brooke at Social Butterfly have my undying gratitude for their help in promote this release.

Whitney Barbetti and Leslie McAdam always read my early drafts, and their enthusiasm gives me that extra boost of energy I need as I reach the final stretch of a book. They talk me off the ledge and pat my hair when I'm eyeball-deep in edits and hating life. You two rock!

A huge thanks to my amazing team of beta readers: Victoria Denault, Serena McDonald, Kristie White Bivens, Kelly Latham, Erica Christofferson, Amy Vox Libris, Stacy Kestwick, Becky Grover, and Elizabeth Clinton. I couldn't do what I do without your tough love!

Serena McDonald gets another shout out for being an outstanding PA. She's helped me with my Facebook group and ARC team for years, and I'm so grateful for everything she does for me!

I'm sending a big hug to Staci Hart for her help with my

blurb. I can write a full-length book but struggle with blurbs. It's sad but true.

I really appreciate the daily inspiration from Shop Talkers. They raise the bar, and I'm in awe of their skills and their take-no-prisoners beast mode.

To my readers and the many bloggers who helped promote Logan and Joey's book, I see your posts and likes and comments and appreciate each and every one! Thank you for taking the time to pimp out my books.

Wildcats, I love y'all to pieces! *ass smacks*

Would you like a story for Isaiah, the extreme sport junkie, and Liberty? Let me know!

xo,

Lex

ALSO BY LEX MARTIN

Texas Nights Series

Shameless (Kat & Brady)

Reckless (Tori & Ethan)

Breathless (Joey & Logan)

The Dearest Series:

Dearest Clementine (Clementine & Gavin)

Finding Dandelion (Dani & Jax)

Kissing Madeline (Maddie & Daren)

Cowritten with Leslie McAdam

All About the D (Josh & Evie)

Surprise, Baby! (Kendall & Drew)

ABOUT THE AUTHOR

Lex Martin is the *USA Today* bestselling author of *Shameless*, the *Dearest* series, and *All About the D*, books she hopes her readers love but her parents avoid. To stay up-to-date with her releases, head to her website and subscribe to her newsletter, or join her Facebook group, Lex Martin's Wildcats.

www.lexmartinwrites.com

Made in the USA
Monee, IL
10 July 2020